Taki

the

Reins

Taking
the
Reins

KAT MURRAY

BRAVA

KENSINGTON PUBLISHING CORP.
www.kensingtonbooks.com

BRAVA BOOKS are published by

Kensington Publishing Corp.
119 West 40th Street
New York, NY 10018

All Kensington titles, imprints, and distributed lines are available at special quantity discounts for bulk purchases for sales promotions, premiums, fund-raising, educational, or institutional use.

Special book excerpts or customized printings can also be created to fit specific needs. For details, write or phone the office of the Kensington special sales manager: Kensington Publishing Corp., 119 West 40th Street, New York, NY 10018, attn: Special Sales Department; phone: 1-800-221-2647.

BRAVA and the B logo are Reg. U.S. Pat. & TM Off.

ISBN-13: 978-0-7582-8104-3
ISBN-10: 0-7582-8104-8

First Kensington Trade Paperback Printing: January 2013

10 9 8 7 6 5 4 3 2 1

Printed in the United States of America

Chapter One

Peyton Muldoon hefted the bag of dog food over her shoulder. God, there were times her pride was a big-ass burden. A fifty-pound burden, by the feel of the feed in her arms. Would it really have killed her to ask Tiny to make the run to the store for the forgotten food and supplements?

But she'd been the one to forget, so it was her responsibility to make the second trip. Just like everything else. Responsibility. Her middle freaking name. Too bad it wasn't a family name everyone shared.

She let the bag plop into the oversized shopping cart and navigated it with some effort to the next aisle, then looked up to the highest shelves for the supplements she needed to mix in for her pregnant mares. As she debated her purchase, she heard voices on the other side of the aisle discussing the latest cutting dog. She ignored the voices at first; then her ears rang with the clear twang of one man in particular, as he said her own ranch's name. How could she help but freeze to listen?

It wasn't eavesdropping when people were talking loudly in public, right?

"Red, I need you to be straight with me now. I've been shufflin' back and forth about it, and I'm out of time. Is

Muldoon the right place to go for stud and training or not?"

There was a silence, so long she wondered if Redford Callahan had walked away. But then he spoke.

"Pete, I don't know what to tell you. I think it could be a first-rate operation. But right now . . ." His voice drifted off, and Peyton could imagine that stupid cowboy lifting his hands with a *What can I say?* shrug.

"I'll just read between the lines then," Pete said easily. "Thanks for that. How's the Three Trees colt turning out?"

As the men moved into easier conversation about horse training and then something about pie, Peyton fumed. That rat bastard. She'd known of Red for several years. Everyone knew of him. His training skills had become a valuable commodity in the tristate area. They'd met more than once at events, shows, auctions. And she'd always thought his smugness, his arrogance, was highly inflated. But it took balls to shoot down someone's business like that.

How dare he insinuate that she didn't have what it takes? Okay, he hadn't said it outright. But he'd all but implied it with his silence.

And everyone listened to Red. Anyone who wanted to be right, that is.

Peyton hooked her boot heels on the lowest shelf and stretched high for a small bucket of supplements just out of reach. Damn it, she just wanted to pay for her purchase and leave. Midday, nobody from the feed store was going to be around to help her reach, and she'd rather be stampeded than walk around the aisle and ask for either man's help. She hated being short. In boot heels, five-foot-three didn't mean much. But she'd get the darn supplements by herself. She scooted the cart over and used the bottom rung for her second boot, giving her the extra few inches she needed. Her fingers grasped the edge of the container and she stepped back down as silently as possible, placing it in her cart.

"I'll pass along what you said about the Muldoons, Red. Thanks again for the warning."

No! She bit back the urge to scream, to run between the aisles and stall him, convince him she wasn't just some idiot on a lark, that she knew what she was doing with her ranch, her business. But verbally attacking the man in the middle of the store wasn't going to win her any points in the sanity column.

Peyton swiveled her head to look between the aisles of food, desperately wanting to see if Red and Pete were alone. Please, God, at least let them be the only two over there having this conversation. M-Star couldn't afford any more bumps in the road right now.

From what she could tell, they were blessedly alone. Thank you, God.

But now she was stuck. Peyton stared at a supplement label at eye level, unseeing, wondering how she should handle this. Walk toward the register and hope they didn't notice her? Or go greet the two men and act as if she hadn't heard a word?

Or confront the rat bastards and call them out . . .

Though the last idea had merits—most of them personal—causing a scene of any size wouldn't do a damn thing to help the ranch.

She traced the lid of one bottle, giving herself another few breaths before going with her gut.

"Earth to Peyton Muldoon," a wry voice said from behind.

Her body froze, air caught in her throat. Nothing could be worse than being caught off guard by that one man. While she'd been debating how to make her getaway, he'd wandered over into her aisle. Her body jerked and she turned her head to look at the momentary bane of her existence.

Red Callahan. Horse-trainer extraordinaire. And right now, first-class pain in the ass. She opened her mouth to give him the chewing out of a lifetime, but the moment was ruined when she knocked another bottle off the shelf and fumbled to catch them on the way down.

Hell had to be just like this.

Pete Daugherty rounded the corner and caught sight of her and Red standing together next to her shopping cart. "Peyton. How are ya?"

She studied his face a moment, looking for any sign of guilt or shame at having just talked about her. But nothing showed. Typical. "I'm fine, Mr. Daugherty."

Red reached for the bottle she'd knocked off the shelf. "I'll put that back for you."

Peyton batted his hand away. "I don't need your brand of help, Red. Nobody does."

He just chuckled and stuck his hands in the pockets of his well-worn jeans. No flashy denim outfits or studded cowboy boots for him. At least the man didn't dress as pretentious as he acted. "Suit yourself."

She settled the bottle back on the shelf and gripped her cart handle, resisting the urge to rub the ache forming just under her breastbone. She'd survive.

Her pride, however . . .

Pete nodded, then glanced between her and Red. With a shrug of his shoulders, he wandered off. Probably to gossip about what a fool Peyton was, and how thankful he'd been to receive the warning from Red before he'd gotten stuck with her.

Red's hand wrapped around her bicep, and she jerked away. "Don't touch me."

The corners of his mouth twitched, like he was holding back a smile. The bastard. But then his eyes narrowed, and the corners crinkled from years of being in the sun. It was kind of nice, really. Showed the difference between a real cowboy and a man trying to fake it with fancy boots.

"Sure you didn't bust your head with that bottle when you knocked it down?"

What a gentleman. Be still her heart. "No. I mean yes, I'm sure I didn't bust anything."

"Except your pride, right?" he asked, tongue in cheek.

She didn't answer, mostly because he was right. Didn't need her to confirm it.

He stuck his hands in his pockets again and rocked back on his heels. Another shopper started down the aisle. After a long assessing gaze that traveled down her body and back up again—and left her feeling strangely naked—he inclined his head. "Should probably move on and stop blocking the way so other people can shop."

"Right. Yeah." Much as it pained her to take direction from him, she pushed the cart down the aisle, wincing slightly at the rusty shriek of the left front wheel. When she wanted to turn toward the register, the wheel locked up and she almost tumbled over the handle.

Why was it God was intent on her making a fool of herself in front of Callahan today?

But he didn't say a word, just used the heel of his boot to kick the side of the wheel and get it rolling again.

She could have done that. "I could have done that."

"I know," he said mildly. She had the distinct feeling he was trying not to laugh. And she felt like an idiot, again. If the earth could have opened up a hole right there, she would have gladly jumped in it just to escape the amused grin on Red's face right now.

The one thing she couldn't afford was to look stupid. Not when she needed people to trust her with their horses, and sometimes their livelihood.

"You can go now." She edged closer to the register and

maneuvered around a display of planters as best she could with the oversized cart. "I've got it all under control." The cart, anyway.

He put a hand on the side of her cart, stopping her progress. "This is where you say thank you."

"I'm not going to thank someone who might as well have just put me out of business," she snapped. And immediately wanted to bite her tongue.

"So you were listening in on a private conversation." There was no censure in his voice, only that damn amusement. Like everything she said was funny to him, whether it was a joke or not. It made her feel small, and she hated him all the more for it.

"It's not private if you're talking in the middle of the damn feed store." Peyton clipped a planter with the cart and sent it spinning, then caught it and settled it back on the stack, pressing on.

Of course, thanks to his long legs, Red caught up with her easily. "I don't know what all you heard, but that's not exactly what happened."

"I heard enough, Callahan. So back off." She reached the register and started piling things on the counter. Billy Curry, a high school kid who was known to work several jobs to help his folks out, started ringing up the items. He glanced between her and Red several times from lowered lashes.

"Everything okay, Ms. Muldoon?"

Peyton took a deep breath and let it out. "Yes, thank you, Billy." He didn't deserve her temper, so she did her best to give him a smile. He flashed one back. "You still looking to pick up extra work over the summer?"

His eyes lit up. "Yes, ma'am."

"Call me Peyton, please. Plan to come by the main house once school's out. We can always use another strong man around the ranch."

She watched in sly amusement as his scrawny chest puffed out a little. "Yes, ma'am—I mean, Peyton. Thank you."

"No prob." His eyes darted over her shoulder and back again rapidly, like he was watching for someone. Or something.

She smiled and added, "You should get a stool for people like me. Shorties. I almost bit it trying to reach the supplements on the top shelf." When she loaded everything back in the cart, she turned. Only to find Red still standing there.

"Need a hand with those?"

She pushed around him, though it was hard with a cart loaded down and the wonky wheel fighting her with every move. Pride demanded she do it herself. "No. I think we're done here."

As she pushed the cart out the door, she could have sworn she heard him mutter, "Not likely."

"Hey, Mr. Callahan. How are ya?"

"You get to call her Peyton, you get to call me Red." Red smiled at the lanky teenager. "How are things?"

Billy shrugged his narrow shoulders and rang up some vitamins. "Okay, I guess." His eyes grew huge. "Peyton said she might give me a job this summer."

"Not if you don't keep your grades up. I'd be willing to bet my favorite saddle she asks to see your grades before she lets you near her stables." She would if she was smart about her business, anyway. And she was . . . to an extent.

His shoulders dropped a little. "I do okay."

"Do better. You're a smart kid. Study hard, and you'll do fine." He leaned in and dropped his voice. "I'll let you in on a little secret. When I worked the counter at the feed store in my hometown, I used to bring my schoolwork in with me. During downtime, if all my work was done, the manager wouldn't mind if I cracked a book and made the most of my spare minutes studying between customers."

Billy nodded sagely, apparently appreciating the man-to-man advice. "I just get so tired by the time I get home that studying is hard."

No kidding. Rumor in the small town had it the poor kid worked three part-time jobs to help out his family. Noble as it was, his efforts wouldn't help him a damn in school. "I'm sure Mr. Monroe wouldn't mind if you brought in your books from time to time. Long as the work's done and there are no customers that need you." He'd speak to the manager himself and make sure of it. Shouldn't be an issue. Monroe was a good man and was very fond of the teenagers who worked in his store.

Red left feeling a little lighter than he had walking in. Between helping Billy, even just that small bit, and his verbal tussle with Peyton Muldoon, he was in a downright decent mood.

She was a feisty one, damn sure. Talked before thinking. Reacted at the drop of a hat. And pissier than a she-cat dropped in a cold bath half the time.

But he couldn't help liking her all the more for it. Not to mention his respect for her efforts in bringing her family stud ranch up from the hole her mama—God rest her soul—had tried to drive it into. She was a fighter, that was sure.

Red tossed the bag in the passenger seat of his truck and watched the dust fly up. He could vacuum it out, sure. But why bother when it'd be right back to the same condition three days later. When your life was spent in a barn, your truck was gonna be a mess. No two ways about it. He patted old Bertha's dash, watched more dust and dirt fly in the air, and drove out.

As he passed by the M-Star Ranch, Peyton's place, on the way to Three Trees where he was currently training, he thought again about Peyton and the scene from the feed store.

Sure as shit, she'd overheard him discouraging Pete Daugherty from using her stud ranch and training services. It wasn't the first time he'd done it, either. And he refused to feel guilty about it. Pete was constantly late on paying up for anything, if he ever did. A nice enough guy, sure. But when business was business, bills had to be paid. Sure, if Peyton went into an agreement with Pete and he didn't pay, Peyton would keep his horse. But she didn't need another mouth to feed. She needed steady, dependable business to build up her reputation.

Other cowboys, he knew, only wanted to take advantage of her when she was down and knocking on the door of desperation. In the end, Peyton didn't need that kind of millstone hanging 'round her neck. Not now, when she was trying so hard to get out of the debt her parents had left her.

Not that her efforts would do her any good, if she kept working at it the way she was. But that wasn't his problem. That was Peyton's bag of issues. Sad fact that she had to face it alone, and sadder still that the woman had serious skills with a horse that went unnoticed thanks to her gender. But sometimes life wasn't fair.

Red pulled up to Three Trees thirty minutes later in his beat-up rig. He smiled as he heard the truck sigh, as if with relief, when he hopped down with the vitamins in hand. The vehicle was ancient, and ugly as sin. But it ran, and he had no need for anything nicer. His horse trailer, currently in the garage, was a tricked out piece of work. But that was a completely different story. A horse's comforts were priority number one. He could drive anything, long as it ran well enough.

"Red. Took longer than I thought."

He turned to see Chris Tanner striding his way. And the

regret that he'd be leaving hit harder than he'd thought it would. Tucking his tongue in his cheek, he nodded. "Ran into a few folks at the store." Nothing more needed to be said on that front.

"Well then. Ready to head over?" Tanner inclined his head toward one of the workout areas. "Boys have Fire all saddled up and ready to show off."

"That's the problem," Red said mildly. "Y'all let Fire think he's supposed to show off. Horse has a big head. He's there to work. Do his job."

"So you say. Repeatedly."

"Because it's true. You go back to that mind-set, you go back to the problems."

Tanner just shook his head and took the shortcut through the stable, boot heels clicking on the clean cement floor.

Red didn't bother explaining it again, as he had countless times before. There was no use. The man would either follow through with the training, or he wouldn't. Nothing Red could say would change it at this point. Once his paycheck was cut, his work was done. Crying shame though, how some people refused to accept the help they paid for. Waste. They hired him for the name, the prestige. The ones that used his knowledge walked away with a good deal. The ones who didn't, well . . . The best he could say was it didn't hurt him any. It was their problem if they refused to follow through.

He headed for the barn himself, taking his time, saying hello to each pretty lady that stuck her head over the stall door in greeting. He couldn't hold back a chuckle as he reached the end of the line and Daffodil, his favorite Three Trees mare, nudged him extra hard.

"No treats today. Sorry sweetheart." He would have sworn she rolled her eyes in feminine disappointment before he scratched between her ears. That brought a sigh of contentment. "Maybe later, girl." With a final pat, he headed on toward Tanner, who was standing in front of the workout pen. And he watched in silence as the cowboy led Fire through a series of exercises meant to work both man and horse to the limit.

"Looks good. Right? Looking better every day. I'd say he's just about fixed now. Damn fine horse."

"Nothing was ever wrong with the horse. Just the humans working with him." As usual. Ninety percent of his job was spent fixing human error, not equine.

"Yeah, well, now we've got it all ironed out."

Red just nodded and stayed silent.

"He's gonna be ready for the Premium Rodeo this summer. Right?"

"I think that's a fair assessment. Long as you keep up the work we've started." Red watched as Fire responded to the leg commands, shifting quickly around the obstacle course of barrels and cones, not touching a one.

All it took was knowing the horse wouldn't listen to jerking on the reins to turn the entire situation around. That and a little common sense had Fire on the right track to be a damn fine rodeo horse.

Tanner had also asked Red to take over the stable's training operations, set them up for a successful future. All a part of the Red Callahan experience. But now . . .

"Time for me to move on."

Tanner's moustache quivered. "What the hell you talkin' bout? We're just getting started. With Fire here ready to take some top titles, we're only just beginning. What's this movin' on crap all about?"

"It was always temporary. Said that from the start. That's why we never had the long-term contract. We agreed going in that when I thought it was time, I'd head out. And I gave you the warning three weeks ago." Red leaned back against the rails, hooked one heel over the bottom rung. Every time, they went through this. Same conversation, different owner. "Plus, you have a full-time trainer. I was only ever here for the temporary fixes."

"Three weeks ago? Hell, I didn't know you were serious. Thought you enjoyed it enough to stay. I'll make it worth your while." Clint fingered the tip of his mustache, a gesture Red knew meant the man was thinking too hard. "I'll double what I'm paying ya. Hell, with your already-inflated rates, that's a gold mine for a trainer!"

Red didn't bother to say he'd been offered five times as much in the past. Never mattered. "Sorry, Tanner. I think you've got something good going on here. It's time for me to move on."

Tanner turned his head and spat in the other direction. "You move around too damn much. Don't you ever get tired of not having a spread that's home?"

Red unwound himself from the gate and started back through the barn, ready to collect his things. "Nope. Suits me just fine."

The transient lifestyle was how he'd been raised. No mom. If it wasn't written on his birth certificate, he wouldn't have even known her name. Just followed his father—a rodeo groupie to the core—around from state to state. Never settled down for any length of time. Always had to be ready to pick up and move when the rodeo dried up. Or slip out in the middle of the night because one of his father's infamous cons had blown up in his face. Again.

This lifestyle was his choice. He never took a permanent training position. He was a one-and-done guy. Moving from ranch to ranch, fixing problem horses or helping establish a more effective training regimen. Then moving on when things were back in order.

Finding his saddle and tack, he started to load up his trailer. Though he didn't have a horse of his own—easier to pick up and move that way—he had his own equipment. Too important not to keep his own.

Always set on moving forward, his mind was busy thinking of where to go next. With a few phone calls and well-placed feelers, word would escape that he was back on the market, so to speak. And the offers would once again trickle in. He'd weigh each job, each location, the pay and the opportunities for growth. Didn't matter what state it was in. He had no stakes holding him down.

He headed out, turning east from Tanner's spread. No real reason 'why. Just sounded good. He'd find a decent motel and hole up for a few days while he figured out a new plan. No hurry. He had enough cash to last him a good long while. He wasn't in a rush to find a new job. Just the right one. In the end, it came down to a gut feeling. Always the gut.

And why, just at that moment, did Peyton Muldoon's ornery face, with those eyes blazing, slide into his mind? He'd said the right job. Not the *absolute, no way in hell, don't even think about it, cowboy,* job. The woman had trouble written all over her . . . at least where he was looking.

And he shouldn't be looking at all. That was the problem.

He resolutely kept the truck pointed east, away from the Muldoon spread. He'd head a few towns over before stopping, just to make sure he didn't wander across Peyton's path on not-so-accident.

Trouble was one thing he had no need of.

Chapter Two

"Tim. Tim, come on. There has to be some hole. Isn't that what you people do all day? Find loopholes?"

"You people?" Tim, her family's lawyer, slid his glasses off and gave her the *Watch yourself, missy* look.

Peyton felt the heat rise up the back of her neck. But dammit, this really wasn't the time to play semantics and get caught on PC bull. "So you're saying that even though I've been doing everything for years, even though I'm the only one who stayed . . . doesn't mean a damn. The M-Star is no more mine than it's my brother's. Or my sister's."

"There's a three-way split of the ranch, Peyton. Three siblings, three owners. That's how the whole thing goes down."

"Why didn't I know about this until now? Mama's car accident was two months ago." Not that her absence was felt with anything but relief.

"At the time, you couldn't make direct contact with your brother or sister. I warned you, if you recall, that you needed to get ahold of them. But you said you couldn't."

"Couldn't," she echoed dully.

"I see you're wanting to make some changes, big ones, and that's where the problem comes in."

"Problem." Her voice sounded hollow, even to her own ears.

Tim sighed and replaced his glasses, shuffling through papers until he found what he wanted. "As I said, it's very cut and dry. Daily operations are still well within your control. But the overall responsibility—financial and legal—is split among the three of you. And any major decisions that need to be made must have all three owners in agreement."

"Major decisions. What the hell constitutes a *major decision*? Hiring a new hand? Buying a new horse? Flushing the damn toilet?" Peyton felt the migraine coming a mile away. Already the pressure behind her eyes was building. Gently, she massaged her temples with her fingertips.

"Well, now, that's up for debate. Of course, if your brother and sister agree with all your decisions, then there's never going to be a problem. If they choose to contest it, however . . ."

"What? Then what?"

"Things get . . . well, we'll just say messy." His grim face reflected Peyton's fears.

"They're not even here, Tim." She let her hands drop to the table, fingers curling into fists. "They haven't come back for anything. Not for the funeral, not for birthdays or holidays. Hell, I'm not even sure I know where Trace is, or if he's still riding the rodeo circuit. I know where Bea is . . . but I don't really want to. And she never responded to my call, my e-mail, or my letter about Mama."

"Verbal confirmation is all you'd require, truthfully. If you call them, explain the situation, and if they okay your decision, then it's done. And you can continue running M-Star as you see fit. If I can get in contact with them, I can draw up some more suitable papers that outline exactly what requires a group consensus and what doesn't.

I'll just need their contact info so I can send these papers. They'll need to be signed and notarized. You know that is why they weren't here for the will reading . . . we weren't able to get ahold of them."

"So I have to call them."

"Unless you have a crystal ball that you're not telling me about." Tim chuckled, but sounded weary. He took one of her balled fists in his two bony hands. "I know it's been hard. Your mother wasn't exactly, shall we say, an expert rancher."

Peyton snorted. "She wasn't an expert anything, except a screw up."

"Yes, well. That's all in the past now. And as sorry as I am for her passing—"

Peyton snorted again.

"—she left behind quite a challenge. A ranch she'd been running with no real knowledge or experience, and more debt than should have been allowed. But she also left behind an opportunity. For you to spread your wings and take over like you've always wanted. It's always been you anyway, Peyton, since your father died. You kept the ranch afloat despite your mother's attempts to drive it into the ground. She's not holding you back anymore."

"Except for this stupid condition in the will. Sylvia was barely smart enough to open a box of cereal. How the hell would it occur to my mother to add in some perverse thing like this?"

"These are your father's conditions, sweetheart." Tim sighed and took his glasses off again to pinch the bridge of his nose. "Your mother didn't have a will. When your father came to me for help with his, she simply said she wasn't interested."

Peyton rolled her eyes. "Sounds like Sylvia."

"And she never corrected that oversight. So this was your father's wish."

"Course, when Daddy died, we were all still one big, happy family." Her voice was drowning in sarcasm. It made her shudder to think of her teenage self, so naïve in thinking life would continue on as it had been, even with her father gone.

"It is what it is, Peyton. I can't change it, much as I would like to. This is just something you have to push through."

Peyton let her head fall to the table until her forehead pressed against cool wood. Unfortunately, the position did nothing to alleviate the overwhelming pain inside her skull that now throbbed in time with her heartbeat.

"Can I fix this? Is there something they could sign to . . . I don't know. Waive their rights to the ranch? Or their right to the veto power? Something?"

"There is. Of course, that'd take a little more time. But either way you have to get in contact with them." When she said nothing, he placed a hand on her forearm. "Call them. Just call your brother and sister. Who knows, it could go better than you think."

Peyton seriously doubted that. But why disabuse helpful Tim of the hope? She walked out of the law office feeling worse than when she'd gone in, if that was at all possible. Hopping in the ranch rig, she started the long journey back to the Muldoon spread, thirty minutes outside town.

That morning had already been a rough start. Upon hearing of his loss of employment, her now-former trainer, Samuel Nylen, had thrown an impressive tantrum, trashing both the trainer quarters above the garage and the tack room in the stables, Peyton just felt lucky he'd left before setting fire to anything. She could have called the police—still wondered if she should have—but the ranch didn't need any more negative press. Cleaning the mess up quietly seemed like the better choice, at least in the moment. She would spin it in public as an amicable splitting of ways. If Nylen wanted the chance to find another job, he'd go along.

She wasn't sure which was worse. That he'd been dead weight all along, that he'd thrown a childish hissy fit upon his dismissal, or that he only had the training job in the first place because he had been screwing her mother.

Ah, Sylvia. Her mother dearest could always be counted on for total drama and zero common sense.

Peyton made a mental checklist as she drove. First things first: make sure the ranch hands had set the mess Nylen had made to rights again. Then she had to figure out exactly how to contact her brother and sister. Bea would probably be easy to find. But Trace . . . who knew. If the last cell phone number she had was still active, she'd be shocked. Living the life of a rodeo nomad left much to be desired by way of stability. So she'd have to start making contact with guys she knew from high school. See if they'd seen Trace around.

And then, it was on to finding a new trainer. The trainer could make or break an operation. Word of mouth was the biggest draw for any ranch, and if you had a good one, your ranch reputation would rise by association. Picking an unknown wasn't a death sentence, it was just a slower build. Cheaper, though.

The wrong trainer could kill any hopes of rebuilding M-Star. They were already in a hole, both with reputation and cash, thanks to the horrible business decisions her mother had made over the years. The wrong move here could take years to fix. Years they didn't have.

But there were more immediate issues at hand. Like making sure her brother and sister weren't going to stand in the way of her running the ranch.

And the way this day was going, the odds of that happening were slim to none.

* * *

Peyton pulled up to the main stable and parked her Jeep. Hopping out, she stared for just a moment over the ranch. Her breeding and training operation—focusing on rodeo horses—was her life. From the time she'd first known what the land was used for as a toddler, she knew this was where she'd stay, to work and live. Some might have thought it was crazy that a three-year-old had known what she wanted in life. But Peyton had always known.

She walked around until she found her head hand, Arby, rubbing down a colt. She leaned a shoulder against the wall and watched him work.

Though he was fast approaching seventy, Arby knew almost everything there was to know about horses. Inside, outside, and everything in between, it was like he could read a horse's mind and anticipate its moves before even the horse knew it. But never did he step into the role of trainer, though he likely would have made a first-class one. A simple hand, he always said, was what he was meant to be. All he wanted to be.

She watched his hands, stiff with age, as they smoothed over the restless colt's back, soothing and relaxing the animal.

"How'd he do?"

"Well enough." He continued his work without facing her. "He's got spirit, got a real fire in him. But he needs a firm hand, a good rider, and a great trainer, or he'll run roughshod over anyone we hand him over to."

"Yeah, well, that's something I need to address." Right after the small problem of her siblings and their third interest apiece.

With a final pat, Arby moved out of the stall and closed the door behind him. "Any ideas on where to turn?"

Peyton shook her head and followed him back to the tack room. "No clue. I'll have to start making some calls,

I guess." Calls that likely wouldn't be returned. Because people either thought that she didn't have what it took, because she lacked a dangling sex organ, or because they didn't want to associate with a struggling operation.

None of those facts was in her favor. But she could change one, if only she had the chance.

Without looking up from the bridle he polished, Arby said, "Red Callahan's free. Just left Three Trees the other day, according to word."

Gossip, despite the distance between ranches and town, moved faster than a wildfire with a good wind.

Peyton glared at the brim of his hat. "You're trying to kill me, right? You know what that bastard's been doing to us."

Arby hung the bridle up with meticulous care and grabbed another. "I know you overheard a single conversation that was private, and you have no context for it. And you're more than a little emotional about the whole thing."

"I'm not emotional!" she yelled, then took in a shuddering breath. Okay, so maybe a little emotional. Calmer, she went on. "He was telling Pete Daugherty to avoid our ranch. He all but said we were failing, didn't know what we were doing. It's not the first time I've heard of him discouraging people from using our operation."

"Might have a reason for it," was Arby's calm response.

She shook her head. There wasn't any reason for it that she could see.

"Does the man know horses?"

Peyton kicked the dirt with her boot. "Yes." It was an inarguable fact. Red Callahan, despite her annoyance with his cocky attitude and know-it-all status, really did know his way around getting the best from a horse. She'd seen it in person, year after year at local and national rodeos. And more than that, people trusted him. If Red signed off on a horse, cowboys came running.

Okay, the more she thought about it . . .

"But I don't like him." At least, she didn't care for his attitude. And even more than that, she hated her need for him. Hated being the one in need. She preferred an even playing field.

Arby tipped his hat up, raised a brow, and said, "More than one cowboy you know has an arrogant attitude. Never stopped you from mooning over cowboys in the past." He went back to his polish.

"I do not moon." She flushed at the memory of her younger self, infatuated with any cowboy who had a good seat and good hands. "Shouldn't that be a qualification? That the trainer and the owner get along?"

"Fishin'."

So she was. But Red's attitude hurt her pride more than she wanted to admit. "I have calls to make."

Peyton forced herself to walk slowly across the way to the main house, hoping the good quarter mile would cool her down. Not quite, but by the time she reached the kitchen, her anger wasn't biting either. She stepped in to smell something mouthwatering and welcomed the reason to procrastinate.

In the heart of the home, she found longtime house-keeper and cook Emma. The woman who had all but raised the three Muldoon siblings while Mama was off on another bender and Daddy was busy keeping things to-gether. Short, petite, and frail-looking, Emma was any-thing but. She could take over a platoon of soldiers and have them whimpering like babies in minutes. A quality almost necessary to live in the rough and rugged, male-dominated west.

"What's for dinner?"

"Roast." Emma didn't turn from the counter where she chopped vegetables. "And you know what time dinner is, so don't think you can come slinking in here and start snacking early. You'll ruin your appetite and my work will go to waste."

Peyton bit back a smile. It was the same speech she'd heard since she was a toddler. She held up her hands in surrender. "Wasn't going to grab anything. Just wanted to say hi."

At that, Emma turned and smiled. Several years older than Peyton's own mother had been, Emma was a comfortable, maternal port in the storm, and Peyton had no problem walking into her outstretched arms. She'd take support wherever she could get it.

"I have to call Trace and Bea," she mumbled into Emma's shoulder.

"Why?" Emma pulled back and stared at her. "God knows they should have been here when your Mama passed. Not for her. But for you." Emma smoothed Peyton's hair back and studied her. "Do you need them?"

"Apparently," she bit off. With a sigh, she stepped back and shrugged. Then with a grin, she grabbed a cookie from the cooling rack and darted away before Emma could reach out and slap her fingers.

On the way up to the office, she munched on the cookie and thought about how she was going to convince her brother and sister to waive their veto rights. But first she had to find them.

Red answered his cell phone to just to make the ringing stop.

"What."

"Well, isn't that the sweetest of greetings?"

"Dad?" Hello wake-up call. He shifted up so his back was against the headboard and blinked at the clock on the nightstand. Three fifty-eight in the morning. Joy. "I don't have bail money." He did. But that wasn't the point.

The loud barking laugh blasted the last dregs of sleep from his brain. "No bail necessary. Not this time. Though I wouldn't mind a few thousand to get me through until—"

"No." Red was firm on this, as usual. "No money. Wait." He sat up a little straighter. "Until what?"

"That's what I was trying to tell you." His father sighed the sigh of the long weary. "I'm calling about a job."

"I don't have a job for you." Same old song and dance from dear ole dad.

"Son, you're not hearing right. I mean a job for you. I've been working out here in Idaho on a sweet spread."

Wonder if you bothered to mention your gambling habit to the sucker who hired you.

"Boss is pretty impressed with having Red Callahan's old man on the payroll."

That explained it. "I told you to stop using my name for things." Having made a name for himself in the horse world gave him multiple advantages. But it also had its drawbacks. Somehow, his father managed to find every single one.

"Calm down, boy. No harm done. Now, like I was saying, heard through the grapevine you were taking offers. Boss mentioned there'd be a prime spot for ya. Why don't you hop on over and check it out?"

"And a decent pay raise for you, too, right?" Mac Callahan didn't do anything, period, unless it benefited him in some way. Mostly financially.

"I'm hurt." Mac laid it on thick, pulling out his best *Don't you trust me?* voice. "Maybe I just want to see my boy every day. Do the father-son thing."

"Thing." *You didn't want to do the father-son thing when I was growing up . . . why now?*

Red rubbed a hand over his face, scratched his jaw and winced at the bristle. Laying low for a break was one thing. Looking like a bum was something else entirely. Knowing there was no way he'd get back to sleep now, regardless of the time, he tossed back the covers and stood.

"Yeah. The bonding thing. Come on out. You'll like the place."

The place, as Red could easily guess, was likely nothing more than a two-bit breeding factory turning out half-rate ponies with no bloodlines. In other words, the exact thing he would run as fast the other way from as possible. But with his father's less-than-stellar track record at both being reliable on the job and staying out of trouble with the law, the fact that he found work at all was something of a miracle.

"I'm going to pass." He kept his voice hard, not allowing a hint of anything that might be seen as regret to leak in.

"Already got something lined up?" In true Mac fashion, he'd counted the chips, realized he was low, and moved on with minimal disappointment. That was the thing with his dad. The bastard was too charming for his own good.

"No, nothing lined up yet." He got up to search for his boxers, pulled them on, then put the phone on speaker and set it on the bathroom counter while he splashed some water on his face. Staring at his own reflection, he knew it was time to stop dicking around and pick a spot. A week had passed, and he'd received too many offers to count. Most he'd discounted immediately for one reason or another. A few he'd hedged on, saying he'd give an answer soon. But his gut wasn't talking. Not yet.

One thing was for sure, though. Wallowing in a hotel room didn't agree with him. He had to get out of there.

"Dad? I'm gonna call you back, how's that sound?" Before his father could respond, he snapped the phone shut.

Mac wouldn't care. No hard feelings, ever, with his dad. It was the beauty of their relationship, really. Sure, he got called for more favors and bailouts than any son wanted. But at least when he said no, his dad wasn't likely to hold it against him.

Walking back to the double bed, he debated turning on the TV, but realized nothing would be on at this hour. So he picked up the folder where he'd kept the info on all the ranches that had reached out to him and spread each one over the rumpled bed.

No one ranch, spread, operation, or owner stood out to him as the clear winner. This hadn't happened before. Usually within minutes, he knew exactly where his next move was. He'd made a few wrong turns based on his instinct, but not many. Not enough to discount it as the main motivator for his choices.

Blue Ridge was persistent. The owner had called several times, hinting the offered salary was merely a starting point, open to big negotiations. But it was small, both on land and in drive from the owner. Little room for growth. The man wanted the prestige of having Red work there, but wasn't focused on the future.

Ten Fork was a good size, likely capable of growth. But they already had a good head trainer, and Red knew for a fact that man wasn't going anywhere unless he was pushed out. Two head trainers in one operation spelled disaster. And he didn't care for the fact that the owner might be willing to throw out a vet for someone new.

He stared at the papers until his eyes blurred, then blinked. It was coming down to this, then. He had to make a choice, had to get going. Not for the money, but to satisfy his own drive. A man without a purpose wasn't a man at all, to his way of thinking. And if his gut wasn't going to decide, he'd just have to do it the mature, rational, adult way.

Eeny, meeny, miny, moe it was.

Just as he started to sing the stupid rhyme in his head, a sharp knock startled him. He checked the clock. Only four-thirty. So not housekeeping then. And not a neighbor complaining, since he'd made no noise. Padding to the door, avoiding the window, he peeked through the hole.

And almost fell flat on his ass at the sight.

Yanking the door open, he drawled, "Well, isn't this a surprise."

Peyton Muldoon raised a brow, then rolled her eyes. "I'm sure it is."

He stared at her, drinking her in. Dark gold-with-chestnut locks flowed out from under a dusty, worn hat; a flannel shirt fit her curves like a dream. And he couldn't help but envy the denim that hugged every inch of her hips, down her legs. Christ, she was pretty. She'd hate hearing that though. She'd likely kick him in the nuts for it. He figured that pretty was too feminine for her mind, considering how tough she had to be to make it in the man's world she'd set herself up in.

"What can I do for you, Ms. Muldoon?" His drawl was pronounced, sarcastic, but better she be annoyed than think he was giving her a real once-over.

Her eyes flicked down his body once. Any other woman, he would have been sure he'd gotten a once-over in return. But with Peyton, he doubted it.

"Wanna put some pants on, cowboy?"

Shit. He glanced down, realizing he was in boxers alone. He let the door go and grabbed the first pair of jeans he could find draped over a chair. He hopped on one leg, then the other, doing his best to hustle in. Which only meant that he had to slow down when his foot got caught and caused him to stumble.

A snort sounded behind him, and he took a deep breath. Acting like an idiot wasn't going to make things better. After buckling his belt, he felt more in control. He grabbed a shirt and tossed it on, doing up buttons as he turned to the door, only to find it closed.

"Over here."

He spun and found Peyton sitting at the small table in the corner, boots propped up like she was at home. "Come on in."

"No problem." She waved him over, as if he were the guest. Balls. She had brass ones. "We need to talk."

He finished the last button as he plopped into the opposite chair. "Before five in the morning?"

"Work starts early on the ranch." She narrowed her eyes at him. Red felt suspiciously like she was taking a mental picture. "You look like shit."

That . . . was not what he expected. "Uh, thank you."

She grinned. "I like it."

He was definitely not awake enough for this conversation. Ignoring her, he got back up and walked to the bathroom counter to turn on the complimentary coffeemaker and start brewing a pot.

"You owe me."

No more ignoring. "I owe you? What the hell for?" Had she lost her mind?

With her arms crossed over her stomach, her breasts were pushed up for display. Not that he was looking. He wasn't looking.

"I heard you talking to Pete Daugherty. I've heard there were others. Unfair, since you've never worked for my operation or with any of our animals. You have no clue what we've got to offer."

"I know what you don't have to offer. And I know what your current plan is to grow the ranch, and that it's not right. The intentions are there, but the plan isn't effective."

"You don't know the first thing about what's right for my place." She stood up, eyes blazing, fists pounding on the fake wood table. "You don't have the right to warn Daugherty off. Or anyone."

"Daugherty doesn't pay his bills," he said quietly. Like horses, humans responded faster to quiet authority than shouting and theatrics. And as he guessed, some of the anger seeped out of her stance. "The others, and there weren't as many as you make it sound, were not reputable. Working with them would have shown you were desperate. I wouldn't have suggested them to anyone. Especially not someone whose reputation can't afford another kick in the teeth."

"I didn't know that." She sat back down, a little deflated.

Red poured two cups of coffee, bringing over a few packets of sweetener. He set them down, and Peyton took the mug gratefully and started drinking it black. Just like he figured. He dumped in sugar and gave it time to dissolve. "So remind me why I owe you again?"

She rolled out of the chair and walked over to the bed. Watching her move was something to see. Graceful as a colt, she moved with confidence and strength. But still, somehow, despite her tough exterior, she managed to have a little flirty kick to her hips when she stepped.

She'd hate hearing that as much as she'd hate being called pretty.

Picking up one file, she examined the ranch name on the outside. He debated telling her it was private, but no use in bothering. She'd snarl and tell him to bug off, then just go on doing whatever she wanted anyway. They'd known each other for years—the horse world was a small one, people-wise, not geographically—though they'd spent more time in each others' presence in the past week than they had in a long time.

"Ten Fork. Good place. Big operation." She looked at him. "Gonna take it?"

"Haven't decided yet." And she'd saved him from making the decision based on a nursery rhyme. But no need to share that part. Her seeing him in his boxers was humiliation enough for the day.

She placed the file back down with precise care. "These all the offers you have?"

"All the ones still being considered."

"Popular guy." It wasn't a compliment the way she said it.

He shrugged.

"How about one more?"

Chapter Three

He stared at her, almost afraid to hear her out. "One more what?"

"Offer." She took a deep breath, linked her hands together, and stared at him with a silent dare to look away. "We need a trainer."

No. The answer was obvious. Clear as day. He shouldn't even be in the hotel room with her now. Too dangerous. He needed to say no.

His gut gave a little jump and roll.

Now? Fuck.

She barreled on, completely unaware of his inner turmoil. "The pay will probably suck compared to what you could get elsewhere, but I can give you what every one of these places can't."

"Besides money?" he asked dryly, trying to settle his stomach.

"Well, yeah. I just said that." She rolled her eyes like he was a child speaking out of turn.

Against his better judgment, curiosity won out. "Let's hear the pitch."

Her eyes widened then narrowed, as if she'd already read his mind and sensed his reluctance. "Why, so you can just laugh and toss me out?"

He waved a hand toward the bed. "I haven't made a decision yet. So it's anyone's game. Why should I pick you?"

"Because I need you."

His heart all but stopped in his chest, and dropped down to rattle around in his ribs.

"I need your experience, your reputation. Your hand with the horses. I've got some great two-year-olds, promising colts. And strong breeding lines. And I've got the drive and the commitment to making it work. What I don't have is the clout to get others to take a chance on me and my horses."

Needed him . . . as a trainer. Right.

Time to get your head out of your pants and pay attention, Callahan.

"You don't think they need me?" he asked, jerking a thumb at the files.

"Not like I do. Oh, they might say they need you. But they either have trainers who do well for them, or they don't have the room to grow. Or they don't give a shit about the future, and only want to use you for your name and pretty face."

That's exactly what he'd said earl—wait. "Pretty face?" He couldn't help but smile at that.

She sat on the bed, causing the files to slide around. "Don't get a big head."

Peyton sitting on his bed was definitely not something he needed to be thinking about. "Is there a time limit on the offer?"

"Forty-eight hours."

Bold. Nobody else had handed him a timeline. It'd always been at his convenience. But Peyton Muldoon and boldness went hand in hand.

"I'll think about it." His gut pulled again, in that way he'd learned to listen to. But he wasn't ready yet.

She shrugged, as if the fate of her ranch didn't hinge on his decision. "You do that." Standing, she walked to the door, then shot him a cocky smile. "I'll show myself out." She shut it quietly behind herself.

He waited until he heard an engine—had to be hers—roar to life and take off, fading into the distance. Then he let out a big breath and rubbed a hand just under his sternum.

"Now? Really? With her? Anyone but her."

It was too late. He knew, whether he wanted to admit it to himself or not, the decision was made. Now he just had to make sure that they didn't wind up hating each other on a daily basis.

Good fucking luck with that.

Peyton pulled up the long drive and debated heading right, toward the stable. But truthfully, despite her cut to Red about starting early, she needed a nap. She'd be no good to anyone without some rest. And she'd spent the entire night before tossing and turning, trying to make up her mind whether she was doing the right thing by going to Red, or if she was the world's biggest fool.

Jury, it appeared, was still out on that one. For another forty-seven hours and counting.

But she didn't regret going over there, even if she ended up with nothing but egg on her face. She'd never know if she didn't try, and Red was the best chance she had to save the ranch with minimal fuss.

Besides, if she hadn't gone over there at such an early hour, she never would have scored the prime sight of Red in nothing but his boxers. God, that'd been a treat. It would be so much easier to dislike the man if he had a potbelly, or some weird deformity. But no, he had to look like God's gift to females. All tan, smooth skin pulled tight over hard muscles. And that intriguing little happy trail that led . . .

Led to nowhere good. Time for a mental kick in the ass if *that's* where her mind was heading all on its own.

Pulling up to the ranch house, she stopped short when another rig was in her Jeep's spot. Old, slightly rusted, and dinged in several places, it'd seen better days. Better decades, really. Glancing on down the yard, she saw a horse trailer that didn't belong to the ranch. That, of course, was newer and shiny. Cowboys always took great care with their trailers and equipment. Personal items ranked low on the list, behind anything their animal might need.

But who the hell was this? And why was he—or she—parked in her spot? She whipped around and pulled up next to the rust-bucket-rig and slammed her door shut. Just what she needed. Company, when she was hoping for a nap.

Who the hell came to call at five-thirty in the morning?

After wiping her boots on the mat and toeing them off in the mudroom—Emma could put the fear of God into anyone who muddied up her floors—she started the hunt for the rig owner.

"Emma? You up yet?"

The answer was quick in coming. "Quit your hollering and get in the kitchen. I've got breakfast started in here and I'm not leaving it to chase you down."

She smiled. In a year full of changes, it was great to know that some things didn't change at all. She followed the scent of bacon and eggs to the kitchen. "Emma, do you know whose rig that is out—"

She stopped short, breath cut from her lungs as the figure seated at the kitchen table rose and faced her.

"Hey sis. Long time no see."

Breathe. Breathe, dammit. She whooshed out a breath. "Trace? What the hell are you doing here?"

His grin was slow and easy as he held out his hands. "Wasn't that you who left the angry voicemail saying I needed to get the lead out of my lazy ass and call you back?"

Time to pop her eyes back in her head. "Yeah. But . . . but . . ."

"But you didn't think I'd come on over this way, huh?" He walked toward her, long legs carrying him in a few steps, socks padding quietly over the kitchen tile. He grabbed her in a hug and lifted her straight off her feet. At six feet, he'd always been able to toss her around. It was his favorite pastime as a boy. "Christ, you grew up on me. I missed you, shortie."

"Don't call me that." She beat her fists on his back, but only to give the appearance of resistance. Then, giving up on all hope of remaining aloof, she wrapped her arms and legs around him and squeezed like she would never let go. "I missed you, too," she whispered. Hot tears burned the back of her throat. So long, she'd been holding things together, including herself, with some gum, a shoestring, and a prayer. And with the sight of one friendly face, she was about to crumble.

Then she remembered exactly what it had taken to get him back there, and she straightened. "I'm so mad at you."

"I know. But be mad at me a little later." Trace set her gently down and stepped back. Peyton took the chance to look him over.

He looked leaner, stronger than the last time she'd seen him. But then again, he'd only been nineteen. Lines crinkled around his eyes. Eyes that weren't so naive anymore, so gung-ho, so full of energy. Weary to the bone, that's how he looked. Weary and ready for a break.

"What are you doing here? Aren't you missing something important? Another rodeo, another buckle to chase?"

He rubbed the back of his neck and ambled to the table. She followed and sat down across from him.

"I'm just taking a little breather from the circuit right now. Needed some time off."

Emma snorted.

"Time off? But Trace, the rodeo is your life."

This time, he snorted. "Not quite. I do love the thrill, but the lifestyle's starting to get old."

Another snort from Emma.

"Would someone tell me why everyone keeps sounding like a bull in heat?" Peyton glanced between Trace's wry face and the back of Emma's head at the stove. "What am I missing?"

"You said you needed to talk about the ranch. So, let's talk." Trace crossed one heel over his knee and leaned back, confident in his ability to bring her around.

She wasn't the scrawny teen he left behind, worshipping his every move. "You're dodging."

"Yup."

No bull with Trace. Never was. "Fine. We'll get back to that. More pressing stuff to talk about anyway. Like how you abandoned your favorite sister to the dragon Sylvia."

One more snort from Emma before she turned to place a steaming plate piled high with bacon, eggs, toast, hash browns, and ham in front of Trace.

"Emma, I seriously missed you all these years." Trace leaned over to kiss her cheek.

"Sure could have fooled me, what with you staying gone so long."

He said nothing to that, only pointed to Peyton with his fork before digging in.

Peyton stared at her own slightly less full plate and felt her appetite shrink. "We need to talk about the will."

Trace's easy grin slid off his face. "I don't want to talk about that woman."

That woman. Their mother.

"Well, we have to. She's connected to the issue, although only indirectly, so don't get your tighty whities in a knot. The gist is, Mama didn't have a will. So the provisions in Daddy's will slide on down. After Mama died, the ranch came to—"

"You."

That's what they'd all assumed, apparently. The only one of the three who'd stayed, who'd wanted it. But no. "Not quite. Actually, it's a three-way split. You, me, and Bea."

"Bea?" A pile of eggs plopped back onto his plate as Trace's fork froze halfway to his mouth. "But she doesn't even ride. She doesn't even like to get dirty. She's been to the barn, like, three times in her entire life."

Peyton shook her head. "I know. Trust me, I know. But that's just what it is."

"So what does this mean?"

"Since I'm the only one who has any real interest in the ranch, I'll keep doing what I'm doing. I've got some ideas to work our way out of the debt Mama dug us into. But it's not going to be easy. And also . . ." She took a deep breath, then a sip from the coffee mug Emma sat next to her plate. "Also, you and Bea have equal say in all major decisions regarding the ranch."

His fork clattered to the plate. "No shit."

Emma's hand shot out from nowhere and slapped the back of his head. "Language at the table."

Trace rubbed his head and scowled. "Yes ma'am."

Peyton snickered. She'd been on the receiving end of the manners lesson enough times to know Emma didn't pull her punches. Didn't matter if they were three or thirty-three. Emma ruled the kitchen, and most of the rest of the house, with an iron fist.

"I assume you talked to a lawyer about it."

"I did. It's legit."

"Bea isn't gonna have a clue what to do with this place."

At that, Peyton scowled. "She doesn't have to. She just has to agree with me."

Trace grinned. "That holy terror? She'll argue what color to paint the barn simply because she can. Causing problems just to watch the dust fly was always her favorite thing to do, you know that."

"Thanks for the reminder," she said dryly. "The good news is, if I need to run something by you two, I can just call you and Bea and get confirmation." That reminded her . . . "Speaking of, not that I'm not glad to see your ugly mug. But you want to try again telling me exactly why you're here?"

"Just taking a break. Every cowboy needs a little time to recoup." He took a calm sip of coffee, as if he wasn't hiding a damn thing. She wasn't fooled one bit.

"You know eventually you'll have to tell me."

"Nothing to tell."

"Uh huh. Well, after your break, you can rest assured that you won't have to jot back here every so often for ranch business. I know you like to move around. So you don't have to stay."

"Yeah." He picked up his mug. "Staying. About that—"

A muffled sound from up the stairs caught her ear, and she cocked her head. Trace started to speak, but she held up a hand. "What was that?"

It came again, sharper, louder, and completely unmistakable. The wail of a baby.

Peyton looked around wildly, then over at Emma.

The housekeeper didn't bat an eye. Undoing her apron, she folded it on the counter and left the kitchen, saying, "I'll get him."

"Him?" Her eyes flew back to Trace. "Him who? What is going on? Whose baby is that?"

Her brother took another maddeningly calm sip of coffee. "That'd be mine."

He was five shades of stupid. That's the only reason he could think of to explain why he was listening to his gut again instead of his head. Clearly, his gut wasn't up on the little problem he was having fighting a serious attraction to the current owner of the M-Star.

And yet there he was, pulling up to the first barn, all but asking to get kicked in the teeth. He'd waited around so long for his gut to change its mind that he'd missed Peyton's forty-eight-hour cutoff. Not that he thought she'd really hold him to it. But she'd give him hell just the same, because she could.

Feisty. That's all she was. And it got under his skin more than he ever wanted to admit. He knew he was setting himself up for a big disaster, putting himself in close working proximity to Peyton Muldoon.

He pulled up to a rig that looked like it should have headed to the junk pile years ago. Definitely didn't recognize it, and it was something to remember all right. Hopping down, he saw a horse and rider working out in the main arena and headed that way. From this distance, he couldn't recognize the rider either, but using his sharp detective skills, he figured the man for the owner of the rust-mobile.

The horse, he was glad to see as he came up, was in much better shape. Excellent, actually. The man put the animal through its paces, weaving in and out of an obstacle course set up with barrels, dummies, and traffic cones. Sure-footed, confident, and quick, the horse maneuvered the course like it was born to handle the job. As the exercise ended and horse and rider headed to the side of the arena, he couldn't help but wonder who the hell the guy was. Not a beginner, that was for sure.

Locating Peyton off to the side, he girded his loins, wished he'd worn a cup, and headed over. She had one boot heel hitched up to the bottom rung of the metal gate and her elbows leaning over the top. The position did some interesting things to her backside, plastering the jeans to her bottom in a way he could more than appreciate.

"Peyton." He eased up slowly, giving her ample warning so she couldn't blame him for startling her.

She turned a cool, dispassionate eye toward him. "Callahan. See you finally came sniffing around." Glancing back at the horse and rider exiting the arena from the opposite side, she asked, "All those other ranches rescind their offers? Are we the last stop?"

"First stop." Why lie? She could find out with one call that he'd already said no to every other offer. "Came here to accept the job."

She pushed the gate wide open and started walking to the obstacle course, picking up cones. "Too late."

He paused, gate halfway shut behind him. "Too late for what?"

"I said forty-eight hours. It's been"—she checked her watch, but he'd bet she didn't have to—"fifty-six."

"True." He picked up one of the dummies and walked it to the side where she was stacking cones. "I just needed a little more time."

"Wanted to play hardball. Show me who's boss." Her words were harsh, but she bit the corner of her lip, as if not sure how to play it.

"Actually, no. I just needed the time to think." Or to try to convince himself that his instincts were wrong. Fruitless in practice. He rolled a barrel over, and she hopped up on it.

"Doesn't matter. You're too late."

He understood pride, knew sometimes it stepped in the

way of a good thing. And he was a good thing . . . for the ranch. "You keep saying that, but we know it's not true." He placed a hand on either side of her hips and caged her in. "You need me. Said so yourself. You need anyone, but you really need me. So go ahead and give me hell for taking my sweet time. I can take it. I even deserve it. But when you run out of steam, we can go inside, sit down like adults, and start making a plan."

Her smile was all teeth, and more than a little scary. "I don't say things I don't mean."

He raised a brow.

And her expression turned smug. "I have a trainer."

That knocked him down a few pegs. "You what?"

"Did you stuff cotton in your ears?" She grabbed his chin with one hand, and his breath caught as he wondered what she was going to do with it. "I have a new trainer."

"Bull. No way in hell you could get a trainer that fast. I'm only eight hours late."

She shrugged and dropped her hand. He resisted the urge to pick it up and replace it. Her touching him was a new development. And his body liked it, even as his mind screamed to step away.

"Who?"

Peyton looked to the right, and he followed her eyes to see the mystery rider walking back through the training arena at a fast pace.

"Peyton? This guy bothering you? Need me to take care of him?"

She looked back at Red, her eyes gleaming with mischief.

"Don't you dare," he muttered.

With a sigh, she hopped down and ducked under his arm, body brushing against his. He jerked back like he'd been scalded.

"No, Trace. Not bothering me. He's just a little lost."

Trace? The name was familiar. First or last name?

Reaching Peyton, the man slipped his arm around her shoulders and gave her a squeeze. Red's eyes narrowed in automatic response.

With reluctance, Peyton started the introduction. "Trace, this is Red Callahan."

Red held out a hand, shook it a little more firmly than normal. God, this was insane. He had no business being possessive.

"Red, this is my brother, Trace."

Brother? Well shit in a bag, that was not at all what he'd been expecting. Wait. "Trace Muldoon? Rodeo circuit?"

"One in the same." He tipped his hat in mock salute.

"I'll be damned. Why are you here? There's the big rodeo in Oklahoma next weekend."

The man's face shuttered a little. "Personal business. I'll be sticking close to home for a while."

"I saw you ride in Montana a year ago. You were damn good."

The man nodded in acknowledgment. Red looked back between Trace and Peyton. Despite the almost foot differ-ence in height, he could now see the similarities between the siblings. But hold on. "Trace is your trainer?"

"That's right. You didn't show up, and he did. So it's one point to Trace, zero to Red. Thanks for stopping by though. Good luck with everything." She turned to go but Trace held her still.

"You can't be serious. He's a cowboy. A rider. A damn good one," he added to Trace, "so no offense meant. But you know it's not the same thing. You're going to use your brother as a trainer while he's off the circuit? And when he goes back? Then what?"

"Then it's still none of your concern," she bit out, step-ping toward him. Her body vibrated with anger; her fists were clenched. If he had to guess, even her toes would be curled in her boots. When Peyton Muldoon felt something, it was all or nothing.

"Now, Peyton," Trace began.

She whirled on him. "Don't. Don't even start. You promised."

"But he's here. And you know—"

"Don't tell me what I know. He had his shot and he didn't show up."

"I'm here now," he said quietly, not caring for being talked about like he wasn't there at all. "I'm here, and I'm sorry."

The quiet, sincere apology seemed to kick the wind from her angry sails. She knocked her hat back and blew out a breath. "I didn't think you knew the word sorry."

"I use it sparingly."

"Peyton, can we talk?" When she said nothing, Trace tugged her elbow until she jolted and followed him to another corner of the arena.

Red watched with amusement as Trace bent and spoke in Peyton's ear. She tilted back and said something that had her brother shaking his head. Red stuffed his hands in his pockets and turned his back, giving them the illusion of more privacy. Wandering to another corner, he came upon the office. With the door wide open, he felt no guilt sticking his head in.

A computer, older than Moses, sat on a desk cluttered with papers. Pile had to be two feet deep. Looked like the last trainer did less than nil with paperwork. Not shocking, knowing the kind of man Nylen was. Paperwork was never a favorite, but it was a necessary evil.

"Callahan."

He turned to see Trace walking over, no Peyton in sight.

Trace stopped in front of him, propped his shoulder on the wall, and looked very much at ease. "You're right."

Once again, not what he'd expected. Red mimicked Trace's posture, facing him. "Care to elaborate?"

"I'm a cowboy. Rodeo lover. I can ride 'em. I can't train 'em, not like this ranch needs. I'm not a pro at it. I was willing to give it a shot for Peyton. I love her, and I love this ranch, though I haven't been here for a while. And I would have been better than nothing." He smiled a little at the not-so-glowing recommendation. "But if there's a better offer on the table, she'll grab it."

Red made a show of looking around Trace to the empty building. "Don't see any grabbing."

Trace chuckled. "If you know Peyton at all, you know it's going to kill her to take back her decision. Admitting defeat has never been her strong suit. It's sort of a Muldoon thing. She just needs some time to lick her wounds. She'll get to it." The laughter died from his eyes, and suddenly Red had no problem seeing Trace in the role of big, protective brother. "And when she's ready, you *will* be good to her."

"Will I?" Being a shithead wasn't his plan. But he was curious how far Trace would take the protector role.

"She's had the wind knocked out of her recently, first having the reins of the business handed over so unexpectedly, then Nylen showing just what an asshole he could be. I'm not saying she couldn't use a little humility. But there's humility, and then there's humiliation. Take her prickliness in stride, and it'll go a long way to smoothing the road to good working conditions."

Red nodded once. "I'll take that into consideration."

"You do that." He leaned away a bit. "What's your big plan for the ranch?"

Red scratched his chin, then decided there wasn't any harm in sharing. "She's going after the wrong clientele."

"Wrong?" Trace smiled. "Isn't any client whose check clears the right one?"

Red shook his head. "Selling kid ponies and work horses is fine and all. But if she wants to remake this place's reputation, she needs fewer customers, but quality ones. She needs to be selling the big guys. She isn't doing enough of that. Make the most of the breeding program."

"Well, can't say I"—Trace's cell phone beeped in his pocked and he slipped it out. When he opened it, his eyes darted over the screen before narrowing. "Damn it." He shut the phone with a snap and stuffed it back in his pocket with obvious frustration. Taking off his hat, he ran his fingers through his hair once before slamming it back on his head. "I'm needed at the house. Keep what I said in mind." With that, he was gone.

Red stood for a moment, absorbing what had just happened. Trace was a good cowboy, no doubt about it. He'd watched the man on TV, seen him in person once. But a good horseman didn't always make a trainer. And Trace was wise enough to know his limits.

And he knew his sister well. Red believed the advice about Peyton. But he wasn't really one to give space when he was ready to push. She'd had a good twenty minutes to sulk. Hopefully that was enough time.

Because he was ready for a good long talk with Peyton Muldoon, and this time he was taking the upper hand.

Chapter Four

Peyton slammed her body into the office chair so hard it rocked back. Grabbing the edge of the desk before she tipped over completely, she forced her racing heart to slow down.

Give him another chance, my ass. Damn you, Trace.

Her brother didn't seem to mind she'd have to choke down her pride to do it. Yes, she was aware Trace was only a temporary solution. He'd go back to the rodeo eventually, no matter what he said. It was in his blood, in his heart. So he wasn't a permanent fix.

And it wasn't just pride, she admitted. But fear. Her hand stroked over the desktop, worn and nicked in places. Her father's desk. God, she missed seeing him behind it, even when he would frown and pull at his hair absently going over the books. Not that he'd done that often. The man knew horses. He didn't have a head for business at all.

She'd always wanted to run the ranch with him. And now she had to do it for him. And for herself. But did she truly have what it took to get their feet back on the ground? So many people counting on her. Expecting things from her.

In the bedroom above the office, Peyton could hear Emma through the heating grates, singing in a low, gravelly voice, some lullaby to Trace's son, while she walked the floor. Though it was the child that was supposed to be soothed, Peyton felt her own muscles slacken a little at the comforting sound.

Maybe Trace did intend to set up permanent residence. But that didn't mean he was the best choice for training.

That, unfortunately for all involved, was Redford Callahan. Just her luck.

To keep the madness going—because it was exactly what she needed—she picked up the office phone, reached into the top drawer where she kept the address book, flipped through and found Bea's phone number, and dialed. Again. For the seventeenth time.

But who was counting?

After five rings, the damn thing went to voicemail. Again. Peyton was very quickly coming to loathe the sound of that beep that signaled, once again, she'd failed to reach her irresponsible sister. She'd already left several simple, concise messages explaining the reason Bea needed to call back. This time? She wasn't in the mood for simple *or* concise.

"Beatrice Muldoon. For the love of all that's holy, get your TV starlet ass out of bed and call me back. I'm not kidding around. This is important business. *Business.* You know, that thing I'm busy running while you're getting your makeup done every day? Call. Me."

She hung up the phone hard enough to rattle the whole intercom system. With a few deep breaths, she placed the address book back with delicate care. Nothing would be solved by her losing her shit and flying off the handle.

Good as it felt in the moment.

"That'll bring her in."

She jumped in her seat, then scowled at Trace, who was standing in the doorway to her office. "Bite me."

Instead of taking her suggestion, he slid in and took a seat opposite her on the other side of the desk. "I can't imagine why she would be ignoring you, what with all your friendly conversational skills at work. In fact, I'm not sure how I held off as long as I did."

"You didn't hold off. You came racing back here like your pants were on fire." The reason for which, of course, was being soothed to sleep by the housekeeper upstairs. But neither of them mentioned that. "I have to do it, don't I?"

They might have been apart for the majority of a decade, but he could still read her mind. "Yeah. You do. He's the one for the job, Peyton. You know I can't do this."

"Yes, you can," she argued back. More from wanting to defend her brother—even against himself—than anything. But when he raised a brow and shook his head, she let her shoulders slump. "Well, you could. If you wanted to. You owe me."

"Could," he admitted, "but shouldn't. Training isn't my style and I don't have the clout to raise the M-Star's reputation. I'll help. You know I will. Breaking, working, doing what needs to be done. But the official spot of trainer is not mine to grab. And I told you before, we're not going into what I owe you. I had to go. I've said it before, I'll say it again. I couldn't be here with our mother. I'm sorry that hurt, leaving you behind. But what was I supposed to do, drag a teenager behind me when I left?"

She gritted her teeth at the reminder.

"Not to mention, I've got as much say in the running of this place as you do."

Her blood started to boil, but she kept her mouth shut.

"So I could try getting ahold of Bea. And convince her to go in with me on it. And I'd just end up hiring him without your say so."

It was a sharp slap of a reminder that, while she carried the emotional weight of the ranch on her shoulders, she only had so much power in the actual running of it. For now, anyway.

Peyton nodded tightly, battling back resentment.

"So what do you propose to do to earn your keep?"

He grinned at the reminder of their childhood. One of Emma's Emma-isms was "Earn your keep."

"I figure I'll be heading up the personal relations and marketing department."

Peyton's eyebrows shot up. "Personal relations and marketing department?" she repeated. "We have one of those?" She rolled the chair back a foot and looked under the desk. "Where have they been hiding?"

"It's a small department," he said with a smile. "Department of one."

"We don't need marketing and PR. We need—"

"Customers."

She rolled her eyes. "Yes, that's typically how businesses stay in business. Customers."

"And where are you expecting to find these customers?" Trace leaned forward, forearms on his knees, hands dangling loosely. "What kind of rider would you say the majority of our horses are being sold to?"

"Right now?" She did quick calculations. "Probably hand horses. Or to weekend riders. Kids with their first horse."

"Exactly. A weekend rider is great and all. Easy sales, probably. But they're not paying the bills. Are they?"

She shrugged. "Not completely, no." And it burned her to admit that.

"But who will pay the bills? Think about it, Pey. Who pays top dollar for their ride? Who goes for the quality and doesn't mind paying the price?"

"Rodeo cowboys." She knew it. But how did Trace know what a kid pony would go for instead of . . . damn. "He talked to you, didn't he?"

Trace slid an innocent mask over his face. "He who?"

She sighed. "If Red put this in your mind, I know he's right. I just don't have to like that he's right."

"What are your plans?"

She ran her tongue over her teeth. "I like the business we do now. It's safe. And my thought was getting more of it, so we could get our feet back under us before making any changes . . ."

"But?"

She sighed. "But I know we need to go big. Take the chance. I want to expand and capture more cowboys. I want to breed rodeo stock. The horses that come from long lines of buckle winners. A ranch that trains the champions. But we don't have the reputation yet—"

"Yet." With a coy smile, he sat back, crossed his left boot over his right knee. "But you'll have Red, and you've got me."

"And you are . . ."

He held up his hands. "Word of mouth."

"You're a mouth, all right." She threw a pen at him, but the idea was already starting to take root. "Exactly what are you proposing?"

"I have contacts. I wasn't the biggest, baddest mo'fo on the circuit. But I knew people. They knew me. I wasn't a top winner, but I was consistently in the money. And people know that. They see that consistency and they like it. They envy it. You can have a lucky weekend and take home the belt. But if that's all you have to show for your career . . ."

"Then it wasn't worth much," she finished for him. She knew. Though competing wasn't where she'd set her sights, she was more than aware of the rodeo. Its pull on a young man. The competition. The fame. The glory. The girls.

"So maybe I call up a few friends, tell them I'm settling

down to work on the stud ranch. Mention a few horses that have potential. Drop some lines here, pull a few interested strings there. Work the phone lines. Maybe even take one of our horses to shows somewhere nearby for a weekend and show what we've got."

"And with Trace Muldoon on an M-Star horse, that gives us the advertising." Yes. She was seeing it now.

A low whimper sounded nearby, quickly hushed by Emma. She glanced at the office door that led to the main floor living area. "And while you're gone, what are we going to do with Seth?"

Trace's face morphed into a mask even she couldn't read. "I'll figure it out. I'm not here for free babysitting, Peyton."

"I know that. I'm sorry, that's not what I meant either." She instantly regretted bringing it up. "We'll cross that bridge when we get to it." Curiosity burned in her. "Are you going to tell us about his mom?"

"No." Just one word, sharply bitten off.

She ignored the not-so-subtle warning. "Is she around somewhere? Should we expect her to pop by for—"

"She's not coming. Let it go." With that, he stood up and left her alone in the office.

That went well. Taking a deep breath, she reached for the handset, dialing the phone in the stables. When one of her day guys picked up, she asked him to find Red, who was likely still out in the training ring.

As she hung up the phone, she let her forehead thump down on the desk. Might as well ask Emma to bake her a nice heaping plate of crow for lunch.

Red strolled into the main house, not sure which way to turn. The place was bigger than he was used to; most ranches that he worked on only had a business office on the property. But from what he could gather from the men, this was also where the family lived. He stood on the entry mat and took in the first floor.

A set of double staircases were situated directly in front of him, one curving off in each direction. Upstairs, he'd no doubt find the actual family living areas and bedrooms. A quick step to the left showed him the rest of the main floor. The place was a showroom, clean as a whistle, and almost startling in its sterile, museum-style. Not the sort of place where a guy could prop his feet up at the end of the day. Nothing about it appeared to say "A family lives and loves here."

He took another step forward and nearly jumped out of his boots when something squeaked. Looking down, he saw some sort of blue plush stuffed animal under the arch of his boot. He bent down and scooped it up. Definitely not a dog toy. No teeth marks, no ripped stitches or slobber. A little worn in places, but more likely from the constant loving of little hands than some animal gnawing on it.

Peyton had a kid? How did he not know that? Was she involved with someone? Had the father left her and the child behind? Unexplained anger had his hands balling into fists until the toy squeaked in protest. He took another two steps before a tiny woman, barely five feet if he had to guess, bustled out of what appeared to be the kitchen.

"Don't you dare take another step without removing your boots, young man."

On the other side of sixty, at least, she barreled at him, using one hand to untie the apron wrapped around her waist, and holding what looked like a cucumber in the other. She waved the vegetable in his direction. "I just mopped this floor and I will not have mud on it. You hear me?"

Frail his ass. She was about to whoop him good. He smiled at the thought. "Yes, ma'am." Contritely, he toed off his boots and pushed them to the side where a mat extended along the baseboard; a whole host of other boots were lined up there already.

"You just remember that rule from now on. I won't have . . . oh." Her face softened and she reached one hand out. "You found Danny."

"I found who?" When she gently took the stuffed dragon from his hand, he realized she meant the toy and chuckled. "Scared the dickens out of me when I stepped on him. Not too bad, for a guard dragon."

She tucked the toy in the crook of her arm. "Thank the Lord. I've been looking everywhere for this thing. He's been so fussy, and I know he wants his Danny."

"Who's he belong to?" he asked, though it was obvious she was talking about a child. He wanted more info. A name. A hint of who the *child* belonged to.

She stroked the dragon's tail for a moment, then snapped back to her former militant posture. "I expect she'll be waiting. I won't keep you."

He nodded, understanding the topic of Danny's owner was now closed for discussion. "Could you point me in the right direction?"

She waved a hand toward a closed door off of the sitting area which boasted fine leather couches, oversized armchairs that invited you to sink in, and a fireplace. Oh, and an infant swing designed to look like an elephant. He chuckled at that. All the fancier surroundings, the posh furniture, the large watercolors, and abstract art hanging on the walls . . . and a child's toy. The two seemed in contrast, but he appreciated it. Made the area seem more approachable.

He knocked on the door, which was cracked a bit, and heard a feminine voice bid him enter. And walking in, he paused a moment to watch her work.

Peyton Muldoon, little queen of her realm, sat behind a

large oak desk that dwarfed her. The desk was obviously built for work, not show, though it was an attractive piece of furniture in itself. Bookshelves lined one entire wall, and he saw all manner of books sitting there. From veterinary help manuals to horse genealogy to . . . was that the latest best-selling thriller novel?

Peyton Muldoon. So many layers.

"Done studying my office?"

Her words jarred him back to the present. "Sure am." Why bother denying?

She sat back, laced her fingers together over her stomach. One of her braids, which made her hair look even darker than usual, flipped over her shoulder. "You probably know what I'm going to say."

He sat down in the chair opposite and mirrored her posture. "How about we not go down the assumption road and just talk in real time?"

"Fine. I'm offering you the job."

"Done."

"Comes with the trainer room, which is an apartment built over the equipment barn. Sounds primitive but it's actually pretty nice."

"Works for me." An apartment within arm's reach of the facility, where he wouldn't have to fight off bedbugs or be awoken by the prostitute next door with her john at three in the morning? It was his childhood dream come true. Not that she needed to know that.

Leaning forward, she pushed a paper across the desk. "Here's the salary information, as well as the other typical hiring info you'll need."

He was supposed to be grabbing for the paper. But instead he couldn't stop looking at her shirt to see if it was a figment of his imagination, or did he catch a hint of her cleavage when she leaned over . . .

"Callahan."

"Hmm?"

She gave him a sugary smile. "Like I said before, the pay's likely not what you're used to."

She thought he'd been staring at the hiring information, not her chest. Good enough for him. "I'm fine with it. Don't need much. Place to park my trailer and somewhere to set my boots at night."

One disbelieving brow winged up. "Not going to negotiate better pay? Better benefits?"

"There are no benefits."

"As I said . . ." She sighed and raised her hands. "Fine. Here's the contract. Go ahead and sign your life away." As he reached for the second paper she slid across the desk, she snatched it back, paper fluttering in the air. He looked up into her eyes, all kidding and amusement gone. "You realize this is a permanent position we're offering. Not one of your *here today, gone tomorrow* gigs? You're being brought in to build the brand. Not just fix a singular problem."

"Yeah. I know." His hand snaked out and tried to pull the paper, but she held it firmly.

"If you get a better offer next week and quit on me, I'm not going to be happy. There's an easy-out clause in here, despite my better judgment, but my lawyer insisted it was for both our benefits. And I'm gonna be pissed if you use it soon after starting."

"You don't seem all that happy with me right now." He tugged again, but it was like she'd glued the page to the wood. "I need this back so I can sign it, you know."

"Right." She let up and settled back. And, he couldn't help but notice, she watched with an eagle eye as his pen scratched across the surface of the page with his signature and date.

"Good. Now that that's done, time for a tour." She stood and grabbed her hat from one of the bookshelves.

As she walked by him, he was eye level with her waist. Dang, she was a tiny thing.

She turned to open the door, and he got a nice view of her backside.

Not tiny everywhere. Curves where it counted. He liked that in a woman.

"Let's go, cowboy. I've got things to do later on."

He debated a moment telling her he'd already done his research, knew the general outline of the ranch. But that seemed imprudent, so he meekly stood and followed her out, slipping on his boots next to her at the front door and following her out toward the stables.

With a view like that, he might just follow her off a cliff.

"So what did you think of the place?"

During their tour, Peyton had spoken with such pride, such loyalty to her ranch. And she did have reason to be pleased, Red could admit.

"Nice area, big but not unmanageable. Seems like your staff knows what they're doing"—though he'd double-check that himself—"and clean. I highly recommend investing in some surveillance cameras in the breeding section, especially in the foaling stalls. Owners like the security, and it makes the operation easier to monitor." He smiled a little. "Upgrades matter to potential buyers, whether you're talking about cars or horses."

She scowled as she approached a building at the back of the property, the last in a circle of buildings that made up the business. "I know. They're just expensive. It's on the list. And finally," she said, her tone telling him she wasn't about to go into the budget with him, "we have the equipment garage." Peyton yanked hard on the door handle to the large building, sliding the door along the dirty floor with effort.

Red would offer to help, but knowing Peyton, she'd

bite him. So he slipped his hands in his pockets and rocked back on his heels, waiting patiently.

"I hate when you do that." She dusted her hands off on the thighs of her jeans and shook her head.

"Do what?"

"Do that patient thing." She waved a hand at his body like that was going to give him any clues. "The whole 'I could stand here all day, I'm fine' thing. Nobody has that much patience."

"I hear it's a virtue, especially working with the stock."

"Well, you're not with animals now. You're with a human." She stepped inside, into the much cooler, shady interior of the barn.

"Yes, I am." Though after spending a good hour in her presence, he was feeling a little animalistic himself.

"Here's where we keep all the big equipment. Also where all the ranch trucks and trailers go at the end of the night." She turned a tight circle. "Though we're thinking of building a smaller one, more garage-style, for just the trucks. Seems impractical to have them settling in next to the tractors."

"If you want an opinion on where to put the building, let me know," he offered mildly.

She gave him a surprised glance, but nodded. "Thanks. Over on that side of the barn, on the outside, there's a set of stairs that lead up to your apartment. Remind me to give you the key later."

"Will do."

"Peyton? You in here?"

Both turned, but looking out from the darkened barn with the sun shining at the angle it was, it was impossible for Red to see who the visitor was.

Not that Peyton needed any help identifying the man. "Hey, Morgan. Come on in."

A man probably in his thirties, taller than Red by at least

two inches but definitely lankier, stepped forward. Long legs carried him in a few steps to Peyton's side. His shirt was new looking, though dusty. And he wore a pair of glasses that looked smudged with dirt.

And he was vaguely familiar, though Red struggled to nail down where he'd seen him before.

"Oh my Lord, you're a mess." Peyton laughed and reached up for his face. The man clearly knew what she was up to, because he bent over enough to give her access. Plucking the glasses off his face, she patted his cheek and started cleaning the lenses off with the corner of her shirt. As she lifted the material up, Red got a glimpse of smooth skin and a hint of rib before she let the cotton go to hand the glasses back.

"Thanks. Thought it looked a little darker today than it should have." He finally—finally—noticed Red standing there like an idiot and held out a hand. "Morgan Browning."

Ah. Now it clicked. One of the area's large breed vets. And apparently, close personal friend of Peyton Muldoon's. "Red Callahan." He shook, feeling like a third wheel and hating the way Peyton smiled at the man. And feeling five kinds of fool that he hated it at all.

"Horse trainer, right? I thought you were over at Three Trees now." Morgan stuffed his hands in his pockets, smiling easily.

"Finished up there. Now I'm here. With Peyton," he added, for no reason at all.

"He's M-Star's trainer now," she clarified when Morgan gave her a confused look. To Red, she added, "Morgan's our vet, so you'll likely get to see him around often enough."

"Convenient for all, since I just live down the way."

"With your parents," she put in with a laugh.

He scowled at her. "Why do you always have to put it

like that? I'm not living in their basement with my mom doing my laundry, thank you very much. I just live on the property. I built my own house on a corner, away from the main house," he explained to Red.

Red nodded, though it didn't matter much to him one way or another. Long as Morgan knew his job and Red could trust the guy with the animals, didn't matter if he lived in a van off the highway. Though the distance was a convenience, to be sure.

"Wait, we didn't have an appointment. What had you stopping by?" Peyton asked.

"Came over to see Trace. Bastard called me, said he's been around for days and he just now lets me know."

"He's been a little busy," Peyton said sardonically.

"Sure has. Cute kid he's got."

She smiled. "Yeah, I lucked out with an adorable nephew."

Nephew. The kid wasn't hers, but Trace's. Interesting. Not that it mattered . . .

Oh hell, it mattered. It all mattered with Peyton. This was exactly what he'd been trying to avoid by not taking the job in the first damn place. Lusting after your boss was an easy way to kill your job, and your reputation.

Time to pull his head out and get started on work.

"If you two don't mind, I'm going to head over to the office and get started on figuring out the filing system, getting things in order, that sort of thing."

Peyton nodded. "Sounds good. Remember to stop by the office for your key later. If I'm not there, I'll leave it with Emma."

He waved good-bye and headed back for the arena and his own office. Something had to cut through the edge of this lust fast. And paperwork was a surefire way to dull his senses, inside and out.

Chapter Five

Peyton watched as Red sauntered out of the barn and toward the training arena where his office was attached. And yeah, sauntered was the only way to describe how he walked. Deceptively easy, as if he didn't have a care in the world and no purpose. But she knew better.

"So that's the new trainer."

"Yup. Like you didn't already know that. Word travels around here too fast for you not to have heard."

"Maybe," he hedged.

She nudged Morgan with her knee, moving the conversation from owner-vet to friend-friend. "What's up with you?"

"Same old, same old. Mom says hi."

She smiled. "I'm gonna have to pop on over there again soon for some more of your mom's pie."

He groaned. "You keep doing that and my mom is going to have worse ideas about us than she already does."

She laughed, amused at the thought of making his life miserable. "Your mom loves you and wants you to settle down with a nice young lady."

"So why she wants me to marry you, God only knows," he shot back.

"I'm convenient and in her line of vision. She'll see it eventually. I'm not for you. You're not for me."

"Too damn bad that never clicked, huh?" He reached out and gave her a brotherly tug on one of her braids. "Convenience factor is through the roof."

Swatting his hand away, she rolled her eyes. "Convenience. Just what every woman is dying to hear."

"You gonna tell me the whole story about hiring Red there?"

With a shrug, she started over toward the stables. Pausing to shut the barn door, she said, "He's our new trainer. We need help. And he's got the reputation to bring people running. Nothing more to it."

After watching her struggle for a moment, Morgan sighed and reached over her shoulder to yank the door. Once started, she was able to slide it shut on her own.

"I thought he never stayed in one place long enough to be associated with one particular outfit. Just a problem fixer and a roamer."

"Maybe I offered him a deal he couldn't refuse." They both knew that was a lie. She hooked an arm through his and tugged him along. "You little snake. What's going on in that mind of yours?"

He grinned. "You don't even wanna know."

"True enough."

His expression grew serious and he hugged her closer. "Just be careful. I'm sure he's a good guy and all. Never heard a bad word about him. But, you know. I'm sorta fond of you."

"Convenience," she sang mockingly.

"Like a sister," he added with a pinch to her ribs. She shrieked and jumped out of arm's reach. "I don't want you to get hurt. Financially, or any other way."

"There's no risk here. He's got the goods." No need to mention she'd be counting the goods he packaged in sexy denim in that mix. "He can deliver. So we're using his name and riding it. It's mutually beneficial. Maybe he's ready to settle down for a while."

"Hmm." Far from sounding convinced, Morgan fell back in step with her.

"While you're here, you mind checking on a colt?"

"You're just using me for my medical bag," he said, his fake pout making him look like an adorable little boy rather than a grown man.

"You bet. I'm a user, baby. Now go get your sexy black bag from your truck. I know you have it with you. I'll meet you in the stall."

With a push, he laughed and loped off easily, long legs carrying him over the distance of the yard with a speed she could only envy.

Being short was so annoying.

More annoying was the fact that she'd missed walking to the stables with Red. After having him around all morning, she was used to his questions, his comments. His presence. Not just annoying, but stupid. She had zero right to get attached to the man like that. It was business between them and nothing more.

A woman in a man's world didn't have room for flings with coworkers. It never ended well. And if the word got out, nobody would take her seriously. Already she had her youth and the ranch's current reputation against her. Personal issues couldn't be added. There was no margin for error anymore.

As she stepped into the stable and saw a number of fuzzy heads pop out over their stall doors to greet her, she knew she'd do almost anything to keep their family ranch afloat.

Just before dawn was his favorite time of day. When things were quiet, people were still asleep, and only the animals could hear him. The air was cooler, sweeter almost, as if the lack of activity kept it pure, and the soft light from the rising sun made everything look a little more romantic.

Not that he was about to admit any of that. A poet, he was not. But as Red dressed for the day, he knew it didn't take a poet to appreciate the fact that he all but had the entire ranch to himself. Which was why he was always up early. Partly to have the day to himself. Some people needed coffee to get their day started right. He just needed a few minutes of quiet.

Of course, since it was his first full day at M-Star, he wouldn't mind the time alone to get his feet under him, either.

But, to his shock, as he headed to the stables, he realized he wasn't the only one up that morning. Not by a long shot. The stables buzzed with activity. The day workers were already bringing feed and water to the horses. Two were being led to the hot walk ring.

In the barn, he found the man named Tiny, a man likely in his late forties and starting to develop the middle age spread around his waist, brushing a mare, crooning to her like she was a lover he wanted to coax back into bed rather than a seven-hundred pound temperamental horse trying to take a chunk out of his butt for his trouble.

"Now, sweetheart, you know it feels good," he said, his voice still gravelly with sleep. "Why do we gotta go through this every morning?"

Red leaned against the outer stall post and watched as his competent hands worked quickly, efficiently, getting the job done while nimbly avoiding the snipping teeth.

"Got your hands full," he commented idly when Tiny caught sight of him from the corner of his eye.

"She's got fight in 'er. But I've always been partial to the ones with fight." Tiny smiled and patted the mare's neck, jerking his hand away a second before teeth clipped where it had just been. "Destiny here's one of our best breeders. Puts out the feisty fillies and the arrogant colts."

She wasn't much of a looker as far as coloring went, but Red could always see past that. Sometimes the sheer spirit of a horse mattered most.

"People always up and around this early?"

"Mostly. Work goes in shifts. You got the few of us up here now, getting the day started. Few more show up in a couple hours, then we're off and the latecomers stay through the day."

"You like working for M-Star?"

Tiny gave him the side eye. "This an interview?"

"Not at all. Trying to get a feel for things."

Tiny was quiet for a moment, the only sound the shuffling of the horse's hooves in the hay and the brush smoothing over her flanks. "Working for Peyton's mama was a hell of its own kind, for just about everyone. But her daddy was always a good man, good to the staff, though I think he had more heart than business sense. The horses were his life. The books, not so much."

It jived with everything else he'd heard about the ranch.

"I like working for Peyton. Kid's nearly half my age and knows what she's doing. Got ideas to expand, wants to make this place a real draw. Not just survive."

Red nodded. "I'm just gonna observe, find the rhythm for the day." He wasn't asking permission, but smiled when Tiny nodded and went back to cooing at his four-legged female companion.

Three hours later, he made his way to his office, having developed a sense of how things were run. A few things he would change. But the basic flow was something he appreciated. What he appreciated even more was that he continually caught glimpses of Peyton from the corner of his eye. Walking this way, talking to that hand, checking on a horse or slipping treats when she thought nobody was watching. An owner in the middle of things, not just sitting on her throne away from the dirty work.

Heading back to his office, he flipped through the books, comparing the figures from several years ago, the trainer before Nylen, and then all of Nylen's records. And one glaring inconsistency popped out, over and over again.

"Damn." The man had been systematically skimming from the feed fund. It wasn't the first time Red had seen it. But to this level . . . another story entirely. Anyone who took five minutes to double check his records would have seen this. The arrogant bastard hadn't even bothered to do more than a half-assed job hiding it.

A knock at the open door had him looking up. Peyton stood at the threshold, waiting for him to ask her in, a small smile tilting her lips.

Damn. Again. She looked fresh and flustered all at once. Her face was free of makeup, hair in those pigtail braids that fit under her hat. But she was dusty, and had a smear of dirt over one cheek, like she'd wiped at her face with her sleeve and only made the problem worse.

And if she were any other woman, and he were any other man, he'd jerk her inside, slam the door shut, and give himself a lunch hour to remember.

"Can I come in?"

"Yeah. Sure." *Please leave the door open. I can't handle the temptation.*

As if reading his mind, she did. She propped one hip on the corner of his desk, completely unaware that it put her very delicious looking ass within touching distance. He balled one fist against his thigh and kept his voice light. "What can I do for you?"

"I wanted to make sure you were settling in okay. That the guys were all treating you well enough, being helpful."

The lightness of her voice caught him off guard. It was

as if she was determined to play nice. He could get behind that game plan. "I do have one question, actually. Did anyone ever check over Nylen's books while he was around?"

Her easygoing smile faded and her mouth set in a hard, grim line. "No. Not that I know of. I asked once or twice to check, but I was denied."

"And you let him get away with that?" he asked, then immediately regretted it when fire flashed in her eyes. "You're the owner."

"Now, I am. Until two months ago, I had no authority on this place. It was the Sylvia Muldoon show, nonstop." She stood quickly, the rickety desk shifting a little under her push off. "I asked, he said no. He kept the door locked when he wasn't around. And my mother was sleeping with the jackass, so she wasn't exactly much help either."

That was news.

She laughed at his wide-eyed surprise. "Right. That one hasn't made the rounds yet, and I doubt many would be suspicious, since Nylen wasn't really up to my mom's usual standard. But apparently Mama was desperate. Or maybe he was passing out kickbacks on what he skimmed." She nodded. "Yeah, I knew. Or suspected anyway. But without the books, no way to know for sure. Plus, what was I going to do about it? Not my ranch, legally. Once my mother was gone, I managed to get the key and came in here to look. Found the proof I needed, told him to get his sorry ass out of town."

He settled back, trying to quickly make sense of the whole thing. "Why not involve the police?"

"I just wanted him gone."

"It's not too late." He lifted the book in his hand. "You report him, and we might at least get some of this money back."

Her eyes narrowed. "And risk having the word out

there? It already looks bad enough he left so quickly. I don't need more negative press. We're struggling to rise from the ashes as it is." Leaning over, she placed her palms on the desk and closed in until she was inches from his face. "Before my mother died, I was blocked from every opportunity to make this place better. Now that she's gone, I still don't have full authority, thanks to my two siblings. But I did my best then. And I'm doing my best now."

With that parting shot, she stood and walked out, shutting the door behind her.

Oddly, the action was not nearly as erotic when she was on the other side of it.

And hell, he'd just screwed that one to Kansas and back. She was still touchy on the subject, and he couldn't blame her. She'd see it as the ultimate slap in the face that someone was stealing out from under her nose and she had no control over it. He hadn't meant to accuse, just to get a handle on how it'd gone on for so long. But it was obviously still a raw wound. And knowing he'd inadvertently poured salt into that wound tore at his gut in ways he didn't quite understand.

Time to make amends.

Peyton let Lilly Mae's graying nose snuffle under her arm in search of more treats even though it tickled. Wrapping her arms around the old horse's neck, she breathed in the familiar scent of horse and hay and feed and instantly felt her heart rate drop from its formerly racing status.

"Big mistake," she muttered into the horse's mane. "I let him get to me. Lost my cool. Stupid."

Lilly Mae made a soft nickering sound in response. Peyton smiled and decided to take the noise as an *It's okay, you'll do better next time.*

"She's sweet."

Her skin prickled at the sound of Red's voice, but she didn't look up. A new tension momentarily vibrated through Lilly Mae's muscles, but she calmed down quickly when there was no threat.

"She's mine." With a scratch between the ears, she stepped back and grabbed a brush, intent on doing something with her hands while they talked. "I've had her almost my whole life. Learned to ride on her. She's ancient, but she's my favorite." Leaning forward, she mock whispered, "Don't tell the other girls," into Lilly's ear.

Red chuckled and stepped forward cautiously, holding out a hand for Lilly Mae to sniff and nuzzle. "Nice. Bet you're the queen around here, aren't you?"

Peyton took it as the peace offering it was. "I sure am. Oh, you meant Lilly." She grinned when he smiled.

"Thought I might find you riding some two-year-old around the ring for a hard workout to work off the tension."

"Too pissed for that. Does nobody any good when you can't keep a cool head to train a stubborn horse. Especially an arrogant two-year-old."

"Glad to hear it. Good instincts." Lilly Mae stepped forward, bumping into him hard enough to send him back a step, shoulder hitting the nearest wooden post. "Well, hey now. I didn't mean to ignore you, I'm sorry." He scratched her between the ears, smoothing down to her nose where he rubbed with gentle thumbs. Lilly Mae sighed with delight and took another step into him, all but snuggling against his chest.

"Floozy," Peyton muttered.

Red just grinned. "The ladies know what they like."

She rolled her eyes, but watched from behind lowered lashes as he charmed her horse. He had such gentle hands, not at all like Nylen's. Strong, she knew they could control a horse with a simple tug of one rein, distract a rearing stallion with one wave. But then lovingly caress the velvety softness of a sweet old mare well past her prime.

Lilly Mae's rump bumped her and she snapped out of the trance. Admiring his hands? Jesus, what was her deal?

"I'm sorry. I never meant to imply you weren't doing your job or taking things seriously. Just trying to get a handle on the situation around the ranch."

Peyton nodded and tapped the brush against her thigh, stirring the dust a little. "I realized that after about five minutes. It's still sore with me, here." She fisted one hand against her breast bone and tapped once. "But I'm working on it."

Another minute passed with only Lilly Mae's rhythmic breathing and happy snuffling to break the silence.

"I haven't seen the outer perimeter of the ranch yet. Wanna saddle up and show me around?"

A leisurely ride to get her mind off things, give her some time to compose herself and still get ranch business done? Sign her up.

"Yes, Mr. Schneider. Absolutely. No, all our work is done out in the open. You're more than welcome to come on over and take a peek." Peyton tapped the edge of her pen on the desk, listening to the potential client's hemming and hawing. "Naturally. We have an open door policy to all potential clients. Yes, I realize not all—yes, this is a new policy. I understand we were more closed up in the past."

Back when Mommy Dearest was running things.

After another moment of the man's indecision, she sighed and dropped the pen. "Have you met our new trainer yet? Redford Calla—yes. That Red. Uh huh. Same one."

She rubbed at the throbbing between her temples with her thumb and forefinger.

"Of course. I'm sure Red would love to speak with you on that subject. Not a problem. Let me patch you over to his office phone. If he's not in, you can leave a voicemail for him. Does that sound all right? Excellent, hold on just one moment."

Peyton clicked hold, then a few more buttons to send Mr. Schneider over to Red's office phone. Odds were, he wouldn't be in, but the voicemail system always made people feel like the M-Star was a more legitimate business. She never understood why. Jotting down the question and the man's name and phone number just in case the phone system failed, she pinned it to her corkboard as a reminder to pass off to Red when she ran into him next.

Emma walked in just as she was making a final note for her own records about the call. "Potential client?"

"Yup. Wasn't overly certain about things until I mentioned Red's name. Then it was all 'Oh, that's great! When can I come by? Can't wait to get there!' " Peyton snorted. "The man doesn't even sound like he knows which way to saddle a horse, but he's heard of Red and suddenly we're sent from the bottom of the barrel to the top of his list." It still burned that she had to use someone else's reputation to bump her own. But she'd do what she had to.

Emma wiped her hands on the apron tied around her waist and eyed her. "Correct me if I'm wrong, but wasn't that the entire purpose of hiring Redford?"

Peyton smiled. "You know, I think you're the only person who calls him that on a casual basis."

"It's his name, isn't it?"

"That it is. And yes. It's why we hired him. And he's done some amazing work in the last two weeks." The fact that Peyton had been sneaking over to watch him work with the horses more than she should have been was only a little lowering. "It's just a bit humbling, being reminded that our own reputation isn't doing the job."

"That'll change," Emma assured her. "Now, do me a favor and take a tray up to your brother."

"He's got legs," she whined in a childlike voice. "Make him come down and get it."

"He's got Seth with him upstairs. Be a good sister and just run it up."

"Fine," she muttered, but inwardly was pleased to see the baby. Not that she'd admit it, hell no. But that little boy was her new favorite thing in life. Except when he needed a diaper change. Her auntie skills only extended so far.

She passed by the living room to grab the tray in the kitchen, getting a glimpse of the training yard and Red working a yearling.

Seth isn't your only new favorite thing . . .

Ugh. Definitely not what she should be thinking right now. She grabbed the tray Emma had left on the kitchen counter and hustled back through the sitting area and toward the double stairs. She hated the first floor, except for the kitchen and her office. Her mother felt that the appearance of wealth was the way to woo potential customers, so she'd turned the place into a gaudy palace, with floors everyone was scared to walk on, uncomfortable furniture, and artwork nobody liked, simply because they looked—in Sylvia's word—artsy.

Peyton had another word for it. Ugly.

The upstairs, though, was the family's haven. Comfort reigned and the main purpose of the space was to be lived in. The staircases opened into the family living area, then broke off into several bedrooms.

Trace and Seth were sprawled on the carpeted floor of the family area. Well, Trace was sprawled. Seth lay facedown on a quilt spread out on the floor, screaming his head off and flailing his arms.

"Should he be eating the quilt like that? I think a nice bottle would be better, don't you?" She put the tray down on the coffee table and settled on the edge of the couch to watch.

"It's called tummy time. It's supposed to help with crawling and neck strength and crap," Trace replied testily. But when he reached out to rub his son's back, his movements were smooth and soft. "He's not a fan, but the book says it's good for him."

As she watched, Seth struggled to raise his head, arms helplessly pushing against the blanket to support his upper body. Tears streaked his cheeks and his gums were showing as he wailed in protest.

"What book was this, 101 Ways To Torment Your Child?"

"Okay, dude. All right. Come here." Rolling onto his back, Trace grabbed Seth and plopped him stomach-down over his chest so they were nose to nose. Instantly the crying stopped and a gurgle of happiness sounded.

"Why is it he hated being on his stomach on the blanket, but that's fine?"

"Face to face contact, best I can tell." Trace smiled and ran one fingertip down his son's cheek. "I don't really mind. I'd rather hang with the guy this way than listen to him cry anyway."

Watching the tender father-son moment had Peyton swallowing back tears. Being an aunt was something she hadn't thought of before, though she was catching on easily. A kid as cute as Seth made the aunt gig a no-brainer. Watching her brother as a father was a daily source of amazement. Not that he didn't have it in him. But knowing he was capable and seeing it in action were two totally different things.

The number of books he read on the subject of child-rearing was almost comical. He constantly asked Emma for her advice, which she was more than willing to impart. And he didn't try to foist the kid off on the older woman more than necessary, choosing to stay home rather than run wild in town at night. More than once she'd heard him singing a soft sweet country lullaby to Seth when he was fussy at night.

"Still not going to mention his mother?"

"Nope."

It'd become a daily question and answer session, and neither was angry when the other spoke their part. She figured eventually, he'd give up the goods. When he was good and ready.

He shifted a little, his voice dropping to a lower pitch. "I think I'm going to take Ninja with me to a smaller rodeo next weekend, if you don't mind. I've got a few guys who are coming through. Not many, it's small stakes. But I figure it'd be a good trial for me to figure out how to sell the biz without scaring people away. Plus," he added, rubbing a thumb over his son's downy, nearly bald head, "it's close by, so I'll only be gone overnight, I hope."

"Why not Lonestar? He's got better coloring, might catch more eyes. Plus, for roping, he stands at attention quicker."

"I've had more time with Ninja," he countered.

"Good point."

"Can you keep Seth? It's not fair for me to ask Emma to give up her weekend, and—"

"Say no more, brother." She watched as the child's eyes closed, and his mouth went slack. As if the mere sound of his father's voice and the rhythm of his chest rising and falling was enough to lull him to sleep. "I've got plenty of time for my favorite nephew."

"Thanks." They both watched as Seth's arm, normally ungainly and uncoordinated, slowly drifted up with precision and his thumb landed in his mouth. "I didn't think I'd enjoy being a dad this much," he whispered. "This wasn't the plan at all."

"Yeah." She leaned forward and traced one finger down the baby's back, rubbing circles over the onesie he wore. "Just wait until he's two."

Trace snorted softly. "Thanks."

"I'm your sister. It's my job."

Chapter Six

Peyton stumbled down the stairs at an ungodly early hour. No matter how many years she'd been doing it, or how many years she had to go, early mornings were not her thing. She dragged her heels through the kitchen, popping an English muffin in the toaster and regretting she didn't have time for one of Emma's full-course breakfasts.

The woman in question wandered in a moment later as she was slathering butter and jam over the bottom muffin, slapping the top over that and grabbing a paper towel to wrap it up in.

"That's not breakfast."

"It is when you're on the run." Peyton saluted her with the sandwich. "Where's the munchkin?"

"Still asleep." Emma motioned to the baby monitor clipped to her belt.

"If you've got that, where's Trace?"

"Your brother was up an hour ago. Said he wanted to get Red's opinion on the horse he's taking with him next weekend."

"Ah." She nodded and headed for the door to slip her boots on, the housekeeper hot on her heels.

"You gonna do anything about that man?"

She glanced back at Emma, one boot half on. "Which

one? There's about a dozen of them roaming around here at any given time."

Emma's face said she wasn't a stupid woman. "Don't give me that. Redford Callahan. That boy's a looker, sure as I'm standing here. Why, if I were thirty years younger, I'd—"

Peyton shoved the sandwich in her mouth and plugged her ears with her fingers, shaking her head violently and moaning around the muffin.

She watched as Emma laughed and turned back to the kitchen. With a final shudder, Peyton walked out the door and shut it quietly. Normally she'd let it slam behind her, but Seth had gotten her in the habit of taking care with doors. Pointing her boots in the direction of the training arena, she took a moment to take in a calming breath. Yes, mornings weren't her favorite. And yes, she'd still rather be snuggled in bed under her quilt, dreaming whatever she'd had on her mind before she woke with a smile on her lips and no clue what had put it there. But there was something to be said for the peace that came when the rest of the world wasn't quite awake yet.

She just wished she didn't have to be awake herself to experience it.

Nearing the barn, she heard the unmistakable sounds of Red calling out commands. She entered, waited for her eyes to adjust to the darkened interior after stepping out of the sun, and narrowed her eyes on Trace working to control a three-year-old paint named Lad—the horse she'd been working with recently, in hopes of using him in some cutting competitions.

Trace pulled the horse up to a full stop, both rider and animal's breath turning into steam in the cool morning air.

"Feel that?" Red asked quietly from his perch on top of the metal gate.

"No." Trace looked confused a moment before Lad

shied and took a few quick steps to the side before he could control him again.

"He signaled his discomfort before he made the move. That's when you have the chance to make the difference. Before they take flight or react. You have to be more in tune with the horse."

"Easier said than done when it's not your usual mount," Trace shot back, obviously annoyed.

"Course it is," Red replied easily, not at all bothered by the snippy attitude. "But that's your job as the rider. Wanna make you both look good? Pay attention. Still your own body, cancel out your own mind."

Trace shook his head but brought Lad to a full stop again. Peyton walked up quietly behind Red, listened to him talk to himself in low, almost nonexistent tones.

"There. Right there. The ears first, then the—yes. Yes. Now watch how his—got it." Jumping down from the rail, he approached horse and rider. "Much better. You felt it that time."

"Yeah." Trace gave Lad a nice pat on the neck. "Just had to do that mind thing you talked about first. Never thought about it that way before."

Wrapping one hand around the horse's bridle, Red nodded. "Most don't. You ride a horse long enough, you come to expect their moves. But a brand-new horse doesn't work that way. Gotta make the effort. Easier for me to see it on the ground sometimes."

"Nice work, you two." Impressed, Peyton bent at the waist, slid between two railings, and approached as well, coming to the other side of Lad. "I think this is the most still I've ever seen this guy."

"Just needs some attention. Don't you, boy?" Trace gave him another affectionate pat.

"Mind if I see you on Ninja next? I want to take a few

pictures to put up on the website before you head out to the event."

Trace glanced at Red before looking back at her. "Uh, right. First, we were thinking—well, actually I wasn't thinking but we started talking and then the topic got brought up— Actually it's more like—"

"He's taking Lad, not Ninja," Red cut in. "Might as well grab your camera since they'll be working for a while yet."

"What?" Blindsided, Peyton took a step back. "Is Ninja okay?"

"Yeah, he's fine," Trace assured her quickly. "It's just Red thought that Lad might give a more . . ." He shrugged. "You tell her, it was your idea."

Red smiled at the accusation in Trace's tone. "You were doing fine."

"Someone tell me something." When neither man spoke, she shoved one braid over her shoulder, away from her neck where it tickled. "We'd already decided on Ninja."

"I'm the expert you hired to help get things back on track."

"They're my horses. And Trace has been working with Ninja."

"It's my job."

Narrowing her eyes at him, she almost bit out a laugh when Red mirrored the expression back at her. "Trace?"

Trace held his hands up in the sign of surrender. "I'm staying out of this one."

Lad took a few quick steps to the left, bumping Red out of his way. Sensing the horse was picking up on her agitation, Peyton moved back a few more feet and tried a calming breath. "Let's take this into the office."

"Sure thing." Red released the bridle and made a circle motion with his hand. "Keep working on those circuits, and this time shut your mind off to the garbage and tune in to him. See how much better that works for you."

"Got it." Trace led Lad over to another corner of the ring as Peyton stalked off to the trainer office, Red trailing behind.

She waited until he shut the door and leaned against it, arms crossed, like he didn't have a care in the world. Oh, what she wouldn't give to kick his arrogant legs out from under him . . .

"I can't do my job if you don't trust me."

She stared at him a moment. "Trust?"

He nodded. "Trust."

"Huh." She walked to the side of his desk and stared at the blank wall. No pictures up, no framed awards or certificates. Nothing tangible to prove his success. Nothing that made the space his. "Trust is . . . not easy. I haven't been able to trust anyone with this place. Daddy, God bless him, wasn't sure what to do with the business. Mama was worthless. Nylen was a cheat and a jackass. When I could have used some help, my brother and sister took off. All the people in my life I was supposed to be able to trust. So sure, we can talk about trust until the cows come home. But in the end all you'll have is a pasture full of cows and nothing more. This place is my responsibility."

"And I can appreciate that. But you hired me for a reason. And it wasn't to stand around looking pretty and filling out forms. It's for the horses. I chose Lad for a reason. He's going to show better."

"He's not as experienced. Hasn't been tested before. Ninja's calmer."

"That's the problem. If Trace can keep Lad's focus straight, then the horse is going to show like nobody's business."

She scoffed. "And if he eases up for even a second?"

Red nodded. "Yeah, Lad will run away with him, I know. But Trace can handle it."

"So either a spectacular showing, or a dismal failure." She held out her hands. "You want me to bet our reputation on it."

"Your brother can handle it."

She ran a hand over the top of her hair, pushing the flyaway strands back from her face. "Go big or go home, huh?" She lifted one shoulder. "Trust. Fine. Let's go with it."

As she walked past him to open the office door, his quiet question stopped her in her tracks.

"How much did that just cost you?"

Hand frozen on the doorknob, she answered without turning around. "The price is dropping." Then she pushed through the door and left the training arena.

Red let his hat fall on the small table by the door of his apartment, too tired to bend over and replace it when it slid to the floor. Toeing one boot off, then the other, he kicked them under the same table to rest with his hat and padded to the kitchenette for a bottle of water.

Gulping half the bottle in one try, he wiped his mouth with one wrist, then looked around the small studio-style apartment. Something felt off.

Had he left that lamp on when he'd walked out the door that morning? He was almost positive he had dressed in the dark and left the same way. And his closet door was cracked open. And one dresser drawer. Walking suspiciously over to the closet, he realized his clothes had been shifted through. Boots on the floor—normally lined up in good order—were scattered and out of place. A few shirts were falling off their hangers. A box on the top shelf containing his buckles was tipped on its side.

Someone had most definitely done a half-assed job of rifling through his stuff. Though he'd be willing to bet they didn't find anything to steal.

If stealing was their main motivation in the first place . . .

His hand squeezed into a fist, plastic crinkling as it was smashed. He set the bottle down on the bedside table and returned the closet to its original tidy order, his temper rising with each minute that passed.

Dammit, this was his own private space. He didn't own the ranch or the stables or even his own office. But his living area was off limits. And the only other person who would have a key to his space would be the infernal Peyton Muldoon.

Not thinking twice, he stomped his feet back in the boots, grabbed his hat, and thundered back down the outside steps, around the barn and toward the house, where he assumed Peyton would be at this hour.

He was half right. He spotted her coming from the stables, angling the same direction as he was heading, back toward the house. But she wasn't alone. The tall vet was with her, and she all but bounced next to him, trying to keep up with his normal walking pace. Her braids tumbled down her back like whipped ropes.

"Pippi freaking Longstocking. Thinks she can just mess with my stuff anytime she wants." He slammed his hat down on his head and kept going until he was about to cut them off. "Muldoon."

She stopped, the vet stopping with her. "What's up, Red?"

"I need to talk to you about my apartment."

He watched her face for signs of guilt, worry, anything that would incriminate. But she merely tilted her head and asked, "Something wrong with the place? If something needs fixing, that'd be Arby's area. He'd know which one of the guys to send over."

Odd. He figured she'd have the world's worst poker face. He seemed as tuned to her moods as he'd told Trace to be with Lad's, whether he wanted to be or not. He'd drag it out of her though. "You could say that." To Browning, he nodded toward the vet's truck. "You could give us some privacy now."

Her eyes widened. "Red! That was rude."

Morgan just smiled and nodded. "No problem." He leaned over to whisper something in Peyton's ear, something that had her grinning, and had Red's hands balling into fists. Then with a mock tip of his hat, Morgan was off.

Peyton watched as he walked away—was she checking him out?—and waited until he was out of earshot before crossing her arms over her chest and staring at Red hard. "What was so important that you had to be completely rude to my favorite vet?"

"Favorite vet, huh? You know, it's not great to mix business with pleasure." Oh hell, this was absolutely not the route he wanted to take this conversation down.

If looks could murder, he'd be a cold son of a bitch on a slab. But while her eyes attempted to kill him from five feet away, her mouth curved in a sardonic smile. "Why thank you, good sir, for your kindly business recommendation. Why, we little ladies just don't know what we're doing out here in the big wild west."

"Can it, Muldoon." He reached out before he could talk himself out of it and snagged her elbow, pulling until she followed along behind.

"Slow down, cowboy, my legs aren't exactly as long as yours," she said on a pant. "Where the hell are you taking me? A cave? You're supposed to club me *before* you drag me there, you know."

"Do you ever stop talking?" he muttered, not expecting an answer.

Which was his mistake, because naturally she couldn't resist. "Talking is my favorite thing to do, just behind annoying conceited cowboys. Now where the hell are you . . . no. I'm not going up to your apartment. Tell me what's wrong with it, and I can send one of the guys to fix it."

He walked around under the stairs, where they were completely cut off from the rest of the ranch. He waited until she stepped back and tugged on her shirt to straighten it, taking more time than necessary to fuss with the thing. "I need to know why you were in my rooms."

"Huh?" An owlish look passed over her face. "When?"

"Today. Sometime this afternoon, I guess. Why? What were you looking for?"

She blinked once, twice. "Nothing."

"You found nothing?"

"No, I mean I wasn't looking for anything. Because I wasn't in your apartment. I didn't go up there. I never go in there. I don't have time to snoop. In case you missed it, I'm always around here doing work. Not to mention, it's rude."

"Damn right it is," he muttered, rubbing a hand over the back of his neck. Sure, she could be lying, but he really didn't think she had it in her to lie convincingly. Which was a good thing for him. But if she hadn't been in his place, then who the hell had?

Sensing his confusion, she pounced. "You want to falsely accuse me of something else while you're at it?"

"Who else has access to the keys?"

"Nobody. They're on my key ring, and it's always with me. I guess if Arby came to me saying something needed fixing, I'd trust him with them. But he hasn't." She shrugged. "I'm sorry you think someone was in there, but it's just not the case."

"What about the old trainer? Nylen?"

"He turned in his keys when he left. Threw them at me, actually," she ended with a mutter, rubbing at her arm as if that's where the metal had struck her.

Red fought back his temper, both at his privacy being violated, and the new, burning anger from thinking about Nylen hurting Peyton. He wanted to kick something for sounding like an idiot. Could it really be so simple as him looking for something to attack over, and finding it? "I'll apologize then, for accusing you."

She nodded. "Next time, maybe you could just wait a little bit first, think it through and make sure the hill you're standing on is worth dying for." She smiled a bit, looked over his shoulder into the distance. "Wow, my dad always used to say that, and it just slipped out completely by accident."

The transformation from tough-minded boss to soft, thoughtful woman punched him in the gut. It was clear the memory of her father superseded any anger she might have felt toward him. She looked almost worthy of a painting, with the fading light hitting her messy braids and framing her face like a halo. He stepped forward, not even aware of what he was doing until he crowded her space. She glanced up and looked startled, backing up until she bumped into the side of the garage.

"Guess I need a lesson of my own in trust, huh?" he asked. Was that his own voice? Lower than normal, a little husky around the edges like he'd had too much whisky and was feeling fine.

"Guess so," she answered, looking a little less like a cornered deer and more like a woman making an important decision. The sort of decision he hoped ended with *Yes, take me home.*

Would she yield if he pressed against her? Open up,

make room for his body in the shelter of her own? Or would she push, fight back, act like there was nothing going on and she wanted no part of it?

He'd be crazy to find out.

Just call him Crazy Callahan.

He was advancing too fast for her to think clearly. Her brain knew a quick sidestep and a shuffle to the right would have her away as fast as she wanted.

Her body didn't take the opportunity. No, instead it was trying to figure out whether it'd be better to stay where it was or lift her arms for better access.

"Crazy," he murmured.

"Hmm?" She tipped her head back, cursing the brim of her hat for blocking a good portion of her view. But she saw enough. Saw the intent telegraphed by those cool silver-gray eyes as easily as if he'd spoken his wants out loud.

And felt a quick burst of shock to realize their intensity was equaled by the tightening of her own nerves, the quickening of her own breath.

She took a chance and lifted her arms and—

Her phone rang.

Stepping back from her faster than if she were a rearing horse, Red gave her space to grab for her cell in her pocket. The realization that she'd almost made a huge, irreversible decision thanks to a healthy moment of lust had her fumbling with the phone, fighting to flip it open without dropping the thing.

"What?" she snapped.

There was a pause, then Emma's dry voice filled her ear. "Thought you might wanna know that fella you spoke to earlier this week, that Mr. Schneider, is on the phone. I've got him on hold. Figured you'd want to take it."

She growled deep in her throat at the timing of it all.

"Or I could tell him to call back later," Emma tried again.

"No." She bit the word off quickly. Dammit, she had no business even giving that a moment's thought. No way could she put off a potential client to stay behind the garage with Red and . . . what? Neck like teenagers? Hardly. "Don't. Tell him I'm coming right now." Closing the phone with a snap, she squeezed her eyes shut a moment to rid herself of the last feeling of hazy anticipation. Not the right time, and definitely not the right guy. When she opened up again, she saw Red standing a good ten feet away, hands in his pockets, posture relaxed. Not at all affected by what might have just happened.

Or maybe you imagined the whole damn thing and he never even considered making a move on you.

"I need to . . ." She pointed toward the direction of the main house, like that was going to tell him anything. But he seemed to get the hint because he nodded and fell in step with her.

"I'm sorry," he said quietly as they came to the stairs that led up to his apartment.

Apologizing for the almost-seduction? Maybe she hadn't imagined it after all . . .

"I had no right to accuse you like that."

Or not. She waved it off. "Don't worry about it. We're all a little on edge right now. I think after Trace gets back from a successful showing next weekend, we'll have a better rhythm down." In more ways than one.

"Agreed."

"It's Schneider on the phone. If he needs to talk to you, are you—"

"Just text me, I'll hustle over or call him right back." Red held up his cell to indicate he'd have it with him. He patted the railing of the stairs. "This is my stop."

"Goodnight, then."

"Peyton." He laid a hand on her arm when she would have continued on past him.

She cursed her skin that prickled under his completely innocent touch. "Yeah?"

"Schneider's an easy sell. Breathe."

Peyton realized her breath was still coming in fast pants, not from stress over the phone call, but leftover nerves from their almost-moment around the corner. But he'd given her an easy out. "Thanks. I've got it."

She turned and walked away, applauding herself when she made it halfway across the yard toward the house before indulging in a quick glance over her shoulder.

He was gone.

And that was good. Because she didn't have the time or the patience to deal with an infatuation. Where was her head? How could she possibly forget for even one minute that her entire life revolved around the ranch and keeping things afloat?

So what if being that close to Red had sent her body into a spin so intense she'd been ready to forget everything she'd worked for.

So what.

Chapter Seven

The morning after what Red privately thought of as the Stupid Almost Mistake with Peyton behind the garage, he finished in the stables and headed out to where he knew Lad and Trace were waiting in the arena. He'd asked them to work for a bit on their own without him watching, trying out the partnership with no outside interference. Building confidence in both rider and horse. Afterward, they'd work out the bugs together.

But when he approached, he noticed a stable hand holding Lad's bridle and Trace standing on the side, his back to Red.

"We'll just wait a few more minutes for Red to get here," Trace told the hand, who nodded.

"No waiting necessary. Taking a break?"

It was then Red realized Trace was wearing a harness or something that strapped over his shoulders. But when Trace turned around, that was no harness he'd ever seen before. Resting against Trace's chest, strapped down tight, was a sleeping baby.

"What the hell?"

Trace glanced down, then gave a shrug. "Emma's sick as a dog and can't keep him."

"Where's your sister then?" He didn't want to treat Peyton like a babysitter, and he knew she had important work to do. But this work was just as important, and without it, they'd *all* look like jackasses at the rodeo. Not to mention, it'd be easier for her to keep an eye on the munchkin in the house while she did paperwork than while Trace was riding, for cripes' sake.

"She's in town running errands."

"Convenient, that," he muttered. "Well . . ." He stared at the black harness that cradled the boy. It actually looked pretty ingenious, though he'd never admit that out loud. "What the hell kind of contraption is that?"

"A Bjorn." When Red gave him a look, he shrugged. "That's what Emma called it. She wears it when she's doing work around the house and he doesn't want to be put down. Suggested I use it while I get stuff done."

"That's all well and good, but you can't ride a horse wearing that thing." He glanced around, saw nobody else nearby but the ranch hand holding Lad's reins. "Can't we hand him over to someone else for now? Or put him down somewhere?"

Trace looked mildly horrified. "Put him down? He's not a sack of potatoes."

"Calm yourself down, Daddy. Lord," he muttered, taking his hat off and beating his leg with it. "What do you suggest, then?"

Trace started the complex process of unhooking the carrier thing and sliding it off his chest without so much as jostling the baby. Red bit back a smile. Trace might look like a rough cowboy, might have the rumored past to back it up. A buckle bunny at every rodeo, all that. But he loved his son in a way Red hadn't seen before, especially while doing it all on his own. Lot of men might take up a serious resentment toward their child for having to go it alone. He would know. His father'd been one of them. But Trace took to fatherhood like a duck to water, from what Red could see.

Trace muttered a soft oath and twisted his left arm until it was caught behind him, the right still supporting the child's weight against his chest. "Uh. Okay. I think I'm stuck. Little help here?"

A slightly awkward duck, then.

Chuckling, Red helped him slip the harness off from the back so Trace could keep a grip on the kid in front.

"So what's the plan?" Red frowned. "You can't afford to give up practice time. The two of you aren't entirely in sync yet. And you've only got a few days before you leave."

"Oh, I know that much. I figured it all out." He walked over to the side where a set of old aluminum bleachers were tucked against the wall, out of the way. A few more maneuvers and the child was out of the sling entirely. He set the harness down on a bench and cradled his son against his shoulder. "I'll ride. You hold him."

"You ride and I'll—oh no. Hell no." Red took a step back, bumping into the metal gate and wincing at the shriek it made. "You don't want me holding him. I don't know what I'm doing."

Understatement. Complete understatement.

"You'll be fine. You've got steady hands. It's easy. Look, he's asleep." Trace took another step toward him, smiling when Red countered with a step back. "You can't seriously be afraid of a tiny kid, right? You take on thousand pound animals all day."

"Any day of the week," he agreed easily. "But I know what I'm doing there. I'm a horse trainer, not a kid trainer."

"Good, cause he doesn't need training. Just holding." He paused. "You want to explain to Peyton why we showed shit this weekend? All because you were scared to hold a baby that was fast asleep the whole time?"

Damn. Dammit all to hell and back. "I'm not explaining crap. Show me how to not break him."

Trace transferred the lightweight bundle into his own arms—Jesus, humans actually started out this small?—explaining the few different ways to hold the kid without losing support of his head. "Use one of those holds and you'll be good." He peered at the sleeping infant cradled in his arms. "Just think of him like a football."

A perverse thought came over him. "Like a football? Somehow I'm thinking you don't want me to punt the kid." When Trace looked uneasy, he rolled his eyes. "Just go get on your horse, Muldoon," he said dryly, not moving a muscle. If he moved, he might jostle the kid and wake him up. And then, only God knew what came next.

"Loosen up," Trace advised, putting one boot in the stirrup and hauling himself up, settling into the saddle with the ease of someone who was born for it. He grinned down, showing some humor about the situation now. "Kids are like animals. They sense fear."

"Then this kid's gonna be sensing a lot," he muttered to himself. To Trace, he said, "Start your warm-up. And pay attention. The faster you get through this circuit without screwing up, the faster you're done."

"Yes, sir." With a mock tip of his hat, Trace turned Lad around to begin their warm-up.

Red watched for a bit, stiff and unsure. Then, when the kid didn't seem to realize someone besides his father was holding him, he grew bolder and started to walk a little, pacing the length of the short side of the arena, checking for better angles to watch the action. When that didn't disturb the child, he went all out and shifted him to his shoulder, settling with slow, steady movements until he found a position that was comfortable for both of them.

"He likes movement. Walking will keep him happier than standing still," Trace called as he made a quick turn, bringing Lad to a full stop, dust flying around the horse's legs.

"Works for me." Red wondered how the hell Trace would handle single fatherhood while working on the ranch. Great place to raise kids, sure. Wide open space to roam, lots of fresh air. Safe and secure. But most ranchers had wives. Someone who stayed home with the kids full-time. He had a sister, naturally, but she had a job of her own and couldn't always drop what she was doing.

No, he had two sisters, he corrected himself. Not that the other one was much help, living out in California.

And for reasons he didn't want to contemplate, that rankled him. That Peyton was carrying the whole load herself. Yes, Trace was helping now, but the majority of the business rested solely on her shoulders. Though she seemed comfortable with the responsibility, it was still a weight she carried alone. Where had her siblings been when she fought against her mama so hard for the right thing? After her mother's death, when she was dealing with grief and anger and a crooked trainer all at once?

Alone. And he hated that knowledge.

He heard the crunch of tires on the packed dirt and looked behind him. From the opened hanger-style doors, he could see Peyton's Jeep pull up. He turned back quickly to watch how Lad handled the extra distraction, but the horse was too busy playing to Trace's signals to even notice.

Excellent.

Peyton's door shut quietly and she approached. He didn't have to turn and watch to know it. He was as tuned in to her presence as Lad was to Trace's, humiliating as that was to admit.

"Aren't you just the sweetest picture," she purred, hopping up to stand on the lowest rung of the gate near him. "The perfect image of domesticity."

"Thank God you're here." Almost as if he realized there was a way out, the fear he'd originally felt when Trace handed over the precious bundle of baby boy bubbled back to the surface. He wasn't about to pretend any longer. It wasn't about showing he was capable of handling the kid. It was about getting the use of his arms back. "Here, take him."

Peyton shook her head and made no move to reach for the kid. "Nope. You're doing just fine. Getting the hang of it."

"I'm not getting the hang of anything." As if sensing his discomfort, the child shifted in his arms, a slow stretch, the way Red always felt in the morning as he woke up. "Okay, not funny anymore. He's waking up."

"Oh no." Peyton grinned at him. "Whatever will we do?"

"This isn't funny," he shot back. "I don't know what to do. Should I put him down?"

She sighed and smiled, rubbing a hand gently over the child's bald head. "Just keep doing what you're doing. You're fine." She gave him a questioning look. "Have you never held a baby before?"

"No. Never. Why should I start now?" Nearly hysterical, he edged toward her. "Just take him."

"But I think you look so cute," she teased, her voice rising a few octaves in what mimicked baby talk. "The baby is a great accessory. Really smoothes out those rough edges. Who's the cutest pretend daddy ever?"

Red's face and neck flushed. "Peyton . . ." Wait, she thought he had rough edges? "I think it's time for this kid to head to his favorite aunt."

"I have paperwork. And phone calls." Her brows lowered. "Where's Emma?"

"Sick." Which was what Red was about to be if this bundle woke up completely and realized he wasn't dear old dad.

Peyton sighed, then apparently decided to take pity on

him. She took another step up and swung easily over the gate despite her height disadvantage, slipping a hand between the baby and his chest and retrieving the kid. The moment he was gone, Red's chest felt cool, like it was missing something. But that was just the loss of heat, he rationalized.

He watched as Peyton cradled the child expertly. She touched a finger to his nose and he opened his eyes, giving her a gummy smile and grabbing for her hand. She smiled back and cooed a nonsense word, which delighted the kid into a giggle.

"Yes, you love your auntie, don't you? Who's your favorite? Me? I think so, too," she sang to him softly.

The coolness faded and warmth spread through his chest, swirling down into his gut the way a shot of good Jack did.

She was meant for this. All of it. Peyton Muldoon was a woman meant to have it all. The ranch she loved, and a family, too. If there was a woman alive who could keep the two running like a well-oiled John Deere, it was she.

For just a moment, he regretted he wasn't a family man. That his life had always been about being as loose and free as possible, from the moment he was born. He'd been destined to live the life of a wanderer. And it was the first time he could ever remember considering any other way.

"Red, quick question," Trace called from behind him.

He turned toward Trace, holding Lad at attention in the center of the ring, waiting for him.

"Yeah. Coming."

Peyton sat still on her bed, book open and ignored in her lap. The night was so quiet without Trace. She almost missed hearing the dull hum of the TV he left on after he passed out, sprawled over the couch like he had when he was a teen.

Funny how she'd gone from loving her solitude and privacy to missing her brother so ferociously in the span of a few weeks.

It was only one night. But she realized she wanted him back home. Which only served as a reminder that they were still one sibling short of a full house. Without thought, she reached for her cell phone and tried once again to reach Bea. Not surprising, she was sent straight to voicemail. But this time, she tried a different tact.

"Bea, it's me. I've asked you to come back so many times, I've lost count. I asked you to come back for Mama. For the ranch. For business. None of that worked. So I'll ask you to come back for me. I miss my sister. Plus, you have a nephew that is dying to meet his Auntie Bea. So come home, please? We need you."

She clicked the end call button, set the phone on the bed in front of her, and stared at it. Why, she had no clue. It wasn't like she expected Bea to hear the voicemail and immediately call back.

Okay, maybe she had. Just a little. But clearly that wasn't going to happen. She set the phone back on her nightstand, then heard Seth start to wake. Peyton checked the nightstand clock. Yup, midnight bottle time. Stuffing the cell in her sweatshirt pocket, she made her way to the mini-fridge in the family living area where they kept the overnight bottles pre-made. She retrieved Seth, changed his diaper, then settled down in the rocking chair Emma had found in the attic along with the crib and waited for him to finish eating.

Which he did, in ten minutes flat. "Greedy as your daddy when it comes to food, aren't you?" she teased softly, putting the child over her shoulder for a burp before laying him back down. But when he proved he wasn't ready to sleep just yet, she sat back in the rocker and gave up on the idea of heading to her room anytime soon.

"You're not so bad to have around, you know," she told him. "I'll admit, I wasn't sure how you'd fit in at first. But you proved me wrong. Even charmed that big old horse trainer, didn't you?" She snickered. "When you weren't busy scaring the piss out of him." She paused a moment, then added, "Don't say piss. Your daddy would skin me. I guess we'll keep you. Yup. You passed your trial run. Long as I don't have to wear that Bjorn thing. No, Auntie Peyton is not signing up for that one. No way. 'Cause Daddy looks silly wearing it, doesn't he? Yes, he does."

Her phone buzzed and she reached in her pocket to grab it.

"It's a text from your daddy." She read the text, then called Trace rather than attempting to text back with her arms full.

"Hey," he answered. "Thought you might be asleep already."

"Nope. I'm up, and so is little man. Wanna say hi?" She held the phone in front of Seth's face, who reached for the pretty glowing toy.

"Hey bud, you up again? Don't give Aunt Peyton any more trouble than you have to, okay?" He paused for a moment and she wondered if they'd been cut off. "Miss you, little man."

Oh, hell. Tears lodged in the back of her throat, and she had to swallow hard to push them down.

"Peyton? You still there?"

She put the phone back to her ear. "Yeah, sorry. I'm here."

"You okay? You sound funny. Are you getting what Emma had? Is Seth?"

"No, we're both fine. So you did well, huh?"

"First in our event," he said smugly. "Met up with a couple of guys I knew through the circuit, told them about the ranch, let one of them ride Lad a little. They were impressed we'd snagged Red Callahan, though neither thought we'd keep him around long enough to advertise him as our official trainer. But that'll come."

"Yes, it will."

"All in all, a good showing for us."

"Nicely played, Trace. Drive safe tomorrow morning, okay?"

"Sure thing. I'm hoping to get an early start, so I should be there before lunch."

They said their good-byes and hung up. Then Peyton looked to see Seth sound asleep in her arms. She stood slowly, walking with even, measured steps to the crib, and settled him down. On the way back to her own room, she did a silent shuffle of happiness that things were falling into place.

Red did his quick walk-through of the breeding stalls at the end of the stables. Designed to be converted into single stalls if necessary, the breeders were two stalls with the dividing wall removed. For their own safety, and the safety of the foal, the pregnant mares were separated from the others and kept in wider confines. Made getting in and out of there to help easy, and the larger space was a comfort for the mamas-to-be.

"Everything looking okay, Steve?" he asked the hand working quietly on polishing tack in the corner.

The young hand nodded. "Everything's fine. Though I think Suzy Q over there is ready to foal soon. Next few days, for sure." He used the rag in his hand to point toward the end stall.

Red walked over to see, and sure enough, Suzy Q was ready to rock and roll. There was a new alertness in her body, a tension he could read easily. She shifted back and forth, doing the pregnant shuffle across the floor of the stall to the other side, then back again. Her breath snorted in and out in impatient huffs, as if to convey her discomfort.

"I know, sweetheart. I know," he said in a soothing tone, though that was a bald-faced lie. What the hell did he know about being pregnant? But that's what all females wanted, to be understood. He pulled out half an apple and offered it, but she only looked at him, as if to say *What, you think that's going to make it all better?*

He chuckled. "I guess it won't. You'll be through it soon enough."

Walking back toward the other side, he stopped by Steve. "You're the one on duty tonight?"

"Yes, sir." The young man nodded emphatically, as if excited by the responsibility. Red wanted to warn him there was nothing exciting about sleeping in the barn, but he wouldn't ruin it for the youth.

"Call if anything starts going on. You know the signs, right?" It never failed; the mares always foaled in the middle of the night.

"I saw last year. I know what to watch for."

Red nodded, but left the back of the barn with a feeling of disquiet. Something wasn't completely well, though he couldn't say if it was the horse herself, or the lack of cameras that he wasn't used to, or his own mind. He sat by the front of the stables on a bale of hay, watching heads peek out at him curiously, waiting to see if he would bring food, or treats, or affection.

Peyton walked into the barn, nearly passing him by before realizing he was there and skidding to a halt. "Hey, you setting up shop or something?"

"Just thinking for a minute."

"I see." She walked to the nearest stall where a gelding

poked his head out, butting against her shoulder in an obvious ploy for some TLC. "Easy, sweetheart. I know you aren't a master in the world of flirting, but that trick doesn't work on the ladies."

Red snorted. "Like it matters to him. He's gelded."

"Still nice to have gentlemanly manners, isn't it, bud?" she cooed, rubbing between the horse's ears. They flickered in what was clearly a sign of pure happiness as he leaned more into her touch.

He wanted those hands sifting through his hair, scratching and scraping his own scalp. And dammit, no, he didn't. He didn't want that at all. Acting like a fool, taking that road. Red rolled his eyes at himself and stood. "I checked on the breeding stalls, and Suzy Q is close to dropping foal."

Peyton nodded absently, her hand sliding down to rub the horse's nose. "I saw her earlier. Tonight, tomorrow at the latest."

From what little he knew, females were a complex breed . . . no matter what species. He wasn't about to bet his money on any one of the fairer sex doing what she was expected to. But he nodded anyway. "The others will be close soon. I'd like to see the schedule of rotation on who stays in the barn overnight."

Peyton shrugged. "That's Arby's thing, so you can ask him."

He would. Then he shrugged in a mirror gesture of her own. "I know a few guys, if you want to call them in to do an analysis of the area, get quotes on how much it'd cost for the closed circuit cameras in here."

She watched him from the corner of her eye, and he already knew what she was thinking. So before she could break down her pride to ask—because that could take all damn day, knowing her stubborn ass—he added, "Free consultations. Just quotes."

She grimaced, as if hating that it even had to be said, but then she sighed. "Yeah. I know. It's something to think about. I know at Ten Fork they have alarm systems for when the ladies lie down. You probably wish we were more advanced."

He shrugged one shoulder. "It's different, that's all. Sometimes technology gets in the way. It doesn't—"

"Encourage you to trust your instincts?" Peyton finished, grinning. "I've always thought that, too. It's great and all, and I know we need the cameras, for marketing as well as sheer practicality. But sometimes I feel like we give too much power to the machines and not enough to ourselves."

Smart woman. At least to his way of thinking. "They all have instructions to call you and me both, right?"

"Yup. In that order." She gave him a cheeky smile.

As he walked away, he muttered, "Stubborn female." But he was smiling, in spite of himself.

The call at one in the morning shocked him out of a deep sleep.

The barn. Suzy Q.

He grabbed for his cell and answered while standing to grab the nearest pair of jeans he could find.

"Son! What's going on with you?"

"Da—Dad?" He stopped, one leg in his jeans, and sat down on the bed. Figured. It just figured Mac would wake him up when he needed sleep the most, to stay sharp when the call from the barn came.

"How many people you got calling you, son?" Mac's gruff voice asked.

"Too many to count," he replied, because being a smart-ass was easier than reminding his father he didn't like to be called *son*. It was too ironic a nickname, since his father resented parenthood more often than not.

"You wound me." The words were slightly slurred and Red rolled his eyes.

"What did you need, Dad?" He pulled the jeans off his leg and shifted to lie back on the bed, staring at the ceiling.

"I wasn't calling for anything. But now that you mention it, a couple hundred for—"

"No."

Mac sighed, taking the instant rejection philosophically. "I really called to see if you landed somewhere. Last we talked, you hadn't found a place yet."

"Yes, I found a place. And so no, I won't be taking you up on the offer to come out there with you." Just like he'd said the last time. Not that being told no ever had any effect whatsoever on Mac Callahan.

"That offer was ages ago. Jackass left me high and dry anyway. I wouldn't let you near him with a ten-foot pole."

"Uh huh." All of which was likely code for *I was drinking on the job and got caught.* Or maybe *I got into it with the law—again—and my employer wouldn't bail me out.* Or the old standby, *Things started going missing and they can't prove it was me . . . but I got let go anyway.*

Variety was the spice of life, as long as the spices were vaguely familiar.

"So I'm hoping you can point me in the right direction."

"Right direction for what?" Red turned to watch the clock tick another minute off. Another minute he wouldn't be sleeping, when being well-rested was integral to his job performance.

What was Peyton doing now? Sleeping? Reading? Thinking of him?

"Where you are, dummy. I need to know how to get there."

Red sat up again, staring into the dark his eyes hadn't quite adjusted to yet. "There . . . where?"

"Wherever you landed for work. I figure any place you found is bound to be a classy operation. Wouldn't kick a man while he's down, yeah? So the way I see it, they'd likely have another spot open for me, being your old man and all."

"No." Jesus Christ, no.

His father laughed, the same rusty sounding laugh he remembered from his childhood. Whether with a hooker in the room next door, conning someone out of their last paycheck, or hanging out with old friends, Mac was usually laughing. For someone who lived on the edge of the law, he had a lot of natural humor.

Maybe that's why Red found so little humorous.

"Boy, now that's not friendly. We can be a package deal. They're bound to trust your dad. Where do they think you got your skills?"

Not from his father, that was for damn sure. Though Mac wasn't terrible in the saddle, he wasn't going to win any rodeos. No, Red learned from practical application and dedication to what he loved.

"Not gonna happen, Dad. This isn't the place for you."

"Of course it is. My place is with my son."

He started to feel a moment of worry. Just a tiny little tic in the corner of his brain. And he knew it wasn't out of self-preservation. Though that was a consideration as well . . .

No, this was from a need to protect Peyton from his con-artist father. She was too far in the hole right now to dig herself out from another disappointment, another setback.

His phone beeped in his ear, and he pulled it away far enough to see the screen.

"Dad, I have to go. The barn is paging me."

"But what about—"

He disconnected the call without a second thought and switched lines. "Callahan."

"Suzy Q's ready," was all Steve said.

He grabbed his jeans and started pulling them on again, realizing they were backward before trying once more, this time the right way. Stuffing sockless feet into his boots, he grabbed his hat and the first shirt he could find, shoving his arms through the holes while jogging down the stairs.

Chapter Eight

Foaling, when going right, was a quick process. The whole thing could be over and done with in under thirty minutes. No time for Red to jack around with making sure he looked pretty for the event.

He jogged across the yard, heading straight for the barn. Peyton must have slept in her clothes, because she had beat him there and looked way more put together than he did.

She glanced at him as they headed to the back where the breeding stalls were. Her eyes lowered to his chest and held there. "You forget something?"

He glanced down and realized he'd forgotten to button up his shirt. "Shit. Sorry."

She smiled, more understanding than amused. "I know. Exciting. No matter how many times I witness it, it's exciting." She waited until he finished buttoning the bottom few buttons, then handed him a digital camera. "Keep the flash off, there's enough light in there. But take pictures."

He held the small digital camera in his large hand. "And what are you going to be doing?"

She lifted her own hand, wrapped around a small video camera. "Filming. Client will get both video and pictures to document the happy occasion."

Smart. Not to mention . . . "Helps in case anyone wants

to sue for wrongdoing." With the lack of video surveillance, it was a necessity.

She winked at him. "You got it." Their tones became more hushed the closer they got to the stall. Steve was already there, standing out of the way while Arby slid the door open just a little.

"She's on the far left," Arby said in a hushed, gravelly tone, tilting his head in that direction for emphasis.

"Thanks, Arby." As she passed by Steve, she gave him an affectionate pat on the arm before stepping in. Red clenched his teeth a little at the obviously lovesick look the young employee shot after her. Being no more than twenty-three, with the maturity to match an eighteen-year-old, Steve didn't have a shot in hell of making Peyton see him as a potential dating prospect. Red knew that well enough. Not to mention, he worked for her. But that didn't seem to make it any easier to not shoot daggers at the kid. Instead he followed Peyton into the stall, quickly taking his place as quietly as he could next to her on the floor, as far away from the laboring mare as possible.

They watched in silence, almost as if the world had left them behind and this stall was a little cocoon of life. Snapping pictures as often as possible, hoping some of them turned out well enough to use, he paused to glance at Peyton.

She balanced the small camera on her knee, pointed at the mare, but she watched over the top, not through the viewfinder. And her expression was one of awe. Totally focused on the process, not even registering his own presence.

After fifteen minutes, Suzy Q's breathing became more labored, and soon enough, he could see two hooves, then a head. Then, the difficult part over, the foal slid into the world. Once more, he glanced over to look at Peyton, and was shocked to see one tear rolling down her cheek. She

didn't wipe it away or pretend it didn't exist. To his surprise, she didn't seem at all embarrassed by it.

They stood together, by silent agreement, getting a better angle on the action as the new mommy cleaned her
baby.

She nodded to the door, and they shuffled out and shut
it behind them, Peyton keeping the camera trained on the
new family even then. She stepped on a bench and continued to film over the top rung as the little one tried to
find its legs, wobbling around before figuring out which
foot went where. Then he, or maybe she, snuggled next
to mama for a first meal. Red took picture after picture, a
little surprised to realize that the process felt much different from behind the camera. Or maybe it was the company.

Finally, she stepped down, closed her camera, and
pointed out of the barn. They walked out together, leaving Arby and Steve behind, before she let out a wild
whoop and jumped up and down.

Her grin was as wide as it could go, the single drying
tear track down her cheek shining silver in the moonlight.
"Holy shit, that never gets old!"

She started walking toward the house, and it seemed
natural to just follow. "Where was Browning? Don't you
need the vet here?"

She shook her head. "I've always felt like both mom
and baby do best when there's as few people present as
possible. Morgan lives about ten minutes away. Easy call to
make. The guy all but sleeps in his clothes during foaling
season. I'll call him first thing in the morning to come
over and give them a good checkup."

She opened the side door of the main house and waited
for him to walk through before following him and lock-
ing it behind her. They toed off their boots and headed for
the office, like it was something they did every night.

Ha. Right. But she walked behind her desk and held out a hand. He gave her the camera, and she went to work uploading the photos to her computer.

"I'll make a disc for them, with both the pics and the video. But for now, I know owners like to have a couple pictures as soon as possible, so I'll send a few of the best shots in an e-mail. Can't blame them for wanting to see right away."

Red sat in the chair opposite the desk and watched her work. Her fingers flew over the keyboard as she typed out a quick note to the owner explaining the details and up-loaded the pictures to attach to the message. Then she hit send, leaned back in the chair, and grinned like a loon.

"Done, done, and done." She spun in the chair once like a little kid. "Want something to drink? I'm way too jazzed to get back to sleep." She didn't wait for his answer before walking past him—no, more like floating—and heading toward the kitchen.

They crossed through the sitting area, with its furniture that looked like it'd never been sat on, past the fireplace that had probably never been used.

"My mother's taste," she said over her shoulder as they hit the kitchen. A decidedly homier room than the rest of the first floor.

"What?" He reached in the fridge behind her and grabbed a bottle of beer. Drinking on the job was never okay. But this was after hours. More like after-after hours.

"I noticed the way you were—you were—" She grunted as she worked on the twist top to her own bottle of beer, then sighed and gave up, holding it out to him. When he popped the top easily and handed it back, she rolled her eyes and took a swig. "Figures. Anyway, the decorating on the first floor. It's all Sylvia's doing. She thought the place needed to look like money to attract money."

"Did it work?" he asked mildly.

She raised a brow, then hitched herself up to sit on the countertop. "If it did, it was before I knew how checking accounts worked. But I'm guessing not." Her head dropped back to the cabinet behind her. "I've loved this place since I knew what it was. Since I realized what it meant to work for it, live for it. Breath it. It's in my blood." She hitched one shoulder. "Was never in Mama's. Or Bea's."

"Bea?"

"Beatrice. My sister. Our sister. I thought Trace had the fever, that he'd stick around. But he lit off at nineteen. This is the first he's been back, except for very short, sporadic visits." She took another sip of beer and let the bottle land back on the counter with a thud. "And why am I going over all this family history with you? Not at all interested, I'm sure."

He was interested. It involved her, and so he was interested. But as he wouldn't say that out loud—for risk of her kicking his nuts up into his throat—he stayed silent.

She stared out the window of the kitchen, overlooking the stables. The building they'd just come from. "This is what I want to do—no, what I need to do—for the rest of my life. You know when you find something like that?"

"I do."

"And you just can't shake it?"

"Yup."

"And it's like, if it doesn't work out, there's no plan B. No backup. No contingency plan. So you have to throw everything you've got into it. All your cards. No holding back." Her eyes glowed as she spoke, and he felt himself drifting closer, like a magnet drawn to its home base.

"So you don't think there's another option. And then things go to shit, and you suddenly wonder why you haven't been practical before this. All the practical people have a plan B. Why don't you?"

He slid another foot forward, moving silently over the tile floor, but it was as if she didn't even remember he was there anymore.

"And then you find the answer of how to keep your dream alive." She looked at him then, eyes bright and cutting straight through him with their clear honesty. "You were the answer, and I didn't even know the question at the time."

That did it. He broke. The adrenaline of the night, the cozy feel of snuggling up in the kitchen with his partner in crime, her words and the look in her eyes—they all mixed together to break every barrier he'd mentally placed between the two of them. Without thought, without plan, without any consideration to an alternative, he let his beer slide next to hers on the counter, framed her face in his hands, and kissed her like it was the last thing he was about to do before he died.

Zero expectations of how she'd handle it. That'd have required some forethought. But what he never would have expected, even with time to plan, was for her to throw herself into the kiss like a drowning woman grabbing onto a raft. No hesitation, not for Peyton Muldoon. She took everything he gave her, every ounce of his desire, and she shot it right back to him. A thin moan, caught low in her throat, escaped, and he couldn't take it any longer. He let his hands skim down to her waist, hauling her against him. Letting her feel the thickness growing behind his zipper. Her legs wrapped around him, heels digging into the backs of his thighs, tugging him even closer until he was flush against the counter, nowhere else to go.

Then, as suddenly as the storm gathered, it broke. She pulled back, gasping for breath, her legs unwrapping from around him and sliding to the front, nudging him away from her.

"Oh my God," she whispered, staring at him.

Yeah. She could say that again. He waited for her to yell at him, slap him, kick him. Something. But she just kept staring with that glazed expression of shock, like she couldn't get over what had just happened.

Which was his cue to leave. Let her figure it out. And then slap him in the morning.

Trying for nonchalant, he nodded to the bottles sitting side by side next to her hip. "Thanks for the beer." Then he turned and walked out of the kitchen toward the side door and out into the chilled night air, on the way back to his apartment.

Which would probably not be his much longer. He'd handed Peyton exactly what she needed to fire his ass on a silver platter. Not that he was worried about where he'd go. What he'd do. There was always a job lurking somewhere for him, even if he had to broaden his geographic search a little. No, the next thing wasn't the issue.

It was that he didn't want to leave.

Peyton woke with the feeling of sand in her eyes. Probably from the fact that she hadn't had them closed for more than an hour total in the past night. First with the foal being born, which was a perfectly exciting and acceptable reason to miss out on sleep.

Then, well . . .

Damn that man!

She'd said it to herself a thousand times. Rinsing her toothbrush out in the sink, she stared hard at her reflection. Mentally willing it to look less exhausted, less haunted.

No hope there.

She should never have brought him back to the house. That was the first mistake. Peyton walked back to her dresser and started braiding one side of her hair, using a tiny elastic band to hold it in place. But inviting him to the house wasn't the big problem. No, that was almost logical. It was business, mostly, at that point. Informing the owner the foal was born. Celebrating with a simple drink. People did it all the time. Good relationships with your staff were key to a smoothly running operation.

And then he'd done that Unthinkable Thing. And she'd liked it. Her hand paused while separating the other half of her hair into thirds. Oh God, it'd felt so good. She couldn't even remember a time when just kissing had been so arousing.

Her own fault, most likely, thanks to the fact that she'd barely dated since college. She just couldn't justify the time spent away from the ranch, not that the pickings were all that great in town anyway.

So maybe that's all it was. Geographic proximity and general hormones. For both of them. If he was a typical man, he'd likely skip out to town on his next night off, find some hoochie wearing a too-tight tube top and use her mercilessly.

She should probably feel sorry for the woman, but the quick pang of jealousy was just further indication that she had no business tangling with Redford Callahan.

Skipping down the stairs, she ran into the kitchen. "Morning, Emma."

"Morning. I knew you were running behind with lots to do, so I made a breakfast sandwich for you." She pointed to a plate on the counter, and Peyton almost moaned in gratitude at the English muffin stacked with egg and bacon and what looked like little bits of sausage, diced red pepper, and cheese.

"You are amazing. A goddess." She dropped a kiss on the older woman's cheek, then wrapped the sandwich in a paper towel. On the way out the door, she detoured to the sitting area, where her nephew lay on his back on a quilt on the floor, rattling a toy. "And you're pretty amazing, too." She bent down to press a kiss to his nose, inhaling his fresh powdery baby scent that she never quite understood how babies managed, then jogged out the door.

"Good morning, Tiny," she called as she walked in through the stables a minute later.

"Ha." The older man huffed as he dragged a feed bucket out of the storage area. "Hardly. You'd think they'd never seen a horse before."

She stopped in her tracks, taking a bite of the sandwich. "Who?"

"The hands." He tilted his head toward the end of the stables, where the breeding stalls were located. "Bunch of goo-goo eyed men. It's just a horse."

She followed his nod and saw several of her men huddled around the stall where their newborn foal resided. Taking a moment to appreciate the amusing fact that grown men were literally cooing over a baby, she walked behind them and cleared her throat. "Guess all the chores are done already?" she asked mildly.

Several guilty heads swiveled in her direction before manly throat clearing and other grunting occurred. A few of the men scratched at their necks or looked away, and Steve's face turned a bright pink. They dispersed, boots shuffling around her and out to the other stalls.

She stifled a laugh, then stepped up on a bucket to get a better view herself. The new little one was prancing almost in place, very proud of the fact that he had full control of his legs at less than twelve-hours-old.

She thought back to her nephew, who didn't even have control of his head quite yet, and laughed.

Morgan walked up next to her. "So this is the new bundle of joy, huh? He got a name yet?"

"Nope. When the owners tell me, then we'll know."

They watched in silence a little longer as he moved around the stall, content to explore his surroundings as long as mama was nearby. "He's got spirit."

Morgan nodded absently, pushing at his glasses a little with one finger. "I'll give him a checkup here in a minute, after I deal with this sprain. Any problems with the delivery?"

"Nope, she was a champ."

The colt walked over to his mother and butted his head against her leg, darting out of the way as soon as he could.

"Cocky little guy, isn't he?" Morgan asked humorously.

"Aren't all men?" she muttered.

"You wound me. I feel I need to stand up for my gender."

"Don't bother. Now, shoo." He took off to examine another horse, leaving her to watch the colt just a little longer. Naturally, she had an excuse. Just watching out for their investment, she reasoned with herself. Couldn't tell the client she'd just let the new baby flounder on his own. Tomorrow they'd turn baby and mama out into the pasture for some serious playtime. But now, she would just watch. Only for another minute or two . . .

"Good looking fella."

A minute too long. The hairs on the back of her neck stood at attention. With a deep breath, she nodded. "Yup. Client was pleased with him. Checked my e-mail this morning. They'll stop by later today to check on the two of them."

Red walked up next to her, draping his arms over the wall. Unlike her, he didn't need a bucket or anything else to stand on in order to see over the door. "Do they all leave the pregnant ones here?"

She shook her head, catching her hat before it fell off and into the stall. "Many just bring their mares here for

breeding, then take them back when pregnancy is confirmed. But not all of them have the time or resources to
handle their expanding ladies, so . . ." She gestured toward
the proud new mama.

Silence reigned for a moment.

"Ever considered AI?"

Artificial Insemination. She grimaced, though she didn't
mean to. "No. I know it has its uses, and that's fine. But
for us . . ." She sighed and rotated, turning her back to the
stall and leaning her shoulders against the wood. "I would
just rather keep some things the same. The mating process
here is as natural as we can make it, while still being safe.
With all the sweat, and the work it takes. The entire teasing game from the beginning, letting him know she's here,
she's the one for him but he can't have her quite yet. The
energy you get when he covers her, keeping on your toes
in case you have a biter and have to separate them. The
pheromones flying around the place . . ." She trailed off,
realizing what she'd said, how it'd come out. And she
glanced, horrified, at Red to see if he was even paying attention.

He was not just paying attention, but honed in on her
with an intensity she hadn't seen in a man's eyes . . . ever.
Like he might jump her the minute her back was turned,
pull her into an empty stall, and cover her like a stallion
with his mate, and damn whoever else was in the stables
and could hear them.

Jesus God in heaven. What had she started? Inching
away, she kept herself facing him. "So, I have . . . stuff.
Work. Things like that."

His eyes tracked her movements, and for a moment she
had the distinct impression of being hunted by Red. A
predator watching for any hint, any slight weakness to
pounce on and bring his prey down.

And it shouldn't turn her on, how intense he was. It should scare the crap out of her. But she felt it, felt it deep inside where she hid all her feminine, girly thoughts and wishes.

"So, let's get in there and see how our new guy is doing." Morgan stepped up, rubbing his hands together. Then, sensing the tension between the two, he paused and pushed his glasses up just a little. "Did I interrupt a conversation? I can come back in a few—"

"Nope." Red cut him off with the single word, but his eyes never left Peyton's. "We're done here." Then he turned and left without another word, without another heated glance in her direction.

Morgan whistled through his teeth. "Peyton, Peyton, Peyton."

"What?" she snapped, finally looking at her friend rather than the trainer walking away.

"You got it bad."

"What's 'it'?"

He poked her in the shoulder, hard. That's what she liked about Morgan. He didn't pull punches—figuratively—with her because she was a female. "Don't play coy. It doesn't fit under your hat."

She rolled her eyes. "Sorry for not being a dopey girl. And just for the record, I have nothing. Bad or otherwise."

"Liar, liar, Wranglers on fire," he sang, unlatching the stall door and sliding it open.

"Bite me."

"You're asking the wrong man, if I'm not mistaken."

Peyton walked away, flipping him the bird over her shoulder when he laughed.

Piss poor timing, Morgan.
Though Red had no clue what might have happened

had the vet not stepped in, he knew it was something important. Something he needed to explore.

The fact that he still had a job spoke volumes. Peyton might feel like he was their only shot, but that wasn't the truth. And she wasn't an idiot. There were other ways to get back on their feet. His reputation might get them there faster, but Peyton wasn't going to sacrifice her own dignity for it.

So she was keeping him around for some other reason.

Knowing he would do nobody any good, he checked with Tiny to see which horse might need some exercise, then saddled up the meanest of the group for a hard ride around the perimeter of the property. He needed the time to think about something other than her. And his mount was enjoying the challenge. Double advantage. Soon enough, his mind cleared and he had to focus his entire attention on keeping the animal in check. The ornery SOB—a five-year-old stallion named Salamander—kept him engaged the entire ride, testing his limits every step of the way.

But an hour later, when he rode back into the stable and started to dismount, his eyes automatically started scanning the area for Peyton.

Clearly he hadn't ridden hard enough, long enough. Probably no way to do that. He was screwed where that woman was concerned. Only confirmed his suspicions from the beginning. Which was why he'd tried to avoid taking the job in the first place.

Now look where it got him.

Trace walked up beside him, Ninja on a lead. "Did you clear your head yet?"

"Hmm?" Red led Salamander, who was trying to take a chunk out of his shoulder with his teeth, to his stall and started the process of unsaddling.

Trace followed suit with Ninja, who was across the way. "I started taking out Salamander when I need to clear my mind. He doesn't give a damn inch, you always have to be present with him. Helps take the mind off whatever it's working on."

"Oh. Right."

"Need to talk about it?"

Was he seriously going to have to have this conversation with her brother? Hell, no. "Nope. Nothing to talk about. How was Ninja?"

Trace smiled, the smile of a man who knew the score and wasn't going to push, even though he could. "Did well. Enjoyed the obstacles for sure. You were right to suggest cutting for this one. Not really my forte, though. That's Peyton's skill. She'll have some good shows with this horse under her."

His head nearly imploded with the sound of her name. He focused on brushing Salamander out.

"I think I need to head into town," said Trace, his voice breaking the silence of the barn.

The statement seemed rhetorical so Red said nothing.

"Want to come with?"

Red lifted his head. "Nope. I have a list though, if you don't mind stopping at the feed store."

Trace laughed and shook his head. "I didn't mean for an errand. I mean for the night. There's a new bar in town that wasn't here when I left all those years ago. I was going to go check it out. Get off the ranch for the night, kick the dust off my boots and forget about horses and business for a few hours. Sound like a plan?"

Red debated only for a moment before nodding once, decisively. "Absolutely."

Chapter Nine

In Red's experience, typical watering holes in a town Marshall's size consisted of a dying jukebox, a dart set missing most of the darts, and two types of beer. Tap, or bottle. The customers were always cowboys, looking to get away from something. Maybe the little woman back home. Or the fact that they were fifty and still working for someone else. The buckle that got away. And the atmosphere would always be dark and smoky, even if nobody smoked indoors anymore.

Jo's Place, as the sign above the front door proclaimed, looked from the outside to be another such watering hole. But stepping inside was a whole new experience. Light filled every inch, not a dark corner to be found. The air was clean, a little sweet smelling. Music played from a decent sound system. And there were women, more than a few. They sat scattered around, in groups or with a man. As the two men made their way to the bar, Red caught sight of more than one drink with a colorful umbrella sticking out.

But while the place clearly appealed to women, the decor was still country, nothing so feminine that would drive a man out the door. Brilliant.

Sitting down, he and Trace waited until a woman walked up, wearing a clean black polo with the bar's name embroidered over the breast pocket. Her long black hair swayed from a ponytail down between her shoulder blades, one black strand caught on the third earring in her right ear.

"What can I get you boys?"

"Bottle," Red said, then was shocked when she handed him a real menu, not a laminated piece of cardboard.

"Domestic is on the left, foreign to the right," she said, leaning in a little, pointing with one finger, the nail painted black.

"Bud for me," Trace drawled, his accent deepening. Red didn't miss the fact that Trace's eyes were glued to the woman's chest, which strained the front of her polo.

"Same," Red answered, handing the menu back. She flashed them both a genuine smile and turned, giving them a moment to appreciate the soft curves hidden under the uniform.

"This is not what I was expecting," Trace said quietly, looking around in awe. "From the few times I snuck in here before I left town, things have definitely changed."

"Disappointed?"

"Nope. Just different. But change is good." He waited until the server set the drinks on the bar. When he reached for his wallet, she shook her head.

"First timers, first round's on the house." With a wink she hurried down to the other side of the bar to take care of a man waving at her.

"How'd she know?" Trace asked. "We look just like every other guy in here."

Red shrugged and took a sip. No point asking questions when free beer was involved.

After a moment, Trace asked, "Mind if I give that a go?" He used his bottle to point at the pretty dark-haired bartender leaning over the front to talk to another patron.

She tucked a strand of hair behind her ear, more earrings in this one than the other.

"You have my blessing."

"Hmm." After his own sip, Trace went on. "Not at all interested? Someone else in here catch your eye?"

"Nope." To cut down the chitchat, Red slapped a hand on his shoulder. "I'm gonna strike up a round of pool. I saw a table in the back. Good luck."

Trace saluted him by raising his bottle, then turned back to study the bartender.

She, on the other hand, didn't spare him a second glance.

Good luck, Red thought again with amusement, making his way to the pool table sitting in a sectioned-off portion of the bar. He racked up the balls and started to chalk his stick. For a moment, he watched as Trace made every effort to catch the bartender's eye while trying to not be obvious. That had failure written all over it. At least, the way Trace was playing it tonight. Change up the game, change up the results.

The stick disappeared from his hand with a harsh tug. Turning, he came face to face with Sam Nylen. Just the bastard he'd love to meet in a dark alley for a fist-to-face conversation. If his own reputation wasn't rolled up with Peyton's—with the M-Star ranch total—he'd give it serious consideration. Instead, he forced a calm into his body and voice. "I think that was mine."

Nylen sneered at him. "Nancy boys get their toys taken away."

Rocking back on his heels, when he would rather be throwing a punch, Red said mildly, "It's always nice to share."

Holding the stick out, Nylen worked hard to look contrite. Red knew the game. The moment he reached for the stick, either the other man would yank it away again like a two-year-old or hit him. It was a toss-up. So he went for the third option—grab another stick from the rack against the wall. Reaching for the chalk, he asked, "So how are things, Nylen? Find work yet?"

"Piss off." Without asking, he leaned over and jabbed at the cue ball, sending it careening at the racked billiard balls, barely clipping the side and making a complete mess of the table. But apparently Nylen thought they were playing the game, because he stood back to watch Red line up a shot.

"Piss off's an interesting way to offer up a friendly game of pool." Red aimed his cue, pulled back slowly and connected right in the middle, knocking in a solid red. "Solids for me, looks like."

"I had a job. I had your job. Then Sylvia had to up and die on me."

"The woman was in a car accident," Red said dryly. "I don't think she did it on purpose." He had no love or admiration for the woman, knowing what she'd done to the ranch, and more important, to Peyton as a daughter. But respect for the dead was something he didn't take lightly.

"She left me without a job."

"Hardly." He paused to send another solid into the corner pocket. "I'm betting if Peyton was happy with your job performance, she wouldn't have let you go when she took over."

A look of satisfaction crossed Nylen's face. It made Red's stomach roil. "Her mama sure was happy with my performance. Didn't mind the work I did in the barn either." He threw his head back, hat falling to the floor as he laughed at what he seemed to think was the world's funniest joke.

Odd, since it had the opposite effect on Red. Quietly, he took another shot, but came up short and shifted away from the table to give Nylen room.

Nylen rushed through his turn again, doing nothing but creating more bizarre angles for them both to navigate. Red sighed and started calculating his turn . . . both with pool and the conversation.

"The way I figure it, that pretty Peyton was jealous."

Red managed to keep from throwing up on his boots at the thought. Barely. He took aim, pulled back on his stick, and winced when something hit the back of his leg from behind.

"Oh, sorry." Nylen stepped back. "Let my cue get away from me."

"Right," he muttered, then took the shot, not caring when he aimed wrong and sent the ball in the wrong direction.

"Her mama always had what Peyton wanted. The ranch. Control." Nylen wiggled his eyebrows. "Me."

"I'm sure that was very hard for her to bear," Red said, though Nylen didn't seem to catch the sarcasm.

"So when she had the chance, she canned my ass. Punishment for not taking her instead of her mother. No matter what she says, I know it was that."

Not because you were stealing? But hey, why be factual? Red knew now what Nylen was getting at. Covering his ass. Laying groundwork in case someone accused him at a later date of stealing. At least one or two other people had to be within earshot of the pool table.

"The fact is, I can see why you took the job," Nylen went on, rubbing chalk over his cue.

Now he was lost. He stared at Nylen, no clue how to advance from here.

"Wasn't no secret I was banging Sylvia. Shit, I'm sure everyone knew."

From the sounds of it, they did, yes. But how tasteful of him to remind everyone listening.

"The way I figure it, you saw the good deal I had going, and once I was out of the way, you wanted some of it yourself."

"The good deal . . ." His hand tightened around the cue, biting into the polished wood. How hard would he have to hit the man with the stick for it to be technically considered assault?

Was there such a thing as justifiable homicide?

"Yeah. You not following me? I had the mom. Now you can have the daughter."

Fuck. There it was. The breaking point.

"You mother fu—"

"Gentlemen." A strong hand clamped down on his shoulder, squeezing hard. "How's the shootin' tonight?"

Trace stood shoulder to shoulder with Red, his presence obviously adding to Nylen's opposition. Though his stance was casual, relaxed, Red didn't miss the tension vibrating his shoulder via the man's grip.

Nylen seemed either oblivious to the additional support, or he really was the world's biggest idiot. "Trace Muldoon. I was just talking about your family."

"Were you." His hand tightened almost imperceptibly on Red's shoulder. "Rehashing good times?"

"I do miss your mama," he said, somehow managing to imply a wealth of dirty thoughts with those five simple words.

"I'm sure you do. But she's gone now." No remorse or sadness lingered in his tone. "And we've got the ranch now. And as I hear it, you were let go."

"I did good work." He tossed the cue down on the table, scattering balls. "Peyton had no right."

"She had every right," Trace argued softly. "And every reason, as I hear it."

Nylen's face flushed an unattractive shade of purple. "I did good work," he snarled again. "That bitch lied, whatever she said. I did good work. She was jealous I didn't get to her fast enough after her mother died. She was just—"

He moved with lethal speed, and Trace let him. Before the sentence was finished, Red had Nylen trapped against the wall, fists gripping around his shirt, lifting him off the ground so only his toes touched.

"I think I must have heard you wrong," Red said softly. "I believe I heard you say something not very nice about Peyton Muldoon. And that can't be right, since I know she's damn near perfect. So maybe you want to try again. And this time, choose wiser words."

Nylen choked out a sound, though it wasn't anything in English. Red's arm ached at holding up the man's weight.

"That's what I thought." He eased the man back down but didn't step away. "See, that's her brother over there, and I'm sure he would love nothing more than to remind you how much he loves his sister. But right now, he's letting me have a turn."

Nylen's eyes widened, reminding him of a cartoon frog. And not the princely kind. "She's got you by the sac, doesn't she?"

He lifted his arm until his elbow was angled against the man's windpipe. "Try again."

Nylen wheezed. "Nice girl," he strangled out.

Trace patted him on the back. "I think our . . . friend . . . is ready to take his leave now."

Letting go and stepping back completely, Red watched as the other man slid down the wall a little.

"I hope there's no problem back here," a stern, feminine voice said from behind them. Red glanced over his shoulder to see the woman from behind the bar standing at the entrance to the pool room, hands on her hips, looking ready to take action if she had to.

"No, no problem at all," Trace said easily. "Mr. Nylen here was just about to leave."

She watched the three of them closely, as if waiting for one of them to give up his hand. When no one said a word, she nodded. "Fine with me. Nylen, Jenna's got your bill rung up at the bar. Cash out and go."

He walked away, wobbling a little, and cursed as he exited the small back room.

The dark-haired bartender crossed her arms over her chest. "I hate fighting. I don't want it in here. And I have no problems calling the cops to remove anyone who throws a punch."

"No punches here," Red promised. No need to mention how closely he'd been tempted.

"Better not be."

"Aw, come on now." Sliding over to stand next to her, Trace gave her a smile that Red could imagine had melted too many hearts in the past. "I'm sure your boss knows what he's in for. Cowboys get a little rowdy sometimes. It all works itself out in the end."

"My boss?" She lifted a brow.

Trace narrowed his eyes. "Yeah. Jo. The boss? Manager? Owner. Whatever you want to call him."

The woman's face split into a wide grin. "I call *him* nonexistent. I'm Jo." With that, she turned and walked back to her post behind the bar.

"Well, that explains why she acts like she owns the place," Trace mused. "Huh."

"I'm guessing that's a strike out for you," Red added.

"You think my sister's damn near perfect?" Trace shot back.

"Tell her I said that, and I'll kill you."

Peyton opened her eyes at the sound of a car pulling up the drive and rolled to her back. The couch wasn't the most comfortable place to sleep, but that was where she'd ended up. And it wasn't because she was waiting to hear how Trace's evening with Red had gone. Nope. Not at all. Not in any way, shape, or—

Oh for the love of God, of course she was waiting up. Not that she was going to admit that to her brother. Wild horses couldn't drag it out of her.

The familiar sounds from their teen years, when Trace was starting to go out and do his own thing and Peyton was still stuck at home, came back to her. The sound of his pickup's engine cutting off. The truck door closing, squeaking a little because the thing was rusted. Kitchen door opening and closing softly, his boots hitting the ground so he could pad silently across the first floor to the stairs and not wake Emma. The seventh stair creaking, which he always forgot about and never skipped as he snuck in.

Though she couldn't see him, she knew when he hit the second floor landing. "Hey."

His face appeared over the top of the couch, arms crossed over the cushions. With a loopy smile, he said, "Hey yourself. What's going on, slumber party?"

She sat up, knocking at his hat with a swipe of her hand. "No, it's easier to hear Seth from out here than my room. Yours is close enough to hear him but mine's not."

"Uh huh." Nobody could see through her bull faster than Trace. Dammit. He walked to the coffee table and picked up the white baby monitor receiver, held it to his ear, shook it a little. "Seems like it's working just fine to me. Does this not fit through your door?"

"Whatever. I fell asleep out here. It's not a big deal." She had fallen asleep, sort of. So that much wasn't a lie. "How was your night?"

He set the receiver down and stuck his hands in his back pockets, waiting.

"Anything interesting go on?"

His jaw ticked, but he said nothing.

"Any hot girls?"

"Jesus, Peyton." He made a face. "Okay. A, I wouldn't tell you if there were, because you're my sister and you don't need to hear about my love life. And B . . ." He smiled, that secret smile he'd always worn as a teenager when he came home from dates. "There might be something I'm working on."

"Something?" she asked with a laugh. "Or someone?"

"Refer back to A." He sat down on the couch beside her, his weight depressing the cushions and making her rock toward him. She slid back toward her own end of the sofa, stretching her legs out along the length. "How was Seth?" he asked.

"Woke up once, around midnight. Took his bottle like a champ and passed right back out."

"Good." Trace stared off into the dark of the room. "Thanks for watching him. I don't want to rely on you and Emma more than I need to, but I just needed a night away."

"It was fine. Easy, even. He's not that difficult . . . at least, at this age. Is it hard?"

"What?"

"Being a dad. Without someone else, I mean."

He shrugged. "I don't know what doing it with someone would feel like. But it's terrifying. And not at all what I expected, though I didn't expect anything so that's a crapshoot in itself. But I'm not giving it up."

The ferocity of his voice took her by surprise. "Of course you're not." Because she sensed he needed it, she changed the subject. "I don't think Bea's ever coming."

"She'll come. When she's ready, she'll come. Bea runs on her own timeline, you know that. Even when we were kids, she was always on her own schedule. That's just how she's built."

"It's rude," she said stubbornly.

"It's Bea," Trace replied. "And honestly, I'm not sure why you're so keen to have her around. You know she doesn't give a crap about the way the ranch is run. She won't have any ideas to help out. Hell, she'll probably just sit around doing nothing and annoy the piss out of you, more than she's doing from a distance."

"But at least she'd be here, trying." Peyton sighed and settled back in the cushions, letting her head droop a little. She really was exhausted. "Maybe you're right. If she's not here, she can't make things difficult as far as decisions. Once she's here, she'll probably try to take shit over that she has no business sticking her hands into."

"Like what?"

"Like painting the barn pink. Or giving all the horses bedazzled halters. Or something else stupid." Peyton scowled when Trace laughed. "You think it's funny, but you know it's true."

"That does sound like something she'd try when she was younger," Trace admitted, wiping tears of laughter away. "But she's older now, probably more mature."

"One can only hope," Peyton muttered.

"And you know this isn't the life she wanted. She ran off at eighteen for a reason. So I don't think you need to worry about this at all. She'll come when she's ready, she'll stay until she's bored, then she'll leave again and not look back. This ranch isn't in her blood like it's in yours."

"And yours."

He shook his head. "The ranch, no. Riding, yeah. But this place . . . it's a house for me. I missed you when I was gone, and Emma. And dad, though he was already gone when I left. Even little Bea–Bea. But I didn't crave the roots this place gives like you did. I didn't have big dreams, big plans for the land. I can work here. But it's not mine. It's yours. Always was."

She nodded, knowing it was true. "Why'd you leave?

Permanently, I mean. I know this place didn't hold much for you, but you just . . . walked away." It was one of the great heartbreaks of her childhood, watching the brother she'd idolized since she could remember walk away and not come back.

His face hardened, the moonlight bouncing off the planes of his cheekbones, his furrowed brow. "I had to get away."

"But if you—"

"I had to. Let's leave it there for now." Clapping hands on his knees, he stood, then held out a hand to help her up. "We need some sleep. I have a lot of work to do tomorrow. And I'm sure you do, though that doesn't really distinguish it from any other day of the week for you."

"I want to keep the ranch, so I do what's necessary." And if she wished she could have a girls' night out, just once in a while, that was her problem. Making dreams come true didn't come cheap. Not that she really had that many girlfriends anyway. Or any, come to think of it.

She walked to her own room, smiling to herself when she heard the soft sounds of Trace crooning to his son in the bedroom-turned-nursery. He might act like a hard, tough cowboy. But that man was mush for his son.

And if she wondered, just for a minute, how quickly Red might turn to mush if he had a son of his own, she pushed the thought aside. Because it wasn't for her to worry about.

She had bigger fish to fry.

Red scowled as he watched Peyton and Ninja workout. She was pulling just a little too hard on the reins. Not painfully so, but ineffective. "Legs, Muldoon, use your legs."

She flipped him the bird as best she could through her leather gloves and adjusted quickly, running Ninja through the course as fast as possible without knocking over any of the obstacles he'd set up. It wasn't a perfect way to practice cutting, but mixing up the workouts helped keep the horse and rider both sharp. Not to mention that practicing with actual cattle was a pain in the ass.

In a live competition, she'd be working with fresh cattle who hadn't been trained or around horses. Cutting one out from the herd and keeping the single animal away from the rest for a set amount of time took nimble footwork and quick reaction times. But it wasn't always practical to practice with the real deal. So footwork drills were used.

When she came to a halt, both she and the gelding were breathing heavily. "How'd we do?"

He liked that. That she asked how they did collectively. So many riders assumed it was their glory alone and ignored that the animal had any part of it. "Not bad, but not great either."

She rolled her eyes and used one finger to flick her hat back farther on her head. Strands of hair damp with sweat stuck to her forehead, curled down around her ears, frayed out from the double braids she always wore. "That was about as helpful as a tornado siren in the middle of a cyclone."

He snickered. "You sounded just like Emma." The housekeeper had a way of creating a phrase that stuck with you for the rest of the day.

She grinned back. "You've been here a while now, you know where I get my best material."

He nodded. "I've got some notes, but let's see you guys run through one more course before we get to it. See if you figure it out on your own first."

Even from his seat, he could see Peyton roll her eyes. With a click of her tongue and a nudge of one knee, she worked her way back to the beginning, waited while one of the hands changed the obstacles a little.

A car drove up the long dirt path, and he turned to watch while the setup went on. Instead of heading directly to the barn, the nondescript black sedan with heavily tinted windows pulled straight up to the front of the main house and parked. A man in a suit stepped out from the driver side, walking around to open the back door before heading to pop the trunk, revealing a set of luggage.

Someone in for a visit. Peyton hadn't mentioned needing the time off, so he doubted she even knew. Maybe the visitor was here for Emma. Or Trace.

A blonde with little to her frame stepped out and around, grabbing the smallest of the luggage bags before heading straight for the front door, leaving the driver with the bulk of the load. She was willowy, and from what he could see at a distance, dressed to impress. No working attire on that one. Heels, light colored skirt and a thin button-down, sleeveless shirt. No plans to get dirty.

"Callahan."

He pivoted, realized Peyton was waiting for him to time her, and that thanks to her angle in the arena, she hadn't seen the car drive up. Debating a moment whether he should mention it or not, he gave the signal to start and punched the stopwatch.

If Peyton was needed, Emma would page her. No sense in disturbing a perfectly good workout for what might be nothing. Could even be a wrong address.

But when he caught the black car pulling back out—sans passenger—a few minutes later, he knew it wasn't a wrong address. Whoever had arrived meant to stay, at least for a while.

Chapter Ten

She was so ready for a shower. After a full day of working with some smaller kids on riding lessons, then her own training from the drill master himself, Peyton was sore as hell. Not at all unexpected, since she spent most of her time on a horse. But the moves Red had her trying, the different angles, the new way of directing, it was a workout in and of itself. Who needed gym equipment when you had a seven-hundred-pound animal controlled by nothing but the squeeze of your knee?

Scratch the shower, she needed a soak in the tub. Effective immediately.

Hopping down from Ninja, she patted his neck. "You did good, boy. We'll keep working on it. You've got a buckle in you, I can feel it."

"You're not bad yourself." Red walked over and gave Ninja some attention, passing him a quarter of an apple.

The compliment shouldn't have meant so much, but instantly her insides warmed and her stomach felt like the whirlpool jets turned on in the tub—all churned up with no place to go. It all seemed so normal, so simple. The little domestic scene of greeting one another after a long day's work. A mild feeling of complacency eased around them, enveloping them in a bubble nobody else could intrude on. "Thanks."

"That's a first."

"What is?" She peered around the horse's neck.

"You, taking a compliment so effortlessly."

And then the bubble popped. "Whatever." She turned on her boot heel to take Ninja back for his rubdown, surprised when Red fell in step with her. "Need something?"

He tucked his hands in his pockets, the already worn, molded denim becoming tighter across his . . . nowhere she should be looking. "Just heading the same direction you are. Thought I'd walk with you."

"Oh." Why did she always feel so awkward around him? What was it about Red that had her fumbling and bumbling all over herself like she did around no other man? She was surrounded by the male half of the species, outnumbered in every direction. She knew how to handle them. They weren't *that* complicated.

Red was something entirely different. He was a man, same as the rest. But how she managed herself around him . . . not at all the same. And she didn't care for it one bit.

Naturally, she concluded, this was his fault.

As they neared the barn, she caught sight of a slender woman standing at the front of the entrance, surrounded by her hands as if she were the storyteller and they were a preschool class of devoted listeners. Her light blond hair was cut into a shag that Peyton knew would annoy the hell out of her. She wore a tight shirt, a khaki-colored skirt, and heels that made her already-tall frame reach skyscraper height. But her back was turned. The woman bent over to hear something Tiny said, her butt popping to one side in an obviously practiced pose.

Peyton scoffed. Who couldn't see through that rehearsed deal? But as she surveyed the rest of the men, she noticed more than one hand's eyes focused in on that par-

ticular area. A few were all but drooling, they were so in-
vested in taking the woman's stock.

One of the barn dogs trotted over, tongue lolling out
the side of his mouth. But when he sniffed the back of her
knee, the woman shooed him away, then rubbed her fingers together like they had something sticky on them.

Peyton walked to Arby, who stood a few yards away
from the crowd.

"Trouble brewing." Arby spat on the dirt just outside
the barn and reached up to rub Ninja between the ears.

"Who is it?"

"Told ya. Trouble."

Which was oh so very helpful. She gave Red a look.
"For you? One of those women from the other night
come to find you?" The moment the words left her mouth,
she regretted them. Could she sound any more like a jealous girlfriend? She was neither jealous, nor his girlfriend.

Not that the reminder eased the churning bubbles in
her gut.

"Hell no." Red's voice was insulted, but his eyes were
giving the stranger a thorough once-over. "But you know,
from this angle it almost looks . . ."

The woman turned slightly, caught sight of them, and
then fully faced them.

Peyton sucked in a breath. Bea.

She hadn't even recognized her own baby sister.

"Peyton!" Rushing over in her heels, as though she
routinely ran marathons in them, Bea leaned down and
gave her a hug. The moment her sister's arms wrapped
around her, Peyton could smell the expensive perfume,
feel the smooth slide of silk from her shirt, hear the easy
way she laughed.

Pulling back, her sister watched Peyton through eyes so
much like her own. That was the kicker. Peyton and Trace

shared the same coloring and face shape, to the point that the family joked they could have been twins. But Beatrice had never looked quite the same. Where they were dark haired, she was a tow-headed blonde. Where Peyton was on the short side with an athletic build that suited her chosen profession well, Beatrice was a willowy five-foot-ten, and had no problem wearing heels to pass the six-foot mark. Where Peyton always considered herself average looking, Bea had movie-star looks, and knew how to use them.

Peyton tried to reply, but all the things she wanted to say, all the years of hurt, of anger, of absolute rage at the past stuck in her throat, surrounded by a layer of tears she'd be damned if she shed in the stable where anyone could see. So she nearly choked as she swallowed them all down.

Red, for once, stepped up to the plate and made her life easier. "Redford Callahan, trainer. How do you do, ma'am?"

"Oh well, lookie here." Bea's smile changed easily from friendly to predatory, placing one manicured hand in his and shaking lightly. "Beatrice Muldoon. But you can call me Bea."

To his credit, Red didn't look all that impressed by her sister. The same couldn't be said for the rest of the hands in the vicinity, who were hanging on her every word, every movement. Peyton scolded them with a quiet look, and most took the hint, bumping into each other on their way to go look busy.

"Welcome home, then. You'll be pleased to see what your sister's been up to these past few months. She's been working hard, turning this place around."

Bea looked around the stables and sniffed a little. "I suppose nothing much can be done about the smell, naturally. But what do I know?" She smiled again easily, crossing her arms loosely over her chest. "I'm more of what you might call an . . . well, an indoor girl myself."

Peyton finally found her voice. "Nice accent," she said dryly. Rather, the lack of. When Beatrice had left the state, her accent had been just as thick as Peyton's. Now, it was nonexistent.

Bea raised a brow. "Not all of us have to sound like cowgirls. It's not a requirement." With a sigh, she stepped around them, giving Ninja an extra-wide berth. "I suppose I should go up to the house and unpack." She put a hand on one hip and posed, glancing around at the few workers still in the vicinity. "Would any of you men mind helping me carry some bags? I've got so much—"

Before she could finish, Steve and another young hand were both off and running toward the house.

"That was sweet of them." Bea wiggled her fingers and walked back toward the house. "We'll catch up later, Peyton!"

Peyton took a chance and glanced up at Red. He—like every other male—was watching her sister walk away. But his face seemed more studious than slobbery. Like he was trying to figure out a thousand piece puzzle and wasn't sure he had all the pieces in front of him yet. That gave her just a little bit of hope for the male species in general . . . and Redford specifically.

Tiny came to take Ninja's halter. "Want me to take care of him, Peyton?"

"Huh? Oh." Normally she did her own dirty work, including taking care of her tack and horse. Her theory was if she played, she paid. But she had something to take care of. "I would really appreciate it this time, Tiny. Thank you."

"Not a problem." He led Ninja back to his stall, where the sounds of leather and brass and blankets being removed filtered through.

"Well." Red leaned back against the outside wall of the barn. "She seems nice."

"She's an actress. She could seem like a circus clown if she wanted to."

Not waiting to hear his response to that, she stormed off toward the house, prepared for a battle.

Red stared after Peyton, who looked less like the graceful swan of her sister and more like a pissed-off pigeon stomping toward the house.

Oddly, he found the pigeon to be the more interesting of the two. Never was much of a swan fan.

Arby leaned on the barn with him, his posture a mirror image, shaking his head. "That's going to be one knock-down-drag-out."

"I thought you knew her sister."

"I knew 'er. Haven't seen her since she was a teenager, though."

Red made a face. "People don't change that much. Why didn't you warn Peyton?" That she was blindsided by her own sister's visit bothered him more than he wanted to admit.

"I did. Said it was Trouble come to visit." He smiled, a wise, crooked smile. "Always did call the youngest one Trouble."

Red shook his head. It wouldn't be worth it to ask more questions. "This will not go well."

Arby spit off to the side and shrugged. "Long time coming. They'll have their come to Jesus talk. Get it out of the way." He gave Red a side glance. "Those two have a lot of issues to work out."

From even their distance, the front door slam was clear as a bell. "Females are a complex species."

"That's why I only deal with the four-legged kind." He spit again, kicked some dust over it, then grinned. "Might get kicked in the junk, but at least the mares do it without talking your ear off first."

Peyton opened the door, nearly jarring her arm out of her shoulder when the heavy old wood kept swinging while she still held on. Slamming it behind her, she watched the circus that had invaded her home.

"Oh, be just a little gentle with that one, please, sweetheart. It's got all my makeup. Don't need any of those bottles breaking."

Steve nodded emphatically as he carted the bag upstairs with a death grip on the handle.

Bea stood at the bottom of the staircase, waving her hands and looking every inch a helpless southern belle who just couldn't manage her own life without a big strapping man there to pick up the pieces.

All that was missing was the big bell-shaped dress and the accent Bea had left behind when she moved to California.

"Are you shitting me?"

Bea turned on her skinny heel and appraised Peyton, clearly finding her wanting. "Nice language, sis."

"Careful, you might lose that sweet veneer you're showing off." When Bea's simple smile slid off her face, Peyton had a moment of satisfaction. "You've got my hands in here, lugging your bags upstairs when they have real work to do?"

"They're heavy. I needed the help." Bea gave a pretty pout, only prompting Peyton to roll her eyes.

"Give it up. I'm not okay with it, and your little lip trick isn't designed to affect my gender anyway."

Bea rolled her eyes right back. "They're ranch hands, Peyton. They're giving me a hand. Get it? And anyway, they volunteered."

"They shouldn't have," she answered loudly, directing

her voice up the stairs. "They have work to do outside in the stables." To her sister, she added, "They're not freaking bellhops. This isn't the Ritz."

Bea was saved from coming up with a sassy answer when the front door flew open again and Trace stood in the doorway.

"Bea? Is that you?"

"Trace!" She took two steps before Trace whooped, jogged to reach her, and pulled her into a bear hug.

Over their brother's shoulder, Bea gave her a smug look. "At least someone is happy to see me."

"I'd be happier if you didn't make a freaking spectacle of your arrival." Peyton shook her head and plopped down on the third step, knowing she wouldn't be going anywhere anytime soon. Bea's *volunteers* thundered down the stairs and by her, mumbling their apologies and taking the side door out to the stables.

"Of course she's happy to see you." Trace pulled her back, held her at arm's length. "I swear, you're as tall as me. Were you this tall when I left?"

Bea bent her knee and popped one foot to the side, displaying her shoe. "Heels help. But no, I was still growing when you left." She took an ineffective, girly swipe at his arm. "Which you shouldn't have done. I missed you."

"Missed you, too, Bea-Bea." He hugged her again, then stepped away. "Has Emma seen you yet?"

"Not yet. I can't believe she's still working here! I thought she'd have retired by now." Bea turned a slow circle, her eyes taking in the furniture and other decor. "Looks like you picked new paintings. There were more portraits of famous dead people when I was here last."

"Sylvia picked the paintings. I never had a say in it." Which was another reminder that when Peyton had time—and the money—she'd need to go through and redo the first floor of the house. Then she almost snorted. *When she had time.* Like, never.

"So where is Emma?"

The woman in question appeared on the stairs, Seth tucked in the crook of one arm. "Peyton, there's a big pile of luggage piled up outside the guest room. The fancy, matching kind. I don't know who you got staying with you but I'm not providing room service."

"It's just me, Emma."

Emma looked at her right, the older woman's eyes widening when she recognized Bea. "Oh my Lord. I thought you'd never come."

Bea laughed and held out her arms. "Of course I came. I couldn't—wait. What's that?"

Peyton followed her line of sight until she came back to Seth. "Uh, it's a baby."

"Yes, but where'd it come from?"

Peyton snickered. "See, when a man and a woman really love each other—"

"Shush." Their sister glanced between the two of them. "Whose is he?"

"He'd be mine." Trace stepped over and gently took his son from Emma so the housekeeper could give Bea a hug. "His name is Seth."

After Emma was done squeezing the breath from Bea, he held out the cooing baby, his intent to pass the child to Bea obvious. "Seth, meet your Auntie Bea."

Bea looked struck with horror and took a step back. Probably didn't want any spit or drool on her designer duds. Peyton shook her head. "Look, if this is turning into a family reunion for real, I have stuff to get done. I'll be back tonight, later." With a hard look at Bea, she added, "Try not to get into any trouble or disturb the workers again."

As she started to close the front door behind her, she heard Bea ask, "What's up her butt?"

Peyton slammed the door a little harder than necessary, for the second time that day, and bit her tongue. There would be enough time for chitchat when the work was finished.

Now she just had to find the motivation to keep on working.

Peyton managed to make it to the arena before her hands started shaking. The whole gang, back together. It was exactly what she'd been calling Bea for, right? All but harassing her to come back and take responsibility for the ranch. Do her part. Be a member of the family instead of pretending her life before the age of eighteen didn't exist.

Peyton glanced around the arena, glad she was alone for the moment.

Bea was back. Bea, who looked so much like their mother, who shared so many of the characteristics that made Sylvia a complete mystery to Peyton. Suddenly, she was ten years old again, desperate for her mother's approval. Knowing it wouldn't happen, but not quite ready to accept the fact that her mother was never going to appreciate her, love her, care about her the way she was. That Sylvia's own little Bea-Bea was the apple of her eye, the perfect princess she'd always wanted, who never got her dresses dirty and never tore the ribbons out of her hair and always kept her Sunday shoes shiny.

Peyton wasn't that girl. Couldn't be that girl if she tried. And the childish resentment toward her mother started bubbling back up, for no reason she could even begin to understand. Sylvia Muldoon had been a selfish woman who didn't have a maternal bone in her body. She hadn't wanted children, she'd wanted live baby dolls that she could parade around and have people coo over. Someone like Bea, who was happy to be fussed over and paraded around.

What had Daddy ever seen in her? Why had he stayed, even after it was obvious she had as much maternal instinct as an animal who eats its own young?

But all kids were born wanting their mother's love, she supposed. Peyton found a dark corner of the arena, tucked away from the bright afternoon light shining in, and settled down between two stacks of orange traffic cones, wrapping her arms around her knees.

Who knew her own sister would bring back so many awful memories? Not that it should matter so much. Hell no. She was an adult, and her self-worth wasn't tied to any one single person's existence. It was just a shock, to see her baby sister all grown up and looking more like her mother than she or Trace ever had. And more than that. The way she moved, the way she tilted her head, how her hands fluttered around as she spoke. It was all Sylvia, whether on purpose or unconsciously done.

Peyton could only pray her sister wasn't half as useless as their mother had been around the ranch. Or as destructive. With a third of the say in ranch operations, she could do more damage than Peyton wanted to admit.

"This is an interesting place to find your boss."

Red's dryly amused voice only made her want to sink farther into the shadows. "I'm doing inventory," she lied, even though they both knew she wasn't. If he was any kind of gentleman, he'd accept it and walk away without questioning.

Naturally, he didn't. "I think we have enough orange cones." Shifting until he slid around a barrel, he sat on top of it, boot heels clicking against the wood. "Wanna try again?"

"Not really," she retorted, then sighed. Clearly he was aware there was an issue. If he wouldn't leave until he got it out of her, then she'd give him something. "It's just weird. I haven't seen Bea since she was eighteen. The day after high school graduation, she took off. Shock to see the kid all grown up."

"That's all?"

She nodded, feeling her throat tighten. *Not now, for the love of Christ. Please not now. Not in front of him.*

Red didn't say anything for a while. Just sat with her, as if silently offering her a shoulder to lean on, without actually having to do the leaning. It was almost nice for a bit.

And then he spoke. "She's nothing like you."

"Yeah. Tall, leggy, blond, beautiful. Who can even believe we're related?" she snapped. Why was it men could never get past a pair of walking tits to see there was more to a woman?

"She's tall, yeah. Blond, that's a fact. Beautiful, I guess. If you like that sort of delicate, fragile look. Like she might crack if you look at her the wrong way."

Men usually did. Made them feel stronger by comparison. More manly.

"Me, never had much use for it." He scratched his chin, took his hat off, and ran a hand through his hair. The strands stuck up every which way and made her smile a little. "It might be nice to look at from a distance. But someone like that, you'd always have to worry about. Me? I prefer something a little more substantial."

She raised a brow.

He shrugged. "Maybe that didn't come out right. But I've just always thought a woman who can saddle a horse faster than me and doesn't mind spending a few nights out in a tent without running water was more my type. The kind that doesn't act like a little hard work will break her in two. And for the love of God, who wears heels to the barn?" He gave her a knowing smile. "Besides, I've always been more partial to brunettes."

Her heart did a slow flip, and she rubbed the heel of her hand over her chest before realizing what she was doing and snatching it away. She stood, coming nose to nose with him. "Is that supposed to mean something?"

He thought about it for a minute. "Probably shouldn't."

Shouldn't. But that didn't answer the question. "Is that supposed to mean something?" she asked again.

He looked at her then, full on, those gray eyes looking more silver in the dark, and he answered, his voice a husky whisper. "Yeah. It is."

The stress of the last hour, the last month, the last year, crashed down on her, and for one moment, all she wanted was simple. Something to take her mind away, where she wasn't the boss, wasn't in charge, wasn't holding the world together with a ball of cheap twine and prayer. And so she did the stupid thing she never should have done, and kissed him.

If she thought he would let her get away with a simple brush of lips, he disabused her of that idea in two seconds flat. His arms came around her, one hand cupping the back of her head, the other on her butt, pulling her close. The heat of his thighs on the outside of hers had her gasping in shock. But that was just the opening he needed to gain entrance with his tongue, tracing along hers, exploring, delving. Tasting.

Oh, God. She was actually being tasted, like a gourmet cupcake by a sugar addict. And any thoughts of breaking it off, of calling it a mistake and turning away, were lost in the simple fact that it wasn't a mistake. Not for her. Not right this moment. It was what she needed. Wanted. Craved.

As his lips cruised down her jaw, all her nerve endings stood up and started a line dance. She jerked as the tip of his tongue traced over her pulse, knocking his hat to the ground. The hand on her butt started to knead, the one behind her head slipping down and around to cup her breast. And she almost stopped breathing. The gentle, tender way he touched her made her knees weak. He might say he wanted someone sturdy, but he treated her like glass. And it made her want to cry with the realization she'd wanted to be treated the same way. At least for a minute.

Voices on the other side of the way, just outside the barn reminded her they weren't in a dark bedroom, lying on a feather-filled mattress with all the time in the world to explore. No, they were seconds away from getting caught by a couple of her men, blowing all her hard work.

"Dammit." Red pulled back before she had a chance to make a decision. Regret creased his brows and he smoothed one thumb down her cheek before his hand fell to his side. "Now is definitely not the time for this."

"No," she breathed, then cleared her throat. "It's not."

Red's voice dropped to a low, gravelly tone she hadn't heard from him before. Something she could recognize as lust. "What I've got in mind where you're concerned requires a soft bed and an entire night. I'm not settling for a wooden barrel and five stolen minutes in some dark corner."

That snapped her back to reality. "No," she said again. The word came out in a short burst of breath. She used the moment to push off, out of reach.

"What—"

"No." Pleased by the force it came out with the second time, she blinked until her own eyes were clear of any lingering lust-haze. "Can't."

"I said that already. Right now isn't the time for—"

"Not now, not ever. We can't."

Red's eyes narrowed. "You're too honest for that. Call it what it is, Peyton. Won't."

"You're right." She nodded and bent to pick up his hat,

making sure their fingers didn't touch as she handed it over. "But it comes out to the same thing. We can't do this again. We won't," she corrected before he could jump down her throat.

Calmer now, he brushed his hat off and settled it on his head. Then the corner of his mouth ticked up. "So you say, boss." With that confusing parting shot, he left her in the darkness.

Literally and figuratively.

Chapter Eleven

"Trace." Peyton stuck her head in Seth's room to find her brother finishing up with Seth's morning dress routine. "I think it's time."

He nodded and gave Seth an absent pat on the bottom. "You're right. It's just gonna piss her off anyway. Might as well let her cool down while we're out of the state. Let me run him down to Emma and I'll be back up."

Peyton waited impatiently in the family room while he took his son to the housekeeper, who Peyton could guess was already in the kitchen. She should be in there, too, grabbing breakfast on her way to get some work done. But thanks to her sister's skill at avoiding confrontation— a trick she'd honed as a child and clearly had only per- fected during their years apart—Peyton realized drastic action was required.

"Okay." Trace hit the top step and nodded. "You go in first."

"Me? Why me?"

"Because you're the girl. If she's sleeping naked or something, I don't wanna walk in on that." Trace pushed her at Bea's bedroom door until she had no choice but to open it and walk through, or be slammed into the wood. She chose the first.

"Bea?" Glancing around the door, she blinked into the

pitch black room. The sun had just started its slow creep up the sky, but at least some light should have shown through the big windows by this time.

Then she noticed the blanket her sister must have draped over the curtain rod, blocking out every inch of the window blinds and effectively turning her room into a cave. No wonder the woman could sleep until noon. Rolling her eyes, Peyton strode into the room and yanked the blanket down.

The room didn't flood with light, which would have been more satisfying. But the noise and small light that did seep in was enough to wake Bea.

"What the . . . hey!" Bea sat up in bed, and Peyton was grateful to see she wore a nightgown. "Put that back! I'm still on Cali time."

"That excuse would have worked a week ago. Now? You're on Lazy time. We need to talk."

Bea huffed and pulled her blankets around her like a queen gathering her skirts before sitting on the royal throne. "Your reasons for doing this at six in the morning are what?"

"To make sure we could actually catch you," Trace's voice came from through the door. "Peyton, is she decent?"

Peyton eyed her sister, who only eyed her back just as suspiciously. "I can't say if she's decent or not, but she's covered."

"Good enough." Trace entered and closed the door behind him, sitting on the bench at the foot of the bed. "Morning, sis."

Bea rolled her eyes. "That's cute over a bowl of cereal at the table. Not so much now."

"Focus, Beatrice." Peyton shook her head. "We need to know your plans."

Bea blinked owlishly, the expression only exaggerated

by her short, white-blond hair spiked around her head like the downy fuzz of a baby bird. "My plan was to sleep past the ass-crack of dawn, but you shot that one to hell. Thanks, by the way."

"Plans for here," she said through gritted teeth. "How long are you staying?"

"Not that we don't want you here," Trace shot in, patting what Peyton assumed was Bea's foot under the covers.

Bea stared at Peyton. "You want me here?"

Not one to lie when it could be avoided, Peyton kept her mouth shut.

"Right. Well, my plans are . . . tenuous," Bea decided. "I mean, I can't stay here forever. Clearly, this isn't where my work is. And my work is important."

"You play a prostitute on a soap opera."

"A rehabilitated prostitute," Bea said with a sniff, ignoring Peyton's snicker. "And just because you don't watch the show doesn't mean it's not important to other people."

A little guilt crept in. It wasn't her idea of real work, but it also wasn't her place to judge. "Sorry."

Bea's shoulders lost a little of their rigidness. "I'm negotiating my contract, and my lack of physical presence is a bargaining chip." She smiled coolly. "I want them to feel what it would be like to make the show go on without me. But you know, they keep begging me to come back. I'm having to fend off their relentless calls to return." To emphasize her point, she nudged her cell phone an inch on the nightstand with one finger.

"So you're here for, what? The foreseeable future?" Peyton held her breath.

"Oh, that sounds so final. I wouldn't say that. Just that I'm enjoying a little time spent with my siblings. And when the timing is right, I'll go back and work out the contract."

Perfect segue. "Speaking of contracts, we need to go over more stuff about the will and the ranch."

"Absolutely. And as soon as I have a few more minutes, we can do that. But for now . . ." In one quick, fluid movement, Bea slid her legs over the side of the bed and stood, her nightgown settling around mid-thigh. Trace cursed under his breath and turned to face the wall.

"Jesus, Bea. Couldn't you sleep in pants like normal people?"

Bea fingered the sleeve. "There is nothing wrong with my sleepwear, except that there's nobody in this place to see it."

"That's my cue to leave." Trace stood and hustled out the door like his Wranglers were on fire, closing it firmly behind him.

Bea laughed softly. "That was easy."

Peyton sighed. "Soon. I know you don't give a damn about the ranch, but soon we need to talk about things."

"Great!" Bea beamed at her. "I have a few fantastic ideas for improvements in this place."

Oh God. Peyton headed for the door. "Over my dead body."

As she closed the door behind her, she heard Bea sing, "It could be arranged, sis!"

The early morning conversation with Bea had accomplished nothing but a headache. As Peyton grabbed a breakfast muffin from the kitchen, she did her best to find something that might remove the headache.

Instead, her mind turned to her trainer. Fail.

Eight weeks since she'd hired the man. Two major make out sessions. This did not bode well for her ability to keep a professional distance between her and Redford Callahan. Her track record thus far was deplorable.

And the fact that she was smiling, even after she knew it was going to end up a total disaster, was only proof that she should have her head examined. So instead, she focused on finding Arby. She checked in the stables first, then his office, where he was busy making notes in an ancient spiral notebook. Propping a shoulder against the doorjamb, she watched his aged hands patiently scrawl over the paper. When he spoke, his voice calmed something inside her.

"Need something? Or you just gonna stare at me and avoid working?"

She smiled. "You know me, lazy as ever. I came to talk about how things will run while we're gone." We being her, Trace, and Red as they headed out to a rodeo the next state over. "The hands know to come to you before following any of Bea's orders. God knows what she might come up with while we're gone just to piss me off."

"Oh, you couldn't begin to imagine," Bea drawled behind her.

Whipping around, the tail of Peyton's hair caught Bea in the face. Her sister took a step back and swatted at her. "Watch that thing, it's lethal. Not to mention completely unstylish." A thoughtful look crossed her younger sister's face. "You should let me cut it for you."

"Touch my hair and die." Peyton rolled her eyes. "I thought you were staying in bed all day."

"Someone was rude and woke me up before I was ready. I couldn't get back to sleep." Bea stared down at the floor where her flats—at least that much was sensible—rested on a pile of dust and remnants of hay. "Is it always this dirty in here?"

"Just don't think to give anyone serious orders while we're gone. We'll be back in a week. I can only imagine what kind of trouble you could come up with in that time, but I'm asking you to keep it simple."

Bea shuddered. "Like I'd be caught dead in the barn anyway."

Peyton looked up and around, brows raised, silently asking *And where the hell do you think you are?*

"Well, not if I can help it," she added quickly. "Trace asked me to come get you. The trailers are hitched and everyone's ready to roll. Just waiting for you." With that, she spun on her heel, which was at least not a killer five-incher destined to get stuck in a floorboard, and headed back toward the house.

"The princess has spoken," Peyton said to Arby with a wink, then waved and turned to follow Bea to the yard where the rigs sat. Trace and Red stood, twin pillars between the two engines, hip-shot and impatient. Her brother tossed a set of keys at her, which she caught in her palm.

"You get silver."

"Dammit!" She stared at the much older truck, silver where the dirt didn't cover, the one that protested going a mile over seventy. They never used it for the horses, only things like luggage. And usually not at all if they could help it. But with the other available truck in the shop, they had no real choice. "Trade me."

"No way." Trace patted his own truck's hood and walked to the driver's side door. "My rig, my ass in the driver's seat."

"Ugh." She watched Red, wondering what his plan was. Ride with her? She could guess he would choose to ride with her, if only just to annoy her to death. His favorite hobby. He watched her back, thoughtful eyes never leaving her. Then he grinned.

"I'm with Trace."

He opened the door through the window and hopped in, a smug smile planted firmly on his lips.

So she'd called that one wrong, apparently. With a sigh,

she unlocked the door and hopped in, coughing at the dust that stirred the air.

It was going to be a long-ass haul to Wyoming.

The sound of the crowd, of the side vendors hocking their trinkets, the horses snorting, cattle braying their displeasure. The smell of leather and dirt, sweat and hay.

God, it was ambrosia. Red settled back in the stands, elbows on the metal seat behind him, and watched another cowboy saddle up. Though neither Peyton nor Trace were in this event, his eyes evaluated every move the cowboy and his horse made. Looking for the weaknesses, the sore spots, the one thing every cowboy had that needed adjustment. It was all pure habit, couldn't stop himself if he wanted to.

The aluminum bleachers clinked as boot heels approached his area, and the structure shifted ever so slightly when a body landed on the seat close to him. Red reluctantly tore his eyes from the arena to see who his guest was.

And then wished he'd kept his eyes forward.

Sam Nylen leered at him from under a dirty, sweat-stained hat. "How are things at the M-Loser Ranch?"

"Piss off." Red faced forward again, shifting his body so his shoulder was blocking Nylen. Any idiot could take the hint that he wasn't in the mood to chat.

Unfortunately, Nylen was a special brand of stupid.

"Couldn't figure out at first why someone of your . . . quality"—he spat the word out like it was a bad joke—"would bother with those losers. Nothing ever good came out of that ranch but a few good bounces on a mattress. And even that's missing now, with Sylvia gone."

Red gritted his teeth, willing himself to not react. Not give the jackass what he wanted.

From the corner of his eye, he could see Nylen scratch his chin with a dusty hand. "I figure there must be some other incentive. I know the pay's not great. The head hand is older than dirt and a jackass to deal with. And the quarters aren't the nicest by a mile. So the way I see it, you must like the management."

"The Muldoons are good people," Red allowed, mostly because he was becoming aware that others were leaning in closer, listening, hanging on every word. He didn't recognize anyone, but that didn't mean the strangers didn't recognize him. Red wouldn't give them the chance to walk away and say he didn't defend his employer.

Nylen grinned, as if that was exactly what he'd hoped for. "I don't know much 'bout that boy, the cowboy. He weren't around when I was there. And there's a younger one that I've never met. But she looked pretty in pictures."

Red watched the arena shift as the first cowboy took his leave, preparing for another rider.

"But that Peyton, she sure was a spitfire."

Do. Not. Engage.

"More horse sense than the rest of the family combined, far as I could tell."

Red nodded agreeably. "She's a good boss."

Nylen chuckled. "I'm guessing that's cause she's got a fine pair of tits."

Red's hands balled—the only thing keeping him from swinging was the scene it would cause.

Nylen seemed to realize he had Red by the short hairs. He couldn't react without causing a scene, which wouldn't do anyone at M-Star any good. "I'd let her boss me around anytime. In bed, anyway."

Red stood slowly, brushing a little dust from the knee of his jeans before straightening slowly. Others were watching. Others would take this conversation away and chew on the gossip for a week. And it would only hurt Peyton if he didn't play it right.

"Well, Nylen," he said, grabbing the post by him and jumping down to the hard packed dirt below the stands. "I'm guessing you'd need the instruction in bed."

He walked away, refusing to smile at the sight of Nylen's red face and pissed gaze until he was well out of sight.

Peyton flung herself at Trace, knocking him back against the rig's side. "We did it!"

"We didn't do anything," he argued with amusement, but he squeezed her in a bear hug all the same. "I don't see any first place trophies coming home with us."

"No." Peyton stepped back and grinned. "But I did grab a third place. And you were kicking some ass, too. Tough competition. But the fact is, we showed our best and I've been talking nonstop to people who want to know more about M-Star. I had one guy whip out his phone and look at our website right in front of me. That's the point!"

Trace tapped her nose. "I've had the same. People asking where I've been, asking about the place, the stock. It's good." He smiled slowly. "Real good."

"Better than good. You both exceeded my expectations."

Peyton's insides melted a little before she had a chance to shore them back up and turn to face Red. "Why, thank you. Good to know you have such high expectations of us."

Red just shook his head and looked at Trace. "Are all women capable of turning a compliment into an insult like that?"

"Every female I know," Trace answered with a smile.

Peyton slugged him in the shoulder. "Nice back up, big brother."

He flicked her hat, sending it flying into the dirt. "Welcome, little sis."

Red picked up her hat and dusted it off, handing it back easily. "If you two are done playing sibling, I wanted to run through the schedule. We're leaving tomorrow morning, around dawn, right?"

Trace started shuffling his feet. A sign, Peyton knew, that he was feeling guilty. "Yeah, about that . . ."

Peyton sighed. "You wanna head home right now, don't you?"

His neck flushed but he nodded resolutely. "I do. I mean, Lad and I are done. You and Ninja are done. And the rest is all mouth work. Right? And scouting to see what's what."

"That's about it." Peyton crossed her arms. "So you want to ditch and run."

"I want to take the horses back with me and make sure everything is okay at the ranch," he corrected. "Plus, you'd still have Red here. Nothing difficult about that. Being away another two days won't kill you. But dammit, I miss my son."

He'd said it, and he looked so fierce about it, she couldn't even tease him. "Okay," she said softly. "Go home and give Seth a hug for me."

"Thanks." He gave her a kiss on the cheek and shook Red's hand, then climbed behind the wheel. As the dust settled after his quick exit, Peyton realized that he had left her with a long drive back and only Red for company.

That could be awkward.

Red stretched out in the passenger seat, laced his fingers behind his head, and closed his eyes. "Sure you don't want me to drive?"

He knew her answer before he'd even asked.

"No. This thing is testy and there's a trick to driving it

properly. Plus," she added, sounding a little testy herself, "just because I'm a woman doesn't mean I don't know how to drive."

"Never said otherwise," he agreed easily, keeping his eyes closed. "Just thought to offer, seeing how we're both tired and it's the middle of the night. You just let me know if you get too tired and need relief."

"Oh." She sounded hesitant, as if regretting her tone of voice. But he didn't open his eyes. "Thank you for the offer."

"Not a problem."

He let his mind drift off just a little, wondering what it would be like if she weren't so stubborn. If she weren't so determined to have absolutely no contact with him that wasn't professional. If he could reach across the bench seat and take her hand, lace his fingers with hers and just hold it on the well-worn, cracked leather seat.

"Shit!"

Well, that wasn't at all the reaction he'd expected. Wait, was he thinking out loud? Jesus.

He cracked one eye open only to suddenly feel the truck swerve and veer across the barely-two-lane road. Peyton's small hands squeezed the steering wheel, her knuckles stark white, as if she hoped the power of her grip alone could control the vehicle.

Her rigid posture wasn't going to do her any good if they ended up in a crash. Though out here, there didn't look like much to crash into. But he took a chance and rubbed a hand over her back. "Easy. It's fine, nobody's around. Let up a little. There we go."

She guided and coaxed and maneuvered with obvious difficulty until the truck rumbled, sputtered, and then finally ground to a halt on the side of the road. Under his hand, he could feel the tension and stress leak out of Peyton's muscles until she went completely lax, letting her head drop down to the steering wheel with a bump.

"Oh my God. I think I just lost ten years of my life."

He'd probably lost twenty, but no need to point that out. "Did we blow a tire?"

She shook her head, forehead still pressed against the wheel. "Something just clutched and the power steering went out." She pounded a fist against the dash. "Damn, thing should have been junked years ago. We just . . ."

No need to finish that sentence. *Couldn't afford to replace it.*

From what Red could see, faint tendrils of smoke snaked out from beneath the hood of the rig. He opened his door, hopping down and closing it before leaning through the open window. "Pop the hood so I can see what's going on. Stay in here in case I need you to start the engine or anything."

She looked relieved. "Do you know a lot about cars?"

No. Nothing. But he figured even he could tell if the problem was minor or major. Slipping out of his button-down work shirt, he wrapped the fabric around his hand and went to open the hood after he heard the faint give of metal, signaling Peyton had pressed the button to pop it. The moment he did, he knew the rig was DOA. The blast of heat and stench of burned . . . something stung his nostrils. He backed away, waving his arms to clear the smoke from his eyes. Rounding the truck to the driver side, he waited for her to roll down the manual window.

"I'm thinking it's a goner."

Peyton once again let her head fall, this time back against the seat. "That would figure. This piece of junk just couldn't get us back home, could it? Just couldn't fight it out to the end. No. We had to break down here in BumFuck Nowhere." She glanced around. "Where are we again?"

He shrugged. "You were driving."

"Fantastic." She grabbed the directions she'd been using from the dash and her cell phone from the cup holder by her feet. "Time to call for reinforcements."

"And who would that be?"

"AAA, duh."

"Sorry sweetheart, but this thing won't be heading to any more rodeos."

Peyton wanted to scream. Then cry. Then kick the son of a bitch for calling her sweetheart like she was some helpless little woman. Though the crying part wouldn't help her maintain her dignity, so she nodded and bit her lip to cut the tears off.

"What broke?"

"What didn't?"

"So it's only good for parts?"

The mechanic who'd showed up on site scoffed. "Love, this thing is barely worth metal scrap. I know a guy who can give you a check tomorrow for what it's worth, but that'll have to keep until morning."

Peyton ran a hand over her quickly fraying braid and shook her head, then nodded. Her mind was too foggy with exhaustion at this point to care. "Great. Fine. So, until then, is there a car rental place around here?"

"Sure is." The robust man hooked his thumbs through the loops of his jeans, where a belt really should have resided, if the droop in his pants was any indication. "Course, that won't be open until morning, either."

And she was back to wanting to scream. "Then what do you suggest we do until morning?" she asked through gritted teeth.

"I can hook up your trailer, drive you out to the motel in town."

The motel. As in, only one. She wasn't far off with her

BumFuck Nowhere comment. Then again, they were driving through Wyoming. What was she expecting?

"That'd be great." Red laid a hand on her shoulder, and though she'd rather chew her arm off than admit it, the weight of his hand was a comfort. "We'd really appreciate the ride. Wouldn't we?" He squeezed gently.

"Yes. Thank you," she said, feeling something like a puppet whose strings were pulled. Peyton waited while Red and the mechanic hitched the small trailer to the mechanic's truck, then climbed into the dusty cab next to Red. When the alternative was to scoot closer to the man in the overalls, Peyton chose the lesser of two evils and slid until she was all but cuddled up against Red's side.

He chuckled low in her ear and looped an arm around her. The infuriating man *would* enjoy this . . .

Chapter Twelve

The mechanic's truck pulled into a poorly lit parking lot in front of the—singular—motel in town. The parking lot was shockingly full, even though there was nothing Red had seen of town to recommend it to travelers. The L had long-since burned out from the motel's neon sign. As he and Peyton slid out of the truck, she muttered, "I think this place was featured as a crime scene on 48 Hours last week."

"Remember which room number?" he asked, then laughed at the face she shot him. They grabbed their bags from the back of the truck and picked up directions to the rental car company in town before waving good-bye to their mechanic.

As they walked in, Peyton coughed a little at the smoky interior of the lobby. "I thought it was illegal to smoke in public places like this."

"I don't think it is in Wyoming." Red glanced around, wondering how a dump like this could actually be a stopping ground for anyone. "Let's just see what's available." He walked to the front desk, looked for a bell, then rapped his knuckles on top of the scarred wood when there wasn't one in sight. "Hello?"

A skinny man with slicked back hair and red, glazed eyes popped his head around the wall. "Yeah?"

Nice customer service. "We need a couple of rooms. Hoping you're not full up."

The man, probably in his forties, slid around the door frame. "Not quite full yet."

"Thank God." Peyton dropped her bag on the ground and slumped against the desk. "Two rooms please."

"Singles?" the man asked, his hand poised with a pen over a registration book. But the glance he gave Peyton was anything but service-like.

"Yes, two singles." Looking relieved, Peyton sagged against the tall counter. Red's back teeth ground together as the clerk's eyes zeroed in on her breasts, now squished against the wood.

"I have a couple of singles left. One on the north side"—he pointed toward the left—"and one facing the back parking lot." He motioned behind him, then gave Peyton a slow smile. "For you, I'd recommend the one in the back. It's more private. What name can I register it under?"

"Muldoon. M-u-l-d—hey!" Peyton yanked against Red's hold as he grabbed her arm and tugged her over to a worn, ripped couch on the other side of the room.

"Just a second," Red said, smiling widely at the desk clerk, who wore a startled expression. "I want to run something by my . . . business partner." She scowled at him but said nothing. Red dropped his voice. "We should get one room."

She stepped away, breaking his hold and crossing her arms over her chest. "You don't have to worry about forking over the big bucks. It's a work expense. M-Star is footing the bill, Callahan."

"Fantastic. But that's not what I was thinking about."

His mind was thinking of security, or lack thereof. Judging by the look of the lobby, the rooms likely didn't even have a dead bolt. No way in hell did he trust the security in this place. And with the motel so full, there were a lot of people to account for.

But Peyton slid him the side eye, not following his train of thought. "Red. You can't be seriously using this as a way to . . ." She waved a hand between them. "You know."

"No," he said through clenched teeth. "I don't know. Spell it out for me."

When her eyes widened, he realized that was the world's worst idea ever. "Forget that. I'm just thinking of safety in numbers, or however that saying goes."

Peyton rolled her eyes. "Thanks, but I'm not the little woman, helpless and alone. Your concern is . . . interesting," she finally decided on. "But unnecessary." With that, she spun on her boot heel and went back to the front desk, where the attendant wasn't even trying to make a show of giving them privacy.

"We'll take the singles."

"Very well." The clerk grinned at her and gave her a wink. "I like a woman who can stand up for herself."

"Uh huh." Peyton bent over to dig in her bag for her wallet with identification, and the clerk practically dislocated his shoulders trying to get a better look at her ass.

Red clenched his fists. *Not mine to protect. Not mine to defend. Not mine to . . .*

Oh hell, it didn't matter whose she was or wasn't. The whole thing creeped him the hell out. Taking a chance, he slid up next to Peyton and gave the clerk the universal stare that all men understand without hesitation.

Mine. Don't touch unless you want to be missing a finger.

The clerk was less than amused. When Peyton straightened and handed him the ID, he made a nice show of looking it over. "Out-of-towners, huh? Traveling from the rodeo, then."

"Yup." Peyton's short tone made it clear she wasn't in the mood to chat.

The man's pen slowed down even further. "We get a lot of rodeo traffic through here. Now you, you are sweet as can be. Did you compete for the rodeo queen?" He ran the tip of his tongue over the edge of his teeth in a disgusting display. "I'd have voted for you."

Peyton hesitated as he held out her ID. "No. I didn't." When she pulled back, the man kept his grip on the driver's license. She pulled harder, but he didn't let go. "Excuse me?"

"Oh. Sorry." Not at all sorry, he barely glanced at Red's ID before tossing it back across the desk. The shiny plastic went sliding over the top and then off the side, clattering on the floor.

"You know," Peyton said suddenly. "I think one room was a better idea."

The desk clerk was noticeably put off. "But I've already started registering you for two rooms."

"Oh, I'm sorry. But we have, you know . . . business things to discuss."

"We do?" Red asked, not wanting to give up the chance to tease, though he couldn't argue with her final choice.

"Yes," she said through clenched teeth. "We do. About that thing you mentioned. You were right."

Red almost choked. "Was I now?"

She gave him a smile that suggested pain was in his immediate future. "You sure were." Turning back to the clerk, she softened the smile a little. "Just one room. But two beds."

Peyton dropped her bag on the far bed, watched it bounce, and waited for a plume of dust or something to poof in the air or for the bed to collapse. But nothing happened. So at least the place wasn't disgusting or deadly . . . with regard to the furniture.

She caught sight of the yellowed lamp shade—the one that wasn't missing—and grimaced. It was a close thing though.

Red set his own bag on one of the two chairs by the tiny table, and scanned the room, hands on his hips. "It'll do."

"Well no kidding. It's the only option." She watched as he shrugged, toed off his boots, set his hat on the table, stretched out on the bed, fully clothed, and shut his eyes. "What, that's it?"

He cracked one eye open. "What's it?"

"You can just go to sleep like that? In this . . . place?" She'd be wired for hours. It really didn't seem fair the man would be able to just pass out like nothing had happened.

He shrugged a little and settled his hands behind his head, eyes shutting again. "I'm used to hotels. Spend enough time in them between work. I'll be just fine for the night."

"The lights are still on."

He smiled without opening his eyes again. "Funny thing about lights. When you close your eyes, it doesn't matter."

Peyton huffed, then realized there was no point in bothering. She sat on the edge of the bed and pulled off her own boots, sighing a little as her sock-clad feet hit the threadbare carpet. Not that her boots weren't comfortable, she'd broken those babies in about two years ago. But even comfortable boots weren't better than bare feet. But she wasn't about to walk on her bare feet on the carpet, so socks it was.

A sound broke through her reverie and she turned her head.

The damn man was snoring. Slightly, very slightly. But

it was an unmistakable sign that he was already dead to the world.

Meanwhile, the simple fact that she would be sleeping next to him—in the same room—would keep her and her hormones up all night long. And no amount of self-lecturing was going to make a difference. If it did, she'd have stopped wanting Red Callahan weeks ago.

She peeked again, watched his chest rise and fall. The relaxed pose, his long body stretched out over the bed, brought all sorts of completely delicious—and absolutely off limits—ideas to mind.

Aaaaand, there she went again, doing that whole *not supposed to think about him but doing it anyway* thing. She rolled her eyes at herself and grabbed a T-shirt and shorts out of her bag. After changing in the bathroom—he might be dead to the world, but she wasn't chancing it—she started to pull back the covers. She held her breath, but a quick scan revealed nothing scary. Before she could slip in, a soft, almost silent knock sounded at the door. Soft enough that Red didn't so much as twitch.

Had to be the wrong room. Ignoring it, she slid into bed. But as she reached for the lamp, the knock sounded again, just a little louder this time. And a careful, quiet whisper through the door.

"Ms. Muldoon?"

Okay, that wasn't a wrong room. She padded across the floor, giving Red's bed a wide berth, and peered out the peephole. The front desk clerk with the slick, thinning hair stood in front of her door, shifting nervously from side to side like a skittish two-year-old before they brought out the saddle for the first time.

Well, shit. She made sure the chain was secured and cracked the door open. "Yes?"

He gave her an apologetic look. "I'm sorry, but the maid on this floor let me know this room didn't have towels." He held up his hands and she saw a few folded white towels in his hands.

"Oh." Peyton didn't remember if the bathroom had towels or not, but a few extra never hurt. Her arm bumped into the door, and she realized she couldn't get through the small crack the chain allowed. After a moment's consideration, Peyton planted her foot a few inches behind the door, released the chain, and opened it wider. Reaching for the towels, she tugged.

But rather than let go, the clerk snatched her wrist and held on in a shockingly firm grip. "Why don't you come out here and get them?"

"What the . . ." She jerked her arm, but keeping her foot planted so the door wouldn't open further didn't give her much leeway. Suddenly she was dragged off her feet and pulled back against something warm and hard. The door opened wider, propped by one thick, slightly hairy, tanned forearm. And Red's voice rumbled from his chest, vibrating through her back.

"Well now, talk about hospitality. The front desk clerk, coming all the way down here just to see if we're doing all right. Oh look. Towels." He drawled the words hard, making a mockery of the conversation. His other arm snaked around her middle, pulling her more tightly against his front, fingers splayed over her abdomen. "Honey, did you call for some room service?"

Honey? Seriously? "No, *dear*," she said through clenched teeth. "I didn't."

Red's voice dropped, lethally soft. "Then I might just be wondering what our friend the desk clerk is doing here, away from his post, when we weren't expecting him."

The man muttered, "My mistake, wrong room," and stepped away, his back running into the metal railing on the other side of the sidewalk.

"Okay, then." Red pulled Peyton to the side and stepped around so he alone was in the doorway. "Nighty night." And with that, he shut the door with a quiet, but decisive click, and locked the dead bolt.

"Jackass," she muttered.

"He wasn't going to win any congeniality awards," Red agreed, leaning back against the door.

"I meant you." She rolled her eyes.

Red ignored that. "And exactly what the hell were you thinking, opening the door to that idiot? Are you trying to get yourself hurt?"

"Please, like that excuse for a man would actually get through the door." But the thought that things could have turned out differently chilled her a little. In her defense, she added, "I can do it myself. I've been taking care of me and my own for long enough."

"Maybe that's the problem."

His soft words caught her attention. "What?"

He eased off the door and took a step her way. "You've been holding it together for years, haven't you?"

"Uh huh." She took a tiny step back. Not out of fear, but because she liked to keep her personal life private.

"Your family. The ranch. All the employees, the stock. Business." Another step closer. "You."

"Me?" She inched back just a little more, and her calf bumped into the edge of his bed.

"You. Taking care of yourself. From what I've seen, that one ranks lowest on your list of priorities."

She shrugged, though the words sliced a little closer to her heart than she wanted them to.

"So who takes care of you then?"

"Nobody. I just said that. I can do it myself."

Those long legs carried him until he stood a spare inch from her. One deep breath and her breasts would brush against his chest.

"Maybe it's time someone gave you a break. A small one, anyway. And took care of you."

Before she could even process that, which would have led to the inevitable question of why, he bent and kissed her. Not a searching kiss, not a testing kiss. A devouring one. A kiss her body responded to without hesitation, even if her mind was still reeling to catch up.

Her arms lifted on their own and wound around his neck, pulling him down lower, closer, into her. Strong, long hands pressed her back until her hips met his, until she couldn't miss the erection straining against the zipper of his jeans. Until she . . .

Until she was close to bursting into flames.

"Let me," he whispered, lips moving to below her ear, over her cheek, her brow, down the bridge of her nose.

"Let you what?" she asked on a gasp of air.

"Let me take care of you. Just for tonight."

There were so many ways he could have ended that request. But it was as if he read her mind, realized how tired she was, how worried and exhausted from carrying the load. And that for one night—just one, she swore—she was ready to set the burden down and allow someone else to carry it.

Just one night.

"Just for tonight," she repeated.

God, thank you. Red wasn't sure how in the good Lord's name he could have stopped his body, now that they'd started on this journey. But he would have pulled back, even if it had killed him.

And sweet baby Jesus, he didn't have to. He could do what he'd been dreaming about, thinking about, craving for weeks now.

Already bent over to accommodate their height difference, he kept bending until she stretched out on his bed, her knees bent over the side. With a little wiggling, she was fully across the mattress. Resting his weight on his forearms, he took a moment to satisfy his mind and stare down at her.

This was definitely not a position he'd thought he'd ever see her in. Time to savor. With soft kisses, he tasted her. The tender skin at her throat, the inside of her elbow, below her ear. When he ran out of exposed skin, he skimmed one hand beneath the hem of her T-shirt and urged her to sit up so he could get rid of it.

No bra. Of course not, she'd been ready for bed. Her breasts were small, firm, perfectly proportioned for her. He filled both hands with the mounds and kneaded.

But Peyton's eyes went from intense, lust-filled blue to a more smoky, uncertain shade. "Never needed a bra for bed. Or anything else, really," she joked. But he heard the uncertainty in her self-deprecation.

"They're perfect. Perfect on you." Red silenced her huff of laughter with another kiss, pulling hard at the tips until she gasped into his mouth and arched for more.

One hand obliged, while the other worked its way down her ribs to investigate the shorts she wore. Which weren't quite shorts at all, but a pair of men's boxers. "Where the hell did these come from?"

The self-confident woman was back, her gaze teasing. "Jealous? Of a pair of shorts?"

He smirked. "Hardly. Since you obviously didn't just walk out of some other man's bed wearing them."

She lifted a shoulder. "They're comfortable."

"True enough." Except when you were packing a hard-on that could pound in fence posts. Then nothing south of the border was comfortable. Sort of like now . . .

He slithered the shorts down, pushing them completely off her feet, and let his hand wander between her thighs. Thighs hard with muscle, thanks to years of daily riding and hard work. No extra stuffing to be found on this woman. But a feminine body nonetheless, with compact curves in the right places. And those curves were driving him five shades of insane.

"Come on, sweetheart." His hand stilled when her thighs clamped shut, barring him from all but the top of her mound. "Open up."

She squeezed her eyes shut, as if making a decision. Then as her eyes opened again, so did her legs. Just enough for him to slip in and feel her damp heat, know she was already wet, excited, anticipating.

One finger trailed down and explored, finding her clit and lingering to touch there. She moaned and pressed against his hand, her own fingers gripping his upper arms like a lifeline.

"There's a spot, huh." He drifted lower, following the slickness until he could slip inside her. "And there's another." He pressed kisses to her mouth, her cheeks, her eyes. "Lots of sweet spots, hidden under that sometimes-sour disposition."

"I'm not candy," she mumbled.

"Of course not." His thumb added to the mix, pressing against her while his finger worked its way in and out, circling around. "Candy's easy to predict. You chew a piece of spearmint gum, you know you'll get that cooling mint sensation."

He worked his mouth down to her breasts. "Now a Fireball, that's straight cinnamon and spice." He circled the tip with his tongue, enjoying the way she squirmed beneath him. "Butterscotch, now there's one I really like. Smooth, creamy flavors mingling together." He pulled at her nipple with his lips, then teeth, listening for the changes in her breathing. "And chocolate will give you that nice sweet treat."

"Oh my God," she moaned as he added a second finger inside her, his thumb upping its pace.

"But Peyton Muldoon, she's a grab bag. Never know what you might get from day to day. Sassy?" He moved to the other breast, giving it just as much attention. "Fiery? Maybe even shy."

He heard it then, that quick hitch that told him she was close, so close.

"I can't tell you how much I've wanted to sample every single flavor of Peyton there is."

It might have been sexy bed talk, but he meant every goddamn word. She pulled at him in ways he could never have anticipated. In ways he didn't always like, didn't always want. But the pull was there, and he was so tired of fighting it. So no more fighting. At least, not that kind.

She arched, gripped the bedding, and cried out her release. And Red knew true triumph, better than any buckle, more worthy than any paycheck, watching Peyton Muldoon lose herself in his arms.

Oh, holy mother of God. Peyton's knuckles ached, and she realized she'd wound her fingers so tightly in the bedspread, they were starting to lose sensation.

The man had a way with more than horses. And he was still dressed. Once she mentally assessed that her limbs would work, she let go of the blanket and propped herself up on her elbows. "Not bad, cowboy."

"Not bad? I think that was better than not bad." His grin lit something in her, something not even physical release could touch. But she pushed it back. This was a one-night-only performance. No time for fires . . . other than the ones they could set between the sheets.

"Well then, let's see what you've got on under that cocky grin." She worked the snaps of his shirt easily enough, only mildly annoyed when she encountered a simple white undershirt. She gripped and tugged until the soft material came loose from his waistband. "Off, off, off."

He chuckled and sat up, pulling at the shirt from behind until it sailed across the room. And she could instantly see his body was nothing to laugh about. Smooth skin, tan muscles, a light dusting of hair, just a little darker than the hair on his head . . .

Thank you, Patron Saint of Cowboys. Whoever the hell you are.

As she attacked his belt buckle, frustration got in her way and she bit back a scream. "Help, please."

"Peyton." His hands covered hers, stilling them. When she looked up, his face was serious. "There's no rush. Slow down. We'll get there."

Technically, she'd already been there once. But she'd like to go back again. Repeatedly.

But the solemn way he stared at her, as if he could tell she was eager to leave the emotion at the door and concentrate on the physical, as if he was ready to call her out on her bullshit at a moment's notice . . . Damn, that fire was starting to spark again.

She ruthlessly tossed water on it. No time, and no choice. "Well then. I've been put in my place." She scooted up until her back was against the headboard. Like a woman bored with the show, she waved a hand at him. "Continue on."

He smirked, but said nothing more. His hand worked the buckle—a buckle much smaller than the dinner-plate sized versions so many cowboys flashed around—and loosened his belt.

"I don't want this to go so fast." He kissed her knee before unsnapping the top of his jeans. "I'm not really in the mood to rush."

"I can tell," she said dryly, but her mouth was practically watering with anticipation.

She really needed to get out more.

His hand paused. "I'm starting to feel like a purchased stud here. Did you want to see my papers first?"

"You have papers?" At his look, she sighed and crawled to her knees. With one hand on either side of his face, she kissed him. "I'm sorry. I didn't mean that as an insult. I'm nervous."

He nuzzled into her neck. "I know." More quietly he added, "We'll figure that out."

She didn't want to know what his idea of "that" was. It didn't matter though, because he pulled away and stood, pushing his jeans to the ground as he did. And suddenly, the idea of calling him a stud seemed applicable all over again. She swallowed once and took her time drinking in the full effect of Redford Callahan, completely naked, and totally erect, right in front of her.

"Yeah. I think I can work with that."

He snorted and gripped the base of his cock. "Well good, because I didn't bring a spare." He crawled over until she was flat on her back, the thick flesh pressing against her hip, so hot she would swear it was a brand.

"I'm done waiting, Peyton."

Waiting. Tonight? Or longer than that. How long had he wanted to get her like this? And no, she scolded herself. Going down that road was too high school, even for her. They were here now, so live in the moment.

He kissed her then, and her mind blanked to anything but the two of them, as if the entire world outside their dingy motel room had melted away into nothingness. If only . . . Then he used his knees to push her legs wider apart, and one hand nudged between her thighs.

Oh, God, he knew exactly how she wanted it, where she wanted it. How to touch her, and when to pull back because it was almost too much. And right before she jumped off another peak, he pulled away entirely.

"What the . . . ? She lifted her head and found him digging through his overnight bag, ass in the air. "What are you doing?"

"Condom."

Shit. "Right. Good." She took the moment to study his backside, the only view she hadn't had so far. And found herself smiling at the severe tan line that separated his back from his butt. The man, if he didn't get sun, would be pale white. But clearly he worked with his shirt off enough to at least keep some color. For some reason, that pale butt made her want to laugh. But she bit her lip, determined not to ruin the moment.

She must not have hid it well though. He turned around and tilted his head to the side. "What?"

Peyton shook her head. "Nothing." She reached for him then, and he came over her, settled between her legs, and his cock nudged against her.

Red's lips rested against her neck, not moving, not pressing. Just a silent reminder he was still with her. That heartbreaking piece of contact had tears pricking her eyes. But she blinked furiously at the ceiling until the moment passed. And as he slid inside her, fully and completely, tenderness was the last thing on her mind.

He rose up on his forearms and grinned down at her. "I'd apologize for how fast this is going to be, but you're already one up. And I've wanted you longer than I'm willing to admit. So I think I'm entitled to break a few speed records." He kissed her, erasing her surprise at hearing him admit that bit of information, and slid out before thrusting back in. Finding a rhythm that set them both on fire . . . the right sort of flame this time.

Gripping his shoulders, she stretched up to meet his every pulse, to work with him, stay with him, just keep up. And when she felt his muscles stiffen beneath her fingers, it was time to give them both a little nudge. Reaching down between them, she touched herself.

"Oh, Jesus," he muttered, the backs of her fingers bumping against his lower abdomen with every push. "Tell me you're close."

No need to answer, as she tightened around him, fluttering with a release she couldn't have held back for anything. And though he might have arched back with his own orgasm, she selfishly grabbed his neck and pulled him down for a kiss instead. Wanting to drown her cries in his mouth. Taste what that level of desire was like, in that heated moment, melting together.

Minutes later, Red pushed up and headed for the bathroom. She indulged herself with one more good look at his butt before it disappeared behind the dividing wall, then she laughed to herself. When had she ever honestly checked out a man's ass before? She was as bad as her teenage summer ranch workers.

But as the seconds passed, the amusement faded and uncertainty crept in, invading the cocoon of pleasure she'd been so comfortably wrapped in. Was she supposed to head to her own bed now? Wait for him in his bed? Go pose provocatively by the table? Pretend that she was asleep and let him choose?

Damn sex and it's post-orgasmic complications. Why did something so good in the moment feel so confusing the next?

Time to move to her own bed. Spending any length of time stretched out next to him, naked, wouldn't foster the "This is the only time" vibe she was looking for.

And oh God. Peyton shifted to sit up and let her face fall into her hands. She'd just slept with her trainer. A man in her employ. Who in the name of Hades would respect someone after that? She'd turned into exactly what every male who avoided doing business with her thought she was.

An emotional, illogical female.

Oh shit. She was her mother.

The very thought had chills running down her spine. She rubbed her arms to ward off the goose bumps, but it didn't help. So she tried reason.

Red wouldn't say anything. He wasn't that kind of guy. Wasn't a big talker to begin with, but he just didn't seem the type to need to brag about any conquests.

Was she a conquest? Another sobering idea.

Cowboys still talked though. Everyone thought women were the worst with gossip, but men could be just as bad. To them, it was "shootin' the shit" and it was conducted around the tack room or in a pool hall. Which made it all seem more manly. But stick them under a pair of hair dryers and a spade was a spade. Gossip was gossip.

And she'd just done something gossip-worthy. Marshall residents could chew on this for a year. Her mother sleeping with the trainer? Old news. Expected, even. But Peyton Muldoon?

"You gave up the reins."

She jumped, losing her grip on the sheet. Grabbing the bedspread to cover her breasts again, she looked at him. "What?"

Confident, at home in his own nakedness, Red lounged against the wall leading to the bathroom. "You're thinking loudly over there. It's amusing, but you're spinning out."

"You can't know that." Could he? "And anyway, not your problem."

"It is, actually." As she started to step out of the bed, he strode over and nudged her back in with his knee. "You agreed to let me take care of you."

"I did agree, and you did take care of me. And it was . . . nice," she finished lamely. Nice?

He snorted, clearly as unimpressed with her word choice as she was. "It was more than nice. But we'll let that go for a minute." He hovered over her, caging her in with long arms and legs. "I'm not done with you yet."

"Maybe I say you are."

"I'm taking the reins. So you need to get over it. For tonight," he clarified, when her eyes narrowed at him. "One night, not a big deal in the grand scheme of things."

She pushed at his shoulder, budging him exactly zero inches. "It is to me. I already made the mistake once."

Something crossed his face—was it hurt?—before he smirked. "I wouldn't call that a mistake. What are you so worried about?" He studied her face a minute. "Are you afraid I'll look at you differently?"

Her silence was easily interpreted.

"Because I won't." He nuzzled into her neck, over her cheek, kissing her nose. "Peyton, I tried my damndest to stay away from you. But you chased me—"

She gasped and pushed at him again.

He grinned, knowing his joke hit a nerve. "And I gave in. So that's the end of it. I figure we earned this one night to let things ride. And in the morning, when we get back to the ranch, nothing happened."

She watched his face, looking for a twitch, a smirk, anything that might hint he was lying. But it seemed he was telling the truth, at least about the morning after.

And really, she'd already given in to temptation once, right? It was like a diet cheat day. If you're going to go, go big.

Cupping his face with her hands, she let the bedspread slither down her body. "Fine. But tomorrow, I'm taking the reins back."

"Gotcha."

Hours later, Red's warm body was wrapped around hers from behind and his arm was draped over her stomach. One of his knees had settled between hers, and his chin was resting over the top of the crown of her head. He had, in effect, completely enveloped her. And it felt so secure, so safe, that for just a moment, she let herself picture coming home every night after a long day, climbing in bed and feeling this secure and safe.

Then, she realized her cheat day posed one massive problem.

Fire begets fire. All this night had done was fan the flame of her need for him. And she couldn't afford the time to put it out.

Chapter Thirteen

R ed pulled the rental up to the dirt patch in front of the main house, thankful they were finally home. The silence on the way back to the ranch had been deafening. And scariest of all, she hadn't even put up a fight when he'd said he would drive the rest of the way. A woman like Peyton didn't give up control like that unless there was a reason.

He stepped out of the Jeep, grateful to see a few hands walking up to help unhook the small trailer.

"Where'd this one come from?" Tiny asked, patting the hood of the rental.

"Silver went to that big scrap heap in the sky a few hours into our commute." Red watched Peyton from the corner of his eye as she slid down from the passenger seat.

"Congratulations on the good week, Peyton." Steve hurried to start unhooking the trailer. "Trace gave us a rundown of the rodeo. Sounds like M-Star had a great showing."

"We did." Peyton grabbed her suitcase from the backseat and let it flop to the ground, ignoring the dust it stirred up. When the hands waited, she shrugged. "What?"

Tiny spoke first. "That's all we get? No stories? No color commentary?"

She smiled a little, though Red could see the strain behind it. "I'll have a full report later, maybe after work's done. I'm a day late though and I need to get back to it."

The younger hands didn't notice any difference, but Red watched Arby give Peyton an assessing glance from a distance. Then his gaze slid to Red and he would have sworn the older man's scowl deepened. But he didn't say a word, just turned for the barn and ambled back.

Well, crap. Not only was Peyton ticked—for what reason, he didn't know—but now Arby was going to be on his case.

"Steve." He tossed the keys at the hand. "When you're done unhitching the trailer, take someone with you and return that in town to the rental place."

"Got it." Steve tucked the keys in his pocket and went back to work.

Red watched as Peyton headed toward the barn, alone and in an obvious mood that told others to give her a wide berth. She could see him from the corner of her eye, he knew it. But she didn't turn to look at him. Didn't wave, didn't call him over for a few words or to ask a question like she always would have before . . .

Before.

Was she right? Had that one night completely ruined their working relationship?

It's only been a day. Calm down. It's not a big deal. Things will settle back into the way they were and you can both move on. You got it out of your blood, satisfied the curiosity, so you can move on.

Only he wasn't a stupid man. Satisfied wasn't what he was at all. Their one night together had only heightened his desire for her. And not just for some physical pleasure, though that could hardly be discounted. The woman attacked sex like she attacked work. Single-minded intensity and focus. God bless her for it.

But in the morning, when they waited at the rental

place for the paperwork to be processed and to be given their vehicle, he'd had the strongest urge to grab for her hand and hold it for a while. Nothing about that was sexual at all. More like a comfortable, easy romance. More like exactly what Peyton would have hated.

Hated? Hell. He snorted to himself as he hefted his own bag and started toward his apartment to unpack. She would have snarled at him like a wild animal being caged.

He'd taken three steps when a truck, a complete rust bucket worse than the rig he and Peyton had left for parts somewhere in eastern Wyoming, crept up the packed dirt drive and parked by the barn. And out popped Bill, the teen from the feed store, surveying the setup cautiously, staying back and out of the way. Smart kid. Seeing that Trace was just finishing up with Lad, he walked over.

"Here for Peyton?"

Bill jerked like he'd been shot, checking around guiltily before finding Red. Hands stuffed in his pockets, he wandered over to meet him. "Yeah. Summer break's coming up, and I'm hoping she will have something for me."

Red sat on that a moment, watched as the boy's eyes lit up while a hand led one of the horses to the hotwalk area. He scratched his chin. "Just wanting some summer cash? Or you interested in the livestock?"

"I'm interested in the—hey. Is that Trace Muldoon?" The boy's eyes nearly popped out of his head. "Jay-zus. I used to watch him all the time on TV."

"Language. And yeah, that's Trace. Hey!" he called, waving a hand. Trace headed over, Lad's lead in his hand.

"What's up?"

Red hitched a thumb to his side. "You've got a fan."

"Always got time for one of those." Wiping a hand on his jeans, Trace held it out to shake with the tongue-tied Bill. "Here to watch?"

"Ho—hoping for a job, actually. Sir."

Trace laughed. "Just Trace. And aren't you a little young for a full-time gig?"

"Oh, it's just for the summer. The last time Peyton was at the feed store she mentioned that I should come by for the summer and see if she had work. You know, mucking out stalls and stuff. Taking care of the tack. Whatever."

Red would have thought the same thing, to give the boy a few easy jobs, shit work nobody else wanted to do. He was eager enough—and likely hungry enough—to do it all without complaint. But now Red had other ideas. "Why don't I take you 'round a little, show you the place before you decide if you want a job."

Bill scoffed, like not wanting the job wasn't even possible, but followed along easily enough. "Sure."

They started at the arena, then wound their way past the garage and the pasture before ending at the barn. As Bill greeted each horse by name—going by the nameplates on the doors—and with a scratch, Red made up his mind.

"How were your grades this year?"

"Huh? Oh." Bill looked over distractedly before going back to inspecting Ninja. "Won't get official grade cards for another week or so. They come in the mail. But I'm expecting all As and Bs. One C, I think."

"A C? In what, gym?"

Bill laughed. "English. I hate all that analysis crap. Can't a guy just read a book and say if he liked it or didn't? Why do we have to talk about the theme and what the author meant and all that?"

Red laughed, remembering his own thoughts in high school being similar. "Can't argue there. But they say it's important. So my suggestion is to bring that grade up next year. Or there might not be a place here next summer."

"Yeah, I can do that." Bill nodded. "So do I have the job?"

"You've got the job." Bill whooped, and Ninja gave him a look that suggested what he could do with his whoop. "Sorry, bud." With a final scratch, Bill followed Red out of the barn. "So what should I do first? Any errands to run? Hay to load?"

"Slow down there. We'll get to it." Red headed back to the arena and his office, Bill chirping the entire way about his excitement. Taking his keys from his pocket, Red went to unlock the door and realized it was propped open. He nudged in and asked Bill to wait outside.

His mind immediately went to Peyton, as the only other person with a key to his office. There were any number of reasons why she would need to get in there. Paperwork and his computer with files, all things she might need access to. But she wasn't inside, and there were no notes or anything to indicate she'd been in there looking for him. And he was pretty sure she would have locked the door behind her, if that's how she'd found it.

Not to mention, after their little blowup over his apartment, he doubted she'd give him any reason to come after her again with questions.

He took a quick survey of the room, saw everything still appeared to be in place, and resigned himself to going through it all with a fine-tooth comb later in the day. Damn, not what his day needed.

"Bill, hey. Didn't hear you drive up."

Speak of the devil. Red heard her voice echo inside the arena.

"Hey, Peyton."

"You come here looking for work? Or are you here about a horse?" she teased, and he finally saw her edge into his view from the office doorway.

"I was here for a job, but Red already hired me!" The boy's excitement was infectious.

"Did he?" Peyton's voice was silky, not a hint of sour. But Red could tell from the way she tilted her head, she wasn't pleased. "I didn't know he was hiring."

Aw, shit.

"Well, looks like we've got another mouth to feed." Peyton batted playfully at the bill of the teen's baseball cap. "Why don't you head home for today and tell your mama what you'll be up to this summer. Come back tomorrow at seven and we'll get started."

Bill started to trot off but she called out, "Hey, Bill! Grades?"

"As and Bs and one C," he yelled back on his way to his truck. "English!"

"Work on it," she advised, just like Red had known she would. And with that, his doorway was filled with pissed-off woman.

Surprisingly, the look she shot him didn't do a damn thing to douse the hard-on he was sporting under his Levi's.

"What was that all about?"

Red shrugged. "Billy's a good kid. Eager. Wants some summer work. Thought he'd be a good addition."

"Yes, I agree with all that." She scowled. "But since when were you hiring around here?"

"Okay, look, if it's the cash you're worried about, I'll pay the kid myself." Since Red had intentions of using Bill mostly as an assistant or apprentice, it was logical anyway. Not that money was ever really a problem for him. Not with the paychecks he was able to demand.

"The money isn't the issue."

"So then . . ." He had no clue what they were even arguing about.

"This is exactly what I was worried about."

"Wait, what?"

"You know, from the other night." At his confused

look, she glanced behind her, then hissed at him, "When we . . . you know."

"Ah. *You know.* Yes." He stifled a laugh. But she wasn't fooled, and stepped fully into the office before closing the door behind her.

"Yes. You damn well do know. And now you're thinking you can make decisions that are my job. This is exactly why I knew from the start it would be a bad idea to get involved."

Red held up his hands to ward off the lecture he knew she was about to start in on. "Hold on now. I hired Billy because I knew you'd already talked to him. Maybe I jumped the gun a little on hiring him. But I knew you'd already suggested he come work for you. I overheard you two in the feed store that day. I already know he's a good kid with a good heart who could use the extra bucks. And I think he's got potential as a horseman, with some encouragement. So, I just went for it." He paused, then judging the temperature of the room, added, "I'm used to making decisions on my own."

"Would you have done this at another ranch? With another owner?"

Fair question. But . . . "I don't know. The fact is—"

"The fact is, you haven't slept with anyone else, so you don't feel that connection with anyone else."

"No." He kept his tone as even as he could, despite his own rising temper. "The fact is, I don't know because not all my employers have been as easy to read as you."

She scoffed.

"I already explained I understood there was a background there between you and Bill. I know the kid myself. Those things combined made this a situation I felt like I could call. I made a decision. I would have done it whether you were an eighty-year-old man or the hot handful you are now."

She rolled her eyes but didn't chastise him for the joke.

"And I know you're a total softie." Yeah, that had her pokering up. She would hate that. "Play the badass owner all you want with other businessmen. I know you're total goo when you want to be with the horses, with the staff when they need it. And that nephew of yours? Don't think I haven't seen you outside with him before on that quilt, cooing and making faces at him." The memory had him smiling.

"So I like animals and kids. Sue me." Arms crossed over her chest—a motion which made her breasts strain at her front buttons and had him thinking once again about dark rooms, soft beds, and low moans—she shook her head. "I don't like this. I don't like second-guessing myself now because of what happened."

He shrugged. "So stop. If you don't like something I'm doing, tell me. I might not listen . . ."

Her lips twitched, holding back a smile.

"But what man does?" At that, he knew he had her. She smiled and dropped into the rickety metal chair in front of his desk.

"I meant to ask, just out of curiosity, but were you in here earlier looking for something?"

"Earlier? No, not today." She glanced around. "I meant to tell you the office looks good. Organized, sort of. At least I could find something if you weren't here. Nylen was a slob."

Red couldn't argue. Though he wasn't OCD-neat about things, he liked order. It was just good business. And as much as he wished his entire job was simply about the horses, he had paperwork like any other guy.

"You knew about the books Nylen was messing with, right?"

Peyton frowned and nodded. "I've got them in the safe up at the house. It's just not something I'm going to bother with. He's not in a position to abuse the trust any longer, so it seems pointless to go after him now. God only knows where he is, anyway. He never left a forwarding address."

Red chose not to mention seeing him at the rodeo or that as of at least a few weeks ago, he'd been in the area. Not a worry Peyton needed.

She slapped her hands over her knees and pushed up to her feet. "So . . ."

"We're good," he answered her unspoken question. "You do your thing, I do mine. And stop worrying."

But as she walked out the door and across the arena out of his sight, Red knew he was the one worrying. Because she might not want a repeat performance of the other night. He, on the other hand, was dying for one. And it could end up as nothing but trouble.

Peyton shook her hands out, erasing the tingling, numb sensation from them as she headed back to the house for some lunch. She hated confrontation, always had. Reminded her too much of her childhood, when she used to try playing peacemaker in the house before she wised up and realized nobody could help the Muldoon clan. Her best bet had always been to stay outside, away from Mama. And so her love of the land had begun.

A familiar rig parked by the house had her smiling. She jogged the last few yards and headed in through the front door, barely remembering to toe off her boots before scooting toward the kitchen.

"Morgan?"

"I'm feeding him," Emma called out, then poked her head around the wall. "You come in here right now and get something to eat, or . . ."

"No need to finish that undoubtedly creative threat. I'm coming." Stepping into the kitchen, her feet skidding a little on the newly-waxed floor, she reached for her nephew, who was riding shotgun on Emma's hip. "Hey fella. How's the cutest little boy in the whole world?"

"I'm doing great, thanks," Morgan replied, a wide grin over his face.

"Har, har. So what brings you here?"

"Was driving past, thought I'd check up on the colt with the sprain."

Peyton frowned. "Thought Arby said it wasn't serious and he would treat it."

"Yup. But I had some free time. Wanted to stop by and take a peek. Not to mention score some of Emma's delicious cooking." He leaned down—way down—and kissed the older woman's cheek. "Best cooking in the county."

"Ha. Tell your own mama that. See how long your backside is sore."

"I'm smarter than that."

"Emma? Have you started lunch yet?" The light, airy scent of her sister's perfume preceded her into the kitchen. Bea leaned against the refrigerator in a practiced pose— though it almost seemed natural—and reached into the cabinet for a water glass. "I'm starving."

"Wouldn't be, if you would eat some breakfast," Emma sniffed, but got down a few plates and started fixing sandwiches.

"Emma," Bea said, tsking. "Eggs, sausage, bacon, grits? Cholesterol city. And there's no treadmill in this house."

Peyton snorted and pulled the end of her braid from Seth's mouth where he gummed on it happily.

"Wanting to keep a decent figure isn't a crime, you know. You could . . . oh." Bea froze, water pitcher hovering over her glass, her eyes taking in Morgan. "I'm sorry, I didn't see you there."

Peyton barely held back another snort. The man was six-foot-four. She hadn't missed a damn thing.

Settling the water back in the fridge, Bea held out a hand. "Bea Muldoon."

Morgan stared at the hand like he had no clue what to do with it. What in God's name was wrong with him? Peyton kicked at his ankle and he jerked his hand forward, shaking Bea's with a little more force than necessary. "Morgan Browning."

"Morgan's our vet," Peyton added, jiggling Seth a little to hear him coo with laughter. "He went to school with Trace, but you two were never at school at the same time. His parents live just down the road."

"Right, the Brownings. Of course. I just didn't put two and two together. So." Hands on hips, Bea surveyed him from head to heel. "That's where you've been keeping the good-looking men."

"I, uh . . . I . . ." Morgan blushed until Peyton thought his ears might burn off.

"Don't play with him," she warned Bea.

"Not playing. Just paying our fine vet a compliment. Anyway, do you mind if I borrow the Jeep, Peyton? I need to run some errands and my car's almost out of gas."

Peyton rolled her eyes. It was like they were teenagers again. Peyton, getting yelled at for letting the car go below half a tank. Bea, stranded halfway to school with no gas and not getting so much as a lecture. "Whatever. But bring it back in one piece."

"What's that supposed to mean?"

"How many cars have you had?"

"That second one was not my fault. Emma, never mind. I'll get lunch in town." Without a good-bye, Bea turned on her impractically high heel and flounced out of the kitchen, her short floral skirt snapping behind her.

"So that's your sister," Morgan said, his voice sounding like his collar was too tight.

"That's my sister," Peyton agreed. "For good and ill."

"She seemed . . . nice."

Emma barked with laughter and reached for Seth, pushing one of the sandwich plates Peyton's way. "Nice. Here, eat this and scoot on out of my kitchen. I've got work to get done."

Chapter Fourteen

Red was ready to call it a day well before he actually could. Though Arby was perfectly capable of treating a simple sprain, he'd seen to the colt's injury himself again after work was done for the day, checking up. He knew it didn't sit well with the older man, having his work double-checked. But Red wasn't about to leave anything to chance. Not to mention, another mare was ready to foal. He'd have to catch some sleep when he could.

Just as he settled on the edge of his bed, ready to pull his boots off, his cell phone rang. Picking it up, assuming it was one of the hands announcing that another horse had gone into labor just as he'd left, he answered without looking.

"Son!" His father's booming voice nearly knocked his tired ass off the bed. "Where you been?"

"Same place I was last time we talked, Dad." Definitely not the night for this. "You know, now isn't a good night to talk. Can we catch up some other time?"

"Well, maybe. But I've been meaning to talk to you for a while now. And I wanted to give you a fair warning about my visit. Though if you don't have time now, I'll just let it be a surprise. How about if we—"

"Stop." *Fuck.* "Stop right there. Visit?"

"Well, 'course! I haven't seen you in months."

Over a year, Red silently corrected.

"Dad, when were you planning on getting here?"

Silence greeted him.

"Dad?"

"I'm . . . close."

Cryptic as always. Mac was good with word games when it suited him.

Red pinched the bridge of his nose. *I will not yell. I will not yell. I will not yell.* "And you were going to tell me . . . when?"

"What do you think this call is for?" his father huffed. "This isn't exactly the warm welcome I imagined, you know. My own flesh and blood . . ."

Red put the phone on speaker and set it down on the bed, upside down to muffle the sound. He took his boots off, pushed them under the bed, then stripped down to his boxers. When the faint buzz of his father's voice stopped, he picked the phone back up.

"This really isn't a good time to visit. I'm sorry, but I can't do this right now."

"Ungrateful. That's what you are, boy. I taught you everything you know about horses, which is how you make a living, if I might remind you, and this is how you treat your own father?"

This is how you treat your own son? "I didn't say you couldn't come to visit ever. Just . . . not right now." Not while so much was up in the air with Peyton. One crisis at a time.

"We'll see if I ever call you again." With that, his father hung up.

Red wasn't concerned. Odds were, he'd receive a call in another week or two, asking for money to be wired to pay off yet another gambling debt, or to post bail, or to get Mac out of some other sort of trouble his father hadn't yet come up with. His mind shuddered to contemplate . . .

When the phone rang again, Red could only think, *Really, Dad? That was fast.* But he saw it was the main house calling, not his father.

"Hello?"

"Red, it's Peyton Muldoon."

He smiled at the professional greeting. Like he wouldn't recognize her voice—or her first name. "What's up? Did Butterscotch go into labor?"

"What? No." She sounded breathless, as if she'd been sprinting laps around the barn. Something in the background made a sort of high-pitched shriek that reminded him of a dolphin documentary he'd watched once.

"What the hell was that?" If that was a horse, something was very wrong.

"That," she said through what he could imagine were clenched teeth, "was my nephew. Who won't stop crying."

"Ah." He waited for her to get to the reason for the call, but she said nothing else. "Peyton?"

"What?"

He held back a laugh. "What'd you need?"

"Oh! Oh my God, I called you. Jesus." He heard a thump. "I just . . . I don't . . ." She broke off; then he heard something that sounded suspiciously like a watery sniffle. And finally, she whispered, "I need help."

"Five minutes." He hung up and reversed the disrobing process until he was taking off at a run for the main house. When he knocked on the front door and nobody answered, he waited a good three minutes, then tried the door. Unlocked.

"Peyton?"

Nothing. He took his boots off—just because Emma wasn't staring right at him didn't mean he was willing to face the woman's wrath later—and wandered through the first floor. Not in her office, nor the kitchen or dining area. Hearing the wailing sound coming from upstairs, and someone walking around, he stood by the foot of the stairs and called her name out again, loudly. But she didn't answer.

Okay then. Into the lioness's den he went. Taking the stairs two at a time, he ignored the carved wood of the railing, the wrought iron that weaved in and out to create the banister, the oil paintings that stared at him like in some creepy haunted house. The entire effect of the first floor and the staircase, he realized, was bizarre and totally out of place for a working ranch. Too glitzy, too obvious. Trying too hard.

Sylvia Muldoon's handiwork, no question about it. There was nothing about the decor that had even a hint of Peyton in it.

But when he stepped up to the second floor, he immediately relaxed. Nothing breakable or priceless there. It felt lived-in. Like a family could breathe there and not worry about spilling soda on the carpet or sitting on a crayon on the couch.

"Peyton?"

She stepped out of a doorway to what he assumed was a bedroom, Trace's son—Seth—held against her shoulder, wailing pitifully.

Peyton's eyes were wide. "I'm sorry. I'm so sorry. I just panicked and Emma's gone for the weekend and isn't answering her phone and Bea isn't here—not that she'd be useful anyway—and I refuse to call Trace and bother him and—"

"Slow down." Taking a chance, he walked to her and smoothed a hand over her hair, now falling from some messy bun thing she'd pulled it back into. "Now breathe."

She gulped in air like a fish on land, and he realized the kid was making her tense, which only made the kid more tense in response. Bad cycle. So he reached over and, as gently as he could, took the child from her. Not entirely sure of himself, he cradled the poor, sad baby against his shoulder, doing his best to mimic the pose she'd held him in. In response to the shift, the kid only screamed louder.

How in the hell did something no bigger than his boot make a sound that loud?

Peyton turned away from him, her hands on her head, and he watched as her shoulders rose and fell. He knew she was trying to compose herself so he walked across the living area with the child. The movement seemed to soothe him, though he didn't stop crying. But at least the volume lowered a few notches.

He glanced over his shoulder and saw Peyton watching him, a little color back in her skin.

"Is he hurt? Or sick?"

She shook her head. "No fever, no injuries. He just won't stop crying. For anything. None of the usual stuff is working."

He jiggled the bundle a little in his arms. "Maybe he just misses his dad?"

"I've had him alone before. I've had him longer than this. I see him daily. I'm not exactly a stranger." Peyton swiped under her eyes. "I would have called the doctor but I felt like an idiot doing that when there's no fever, he's not puking or anything else. He's just pissed off. Which now makes two of us," she ended with a mutter, kicking at the edge of the sofa with her bare foot.

Red gave himself a moment to follow the line of her leg up. She wore short shorts, the hem of which barely peeked out under an oversized Minnesota Twins sweat-shirt that looked older than she was. With the sleeves hanging over her hands, her hair completely disheveled and her eyes looking exhausted, he thought she looked like a sleepy treat he wanted to nibble on for hours while they rolled around under the warm covers.

A high-pitched sound snapped his attention back to the

fifteen-pound pile of anger in his arms. The kid stared up at him, almost pleading to make whatever was upsetting him stop. Though the trick was to figure out what that was.

"So where is Trace? Will he be back soon?" As soon as he asked, he remembered Trace was gone for a two-day event a few hours away. "Never mind. I remembered. Are you sure you shouldn't call him though? It's his kid, after all. He might know what's wrong."

"I refuse. Seth's a baby. I should be smart enough to handle this." Peyton's mulish face made him smile.

"Yeah, but isn't there that whole parental intuition thing? Maybe he'd have better ideas. You're not a mother."

"Thanks for stating that, Captain Obvious." The simple truth seemed to piss her off even more. "I'm going down to get a bottle. He just ate, but I'll offer another one, see if he's going through a growth spurt or something."

She disappeared down the stairs, and Red took the opportunity to sit down and hold the kid on his lap. He'd held Seth once in the barn, but the boy had slept through almost the whole thing. Did he realize he was being held by a stranger now? He wondered how much babies understood, and at what ages.

"Hey," he said quietly, though with all the screaming, the kid might not have even heard him. "I'm Red, a friend of your dad's. And your Aunt Peyton's," he added, though right now his thoughts on her weren't friendly so much as, well, more than friendly. "You mind if I hang out with you a while?"

The child's response was a lip wobble and another cry.

"Yeah, I know, I know." He patted the diapered bottom gently, going on intuition and what little his mind remembered from seeing kids in movies or on TV. "Something's wrong and nobody will listen." He traced the tip of one finger down the boy's nose, over his cheeks, around the pouting lips.

And got quite a shock when the child opened up and bit down. Something sharp poked his skin and he pulled back. When the child wailed at being denied the chance to chomp on Red's finger, Red got a good look at one single white cap in his pink gums.

"You two bonding?" Peyton asked, a bottle in her hands, a more relaxed smile on her mouth. She reached for the child and Red gave him up easily. Maybe she'd just needed a break. Listening to that wailing for hours on end would drive him insane. If it was a moment of peace she needed, he was willing to lend a hand. Though it wasn't his idea of a great night.

"Yeah. That tooth there caught me by surprise."

"Tooth? He doesn't have any teeth," Peyton said, distracted while she attempted to offer Seth a bottle. The kid wasn't having it.

"Then it might be brand new." Red shrugged. "I just know he bit down and I got a poke. Looked inside and there it was." He might not know much about kids, but he knew a tooth when he saw one.

Peyton stared at the baby. "Do you have a tooth?" She angled around until she smiled. "You do! When did that show up, huh?" She glanced at him. "Could that be what the problem is? Teething?"

Red shrugged. "Honey, I know horses, not humans. But it sounds logical. Does Trace have a baby book around here somewhere?"

"Yes!" She all but shoved the kid back in his arms and ran off.

"Well. Another round of manly bonding, then?" Red walked around the room, whispering in the child's ear. Not that it helped. But it was better than nothing. The faintly pleading look Seth sent him, as if begging him to make the pain end, shot through him. "Sorry little guy. I'm not exactly good at this kid thing. If I could go through it for you, I would." He'd do just about anything to wipe the desperate look from the baby's eyes.

"Sweet offer," Peyton said softly behind him.

He turned. "Any clues?"

She held up a book about as thick as a dictionary. "It suggests numbing gel for the gums, or a teething ring that we stick in the freezer for a little bit. Also, some baby Tylenol. I've only got the last one. The other two? I dunno. I guess he's a little early on the teething front so we didn't consider it before."

Red continued walking while she administered a tiny dropper of pain medication to the child. Though it didn't take effect immediately, Red hoped it would kick in soon. Then he had an idea.

"Care if I peek through your freezer for a minute?"

Peyton took Seth back as he held him out. "Uh, yeah, but if you want something to drink, I can go get it for you."

"Not a drink. Just gimme a minute." He hurried down the stairs and into the kitchen. After a quick search of the freezer, he found what he was looking for. Baggies were also easy to find, thanks to Emma's militant organization. The woman was a treasure. Red quickly poked a few holes in one corner of the plastic bag, slipped a frozen slice of peach down there, and hustled back up the stairs.

Peyton glanced at his offering. "Late-night snack? Thanks, but I don't really go for fruit so late at night. I'm more of a midnight ice cream binge eater."

"For him, not you." Not at all sure this would work, he waited for the boy to let out another wail, then took the frozen peach slice in the baggie and held it over his gum right where the tooth was. Seth, suddenly distracted by the new sensation, grabbed for the baggie and started to gum the offered snack. The small holes he'd poked allowed the taste and juices through but kept the fruit inside the bag, keeping the possibility of choking to—Red hoped—an impossibility.

After another minute of crying, the sounds slowly dwindled into soft whimpers. Red settled down on the couch and watched Peyton pace the same invisible track he'd walked earlier with the boy, murmuring things he was desperate to hear. Seth drooled peach juice over her shoulder, but she didn't mind. And as the boy's eyes slowly closed, his chest rising and falling in the sleep of the truly exhausted, she sat down in the armchair next to the couch.

"Is he asleep?" she asked.

"Yup."

She sat silently for another few minutes, then stood and turned. "Grab the bag, if you can," she whispered. When he managed to pry the plastic from the boy's sweaty grip, she disappeared with the child through a doorway—presumably the nursery—and came out a few minutes later empty-handed.

She plopped down in the chair and covered her eyes with her hands. "Seemed so easy, so obvious after you said it. I can't believe I missed something that simple."

"You were exhausted. Sometimes the mind just locks down when you're in a situation like that."

When she didn't say anything, he leaned over and did some fancy maneuvering until she slid onto his lap. Almost as if she were asleep, she curled into him and rested her head on his shoulder. He wondered if she even realized what she was doing. But then again, with the house deadly quiet around them, maybe she didn't figure it mattered. Only Seth was there with them, and he was an unreliable witness.

"Thank you," she mumbled.

Red pressed a kiss to her messy hair. "You're welcome." In moments like these, when she wasn't in her badass ranch owner mood, she was as sweet as a newborn kitten. He liked this Peyton. Warm Snuggly Peyton. Not that he disliked Badass Peyton. It was a good balance.

"What made you so against calling your brother?"

"Felt like I should be able to handle it. The kid's twelve pounds and still poops in his pants. If I can't handle that . . ." No need for her to finish the sentence. He knew where her mind was heading.

"Remember what I said before? You are not the answer to everything that goes on in this place. You are not your family's sole strength. Give your brother and sister more credit."

"With Trace, you might just be right. The business side doesn't even remotely interest him. But he's holding his own, both with the PR side, and with being a father. It's miraculous how easily he's taken to it. Not that it's always fun. But easy in that he enjoys it, he likes it, he looks forward to time with his son. Not all fathers can say that. I see little pieces of our dad in him sometimes."

Red wouldn't argue there. He was a prime example of a father-son dynamic that failed.

"But Bea?" She snorted, air softly brushing against his neck. "She wants nothing to do with this place. Every time I try to pin her down to talk about the realities of the will, she runs off somewhere *important.*" Peyton used air quotes for the last word. "Important for Bea usually implies a manicure or haircut."

Red didn't know her, so he wouldn't jump into that family issue. But rubbing Peyton's back, relaxing on the couch after she'd put the baby back down to—he hoped—sleep for a good long while, any tension he'd been carrying from the long-ass day, the shitty conversation he'd had with his father and the stress of wondering if his dad was a threat to his job . . . it all melted away. And for a moment he could seriously imagine his life like this. Having the quiet, contented moments with Peyton Muldoon every evening after a good, long day's work. Recharging his system, and hers, both in bed and out.

Too bad he knew for sure she would rather slap him and push him out the door head first than even contemplate it.

Peyton shifted, taking care to not squash the family jewels in her movement—a consideration he appreciated—and stood up. That, he assumed, was his cue to make his excuses and head home. But instead, she held out a hand and pulled him off the couch, led him to another bedroom, and closed the door behind her.

Well. Red might just be a slow country son of a bitch from time to time. But even he wasn't dumb enough to turn down this kind of opportunity.

Chapter Fifteen

Big mistake. Big mistake. Big mistake.

And she didn't give a flying Frisbee.

Red had been there, majorly, when she'd been ready to collapse. It burned to call him for help, not because of who he was, but because she needed help, period. But better to call him than her brother. The teasing he would have given her over not being able to handle a baby, she never would have lived down. And he'd been a quick thinker with the frozen peach trick when her own mind had been too exhausted to function at full speed. She wasn't going to forget that.

But it wasn't gratitude that had her pulling him into her room and closing the door. She knew how to say thank you and mean it. She wouldn't use her body when words would work just fine. No, this was pure desire for the man he was. The kind of man who would drop everything and come help a woman take care of a screaming infant. An infant that wasn't his, who he had no prior knowledge to or relation with. And wouldn't use that moment as an opening to tease, to mock, or to hold over her head.

Redford Callahan was a good, honest man. And she needed him like she needed air.

But just for tonight, she reminded herself as she reached

for his shirt. Purely to unwind from the baby stress. Just for now.

Even as the shirt came loose from his waistband, she was calling herself a liar. But if she needed the lie to take what she wanted, so what? It didn't hurt anyone.

Except me.

Shutting down her inner monologue, she concentrated on running her hands over warm male skin and feeling the delight when he shivered and flexed beneath her touch.

"So is this what you always wear to bed?" He reached for and grabbed onto the bottom hem of her ragged sweatshirt. Trace's sweatshirt, actually, but she'd stolen it from him close to fifteen years ago, so she was pretty sure the statute of limitations had long since passed.

"Maybe." Did he wish she wore sexy lingerie to bed every night, just in case of a booty call?

"Hmm. I have to say, as much as it shocks me, seeing this whole oversized shirt, tiny shorts combo on you is massively appealing. Makes me wish it was my shirt you were wearing." He took a nip out of her neck, a possessive bite.

Now she was the one shivering.

Reaching between them, she undid his belt buckle and pushed with frantic hands to lower his jeans. He stepped back and kicked off his boots—no socks . . . he really must have hauled ass to get to the house when she called—and stripped down to his birthday suit.

God, he was beautiful. Though he'd likely disagree. The man wasn't free of blemishes or marks. No, he had scars upon scars. She could easily guess what they were from, too. Ranch work, working with horses, didn't leave you without a few permanent souvenirs. But those marks only made him more beautiful in her eyes. A real man who used his body daily for real work. Not lifting weights in some sterile gym, going through the motions looking for definition. No, these were muscles toned by his job, developed from necessity. Not bulky, but cut all the same.

"I seem to be the one lagging behind this time." She reached for the hem of her sweatshirt but he stilled her hand.

"Let me." She waited, but he didn't strip her shirt off. Just stared at her for a long moment, before scooping her up and tossing her on the bed. She laughed as she bounced and he pounced on her, playfully growling and nuzzling into her neck, working his way down to her breasts, still covered by the shirt. As he nipped, the thick fabric muted the worst of the sting. But she still felt every bite, every bit of contact. And loved it all.

Her hands went instinctively to his hair, fingers gliding through the golden brown locks. It was longer again, like he'd forgotten to bother with a haircut. Not out of any sense of style. Just out of sheer lack of time. The strands felt like little silk threads, like the sort of important material she'd never be able to wear. All that rich, impractical texture just begging to be touched and caressed.

He lifted the bottom of the sweatshirt a little, enough to reveal her stomach, and kissed around her belly button. Then he eased down the shorts she wore until they were completely off. As he pressed her legs wider apart, she clamped them back together.

"What are you doing?" she hissed. "Get back up here."

He smirked, or at least she thought he did in the dark of the bedroom. She wasn't about to turn on a light now just to check. Not while his face was down there. Hell no.

"I'm exploring. Got a problem with that?"

"Maybe. Can't we just do what we did before?" Not the most mature of descriptions, but she was sort of limited in this area of living. She motioned for him to climb his way back up her body, but he didn't budge.

"You're directing again. What'd we talk about last time?"

"That was then. This is now. And Peyton says get back up here."

"Red says no." He pressed a kiss to the crease between her inner thigh and her . . . oh for the love of God. Peyton's head flopped back and she bit her lip to keep from screaming out. In shock, in pleasure, in confusion, she had no clue. Maybe a mix of all three. But she soon realized Red's tongue was good for more than just that sweet drawl he played with.

Dammit. Another moment to add to the catalog she flipped through in her dreams.

All too soon, or maybe not soon enough, she was riding the crest of a seriously intense orgasm. And before she could even lift her hands to play with his hair again, he was sliding up her body and into her. Or almost into her . . .

"Christ. Condom?"

"I . . . oh. No." She didn't have condoms in her room. And why the hell would she? It wasn't like she brought men back to the house she shared with her brother and her housekeeper. This was sort of a first for her. "Hold that thought." Before he could say a word, she slid out from under him and darted into Bea's room. Her uberworldly, super-chic sister would surely have some in her bathroom or bag. But after coming up surprisingly empty, she dashed across the hall to Trace's room. In one of the drawers of his bathroom vanity, she struck gold. After her inability to tear just one off, she brought the whole strip and hustled back to her room, tossing the condoms at Red.

He stared at the strip, holding it up so they all fell out of their folded position. "You know I can only wear one of these at a time, right?"

"Shut up. They wouldn't come apart, so you get to try."

He used his teeth to open one packet without even removing it from the rest of the strip and rolled it on. Then he dragged her back into position under him and entered her with one smooth glide.

They both sighed with relief, though Peyton's heart was doing a jittery dance of its own thanks to her world-record-setting sprint around the house.

"Let's try this a little differently." Before she could ask what that meant, he rolled so she was on top. "Private riding lesson."

She cocked a brow at him, though he likely couldn't see it. "Private lesson, huh?"

"Yup. We'll concentrate on your . . . form." He slid rein-roughened hands up from her ass to her breasts, molding over the flesh and back down again.

She rocked back and forth, loving the instant feedback from his body. The breath that hissed between his teeth, the way his abs tightened under her hands, his own hips surging up as if he couldn't help it.

"My form. Hmm. I've always been told I have such good form. You know, from previous . . . instructors." Was that really her? Flirting like that? Making those not-so-veiled innuendos?

Bea would be so proud.

"Previous instructors, hmm?" His tone thickened. "Gotta tell you, I might have a few tricks up my sleeve you haven't seen yet."

"Maybe so." She was more than willing to let him show her.

And so he did.

With it being Emma's weekend off, and Trace gone as well, and Bea coming home God knew when, Peyton didn't feel all that bad about drifting off after Red returned to the bed from cleaning up. Plenty of time to get him out the door before people were up and around in the morning. And it wasn't as if he had a truck outside that would just scream "booty call, master bedroom."

"That little bit about instructors," Red started, hand running from the top of her bottom to her shoulders and back again. "That was a joke, right?"

"Joke. Sure." She snuggled closer to his heat. He'd stripped her sweatshirt off after the deed was done, saying he wanted skin contact. And now she needed the extra warmth.

"I mean, I know you had some, um, lessons before. And I've had my own share of, uh, students . . ."

"Lovers, Red." Time to put the poor guy out of his misery. She patted his stomach affectionately. "We've both had lovers." Though her last one was, well, a while ago. No need to mention that though.

He sighed with relief. "Yes. Thank you. But I just wanted you to know . . . there's nobody now. Nobody but you."

Oh damn. Shit. Damn. Son of a . . . "Red . . ."

He tugged playfully on her hair. "This is the part where you say, 'There's nobody else for me either, Red.' "

Tread carefully, and watch for road apples. "Red, I'm not . . . I'm not seeing anyone else right now." He deserved that much, and it was the truth. She wasn't about to lie on that one. Plus, too easy to verify. "But that doesn't really matter much, since—"

"It's enough."

"Well, it's not, actually, because this is the last night we're doing that."

He smirked. "You said that the last time. You've got a strange habit of repeating yourself, Peyton."

"This time doesn't count," she said defensively, sitting up and pulling the sweatshirt down over her knees. "It was an emergency."

"The baby screaming bit, I'll buy that. But after?" He shook his head. "Don't do this."

"This what?"

"Don't cheapen this. It happened, we liked it, and I'd like to do it again. I'm guessing you would, too. And we get along."

"We bicker constantly."

"Well, yeah, that's what I mean. You're not afraid to tell me to go fuck myself, and I'm not afraid to push you right back. It works."

Peyton sighed and dug her face into her knees. "Your definition of the term 'get along' is sick."

"Couples that never fight are doing something wrong," he said cheerfully. "Not only are they not growing, but if you ask me, they're missing out on the best part of fighting."

"I'm scared to ask, but what would that be?"

Red's smile turned from simply happy to carnal and a little evil. "The making up, of course."

And even though they weren't really fighting, Peyton thought a little making up wouldn't hurt. Just a little, until she had to roll him out of bed.

Red slid his cart over toward the checkout. "Bill, go have them start ringing the order up, put this on my account, okay? I want to check one more thing before we're done."

"Sure thing, Mr. Callahan!" Bill, whom Red had brought along for his trip to the feed and supply store, raced off with the cart like a NASCAR hopeful.

"It's Red!" he shouted after him, but chuckled. The kid was more eager than anyone else he'd seen. And twice as grateful for the opportunity as kids who were handed their first pony simply for existing. When Billy had realized he'd be shadowing Red, learning and all-around playing personal assistant rather than spending his mornings knee-deep in manure, the kid had all but spun himself dizzy with gratitude.

Red scanned the vitamins, realized they still didn't have the ones he wanted in stock, and resigned himself to ordering online. Though he preferred giving local stores his business whenever possible, he wasn't about to lower his standards on what he gave his horses.

"Son."

Speaking of lowered standards . . . Red turned slowly and stared into the face of Mac Callahan. The year since the last time they'd come face to face had aged the man considerably. He was still handsome, but now showing his age more than he used to. His dad's behavior and constant penchant for finding the next pile of trouble was finally catching up to him.

"So. Found me." Red leaned against the shelf. "I thought I told you now wasn't a good time for a visit."

"Visit? Shit." Mac scratched his belly—a belly just a little rounder than the last time—and shook his head. "I've been working here for over a month now."

It was worse than he'd thought. "Here? The feed store?" Red swiveled his head around as if that'd give him answers.

"Nah, I meant here, in town. I'm down at the tack shop. Good gig, though I always prefer working straight with horses if I can. But work's work."

Red let his hat fall to his side in his hand. "You've been here a month and I never knew. Didn't think to tell me."

"Not like you would've given two shits. Your old man doesn't mean jack squat to you anymore." The heat behind the words petered out before he could finish the second sentence. He shifted weight from one foot to another.

Red waited.

His father ran a hand over his hair, now shot through

with silver threads, his posture almost defeated, reluctant. His eyes didn't quite meet Red's when he said, "I missed you."

Translation: *I missed the open ATM from the Bank of My Son.*

Red silently chastised himself. Maybe his father was trying to turn it around. Maybe with age really did come wisdom. Maybe now, this time, in this place, they could finally start working on mending the fences of the past and—

"I'm hoping you can help your old man out. See, I met up with a few new friends here in town, and there was this game going. And the stakes got away from me. I was conned, I'd swear it, tricked into going higher than I realized. I just need a little something to get me by. Pay the debt. I'll have it back to you before you even—"

Red gave himself a quick *told you so.* "No."

"Ungrateful piece of shit. That's what you are." From vaguely apologetic to offensive in the blink of an eye. Yeah, Red didn't doubt there was a con going on. But his father being the mark? Not likely. "You don't even need money. You got everything you need out there on that ranch with that woman. You probably even have her, don't you? A woman, a job, a place to park your boots at night. Respect. You lucked out and I didn't. That's all that was. You got the good hand and I got the fold. It's pure luck you ended up on top."

Red's hands fisted, crushing the bill of his hat in his right hand. But he didn't care. The insult to Peyton was too blatant to ignore. "You leave her the fuck out of it. Anything you wanna say about me, say it. But the Muldoons? They're untouched by your brand of bad luck, and I'll be damned if that doesn't continue."

"I'm right here. I can touch them if I want." The smug smile was more than a slick move of mouth. It was a promise, a silent threat. Someone else might not see it, but Red knew his father too well to underestimate what that expression meant.

Ice slid through his gut at the thought of his father coming near Peyton, having anything to do with her. And the fear had nothing to do with his job and everything to do with what Red knew Mac was capable of. From small cons to complete ruin, he could chip away at the family business in a million little ways before anyone knew what was happening. And the Muldoons were too raw to handle it.

"You have no right."

His father blustered and Red knew exactly where he was heading next. So he straightened and loomed over his father a few inches.

"Yeah, yeah. I'll save you the time. You put me up on my first pony, taught me to ride, I'm where I am today because of you, blah blah blah." For the first time in, well, ever, Red was finally ready to give his father what he deserved, straight to his face. The mere thought of the man coming close to Peyton gave him all the emotional ammo he needed for the final break. "Don't come crawling to me again. Don't call me for money because you were too drunk or too arrogant and lost it all in a game of chance. Don't ask for a job reference, because the minute someone asks me about you, I'll tell them the truth. Don't step one foot on the M-Star ranch property, because I'll have you arrested. And if I were you, I'd pack up and head out of town as soon as you can. I'll even be generous and give you a two-week break before I go in and tell Mr. Hollins, the tack store owner, all about your multitude of other jobs and why you were fired from them."

He waved a hand toward the door. "Now go hand in your two-week notice, and until you've got Marshall in your rearview mirror, don't give me another thought."

Red sidestepped his father—the only family he had, which was the single thought that kept him from swinging after the insult to Peyton—and walked out the door into the sun to wait for Bill.

"All set, Mr. Callah—I mean, Red. Did you find anything else you needed?" Bill walked up to stand next to him, plastic shopping bags in hand.

"No, nothing else I need in there." Red slammed his hat back on his head and walked out to his rig. On the drive back to the ranch, though, a thought crept through his mind.

His father had been in town for weeks and he hadn't known it. And the man needed money. Mac wasn't above stealing, when it suited him. And stealing from his son, the son who he considered successful through luck alone, would likely suit his father to the ground.

His father had shown up before at ranches where he'd found work. But it was usually with grand fanfare, a big show, trying to give him no opportunity to escape. Never before had Mac snuck in like a thief in the night without making contact.

Thief in the night. Red snorted. Apt term. Red thought back to the old lock his father carried in his bag, the one he practiced picking. The proudest he'd ever seen his father was when Red had picked the lock in record time, beating even his own record. As a child, he'd thought the whole thing a game. As a teen, he saw the potential for disaster. As an adult, well . . .

If his father was snooping around his home or office, looking for money or another way of scoring fast and big, he'd be out of luck.

He resolved to have the locks to both his apartment and his office changed when he had five minutes. No, he'd make five minutes the minute they got back home.

Though his father would have probably used some rudimentary lock-picking tools, he wasn't taking any chances.

Just another reminder to keep from getting too far involved with Peyton. As if Red needed any other reasons. He had some seriously bad blood running through his veins. Damn his luck.

Red made a quick U-turn on the deserted road and headed back into town.

"Small detour on the way home, Bill. We're heading over to the hardware store. I've got a few locks I've been meaning to reinforce."

Chapter Sixteen

Peyton waited until she knew Bea would be in the kitchen. Her sister was like clockwork when it came to her eating. For someone the size of a twig, she could pack it away. Only not when anyone was watching.

Trace followed Peyton into the house, as silent as possible, and both slipped their boots off. When Peyton heard the vacuum upstairs, she knew that accounted for Emma. And the soft scraping of a fork over a plate in the kitchen signaled Bea's location.

Peyton crept on shoeless feet until she could peer around the kitchen door. Bea stood at the sink, shoveling what looked like a leftover piece of the pie Emma had baked for dinner the night before into her mouth.

Not so prissy and girly now, huh? Peyton grinned. "Leave any for us?"

Bea shrieked and dropped the plate, the solid stoneware clanging into the sink. One hand flattened against her chest and she bent over as if catching her breath after a long sprint. "Oh Jesus, Peyton. Don't do that."

Trace walked in behind Peyton and peered into the sink. "Damn, did you clean the entire plate? Emma's gonna kill you."

Bea shoved at Trace's shoulders. "Don't comment on what a woman eats. It's rude."

"Noted." Trace leaned a hip against the counter. "Got some time to talk?"

Bea rolled her eyes and checked her watch. "No, sorry. Big day today."

"Thought you might say that." Without warning, Trace lowered his torso until he could fit one shoulder under Bea's stomach to lift her. She shrieked again and beat her fists against his back while he carried her to the kitchen table.

"Dammit, Trace! This wasn't funny when we were kids and it's not funny now! Put me down!"

"No problem." He dumped her in a chair, catching her by the wrist when she almost flew off the seat. "We're going to have a talk, and if you won't sit still for it, I'm not above getting some rope and practicing my roping skills on you."

Bea huffed, her breath pushing a strand of hair from her eyes, and crossed her arms over her chest. Peyton sighed. It was like looking at Bea ten years ago. A sulky teen who had just found out she couldn't talk or flirt her way out of everything.

"So talk."

Peyton sat down and crossed her ankles, lacing her hands over her stomach. "The ranch is split three ways. You know that now."

"Right." She shifted in her seat, as if about to make a breakaway. But when Trace inched forward to crowd her space, Bea settled down. "I know. I read the papers that lawyer guy gave us."

"Tim," Peyton said, keeping a strangle hold on her patience. "And yes. We are all equal owners, currently."

"And there was something about needing a majority to make big decisions." Bea's pouty mouth curved into a smile that would scare anyone paying attention. "But since that didn't define what made up a small decision, we're entitled to make those ourselves."

"That's something we're going to iron out, with Tim's help." Trace sat down, apparently realizing Bea wasn't going to run.

"So if I wanted to suddenly paint all the tack bright pink, I could. I doubt that's considered a big decision." Bea's grin only widened.

Peyton let her forehead slap the table. "I told you."

"Bea, be serious now." But Trace's voice was amused, as Peyton knew it would be. Even when they were kids, he babied her. Everyone did. Sweet, pretty, doll-like Beatrice. Needs pampering, not as tough and boyish as her sister. Someone has to look out for Bea. "You can't just start making changes. You haven't been here. Hell, I haven't been here. Peyton has."

Bea was silent for a moment, then nodded. "You're right."

Peyton's head snapped up so fast her neck ached. She watched Bea's face for signs of trickery or sarcasm, but for once, her sister seemed to be shooting straight. No games.

"Don't look at me like that," Bea snapped, anger firing her Muldoon-blue eyes to an icy sheen. "I'm not an idiot. This ranch was never mine. I just lived here. And frankly, I don't know the first thing about running a place like this. I'd run it into the ground, the same way Mama tried. Daddy's place deserves better."

Peyton swallowed around the lump in her throat at the mention of their father. "Yes, it does." After a moment, she debated, then pushed on. "I didn't think you even cared for Daddy."

Bea shrugged, but her fingers picked at a seam in the table's wood. "I barely knew the man. I spent all my time indoors with Mama. You two were his shadows."

If Peyton didn't know better, she'd think Bea was upset by that. But years of dealing with her sister had taught her to read between the lines and not take much at face value. "So you're not going to interfere."

"Nope. Just write the check and I'm good to go."

"Check?" Trace and Peyton said at once, looking at each other.

"Sure. To buy me out. Then it's just a fifty-fifty split, unless Trace does the same. But really, ownership looks good on you, bro." She patted his arm condescendingly, and Bea's man-eater, I-don't-care persona slid back into place.

"Bea . . ." Trace looked to Peyton.

"We can't afford to buy you out," Peyton said flatly. Why sugarcoat it? "The place isn't worth much right now. You want a check cut? It wouldn't pay for more than a few months of rent for you out there in Cali."

Bea's mouth dropped. "Seriously?"

"Seriously." Peyton felt a moment's satisfaction at having disturbed her sister's perfect image of how things would work. Petty, and she could admit that. "If you want to wait it out, you can always head back to California and we can notify you when big things are coming up. Eventually, after things are off the ground, we can revisit the idea of buying you out."

"And how long will that be?"

Peyton shrugged. "A few years, give or take. Hard to pinpoint more definitely than that. But it'll be a while."

Bea moaned and let her head drop back so she stared at the ceiling.

"Peyton's right, Bea. If you want to head back home, nothing's stopping you. You don't have to be here. If there are papers to sign or anything like that, we can overnight them to you."

She rolled from the chair with the grace of a dancer. Bea had always wanted to take dance classes, Peyton remembered suddenly. But they couldn't afford them. "I'm going up to my room." She left without another word.

"Well, that went well." Peyton stood and turned back to the fridge to see if Bea had left any pie.

"Think she's upstairs packing?" Trace opened the fridge, poking his head in to survey the contents.

"I couldn't read Bea when we were kids, and I definitely can't read her now after almost a decade apart. Who knows? She might very well just stay here to spite me."

"Us."

"No, me." Peyton grabbed a clean fork and attacked the last of the pie, mostly crust. "She liked you better growing up."

"Because we didn't constantly fight. You two were always snipping at each other."

Peyton thought back, realizing Trace was right. And didn't like how she looked in the mix. "Well, if she stays, we'll have to find something for her to do. Helping Emma or whatever. I don't care. But if she stays, she gets a job."

Emma sailed in, Seth on her hip. "Who's helping Emma?"

"Bea," Peyton said around a mouthful of crust. "If she stays, I mean. I'd give her a job out at the barn but, you know, I don't even think she could tell the front end of a horse from the back."

Emma huffed and used her other hip to bump Peyton away from the sink. "So you won't have her messing things up around your end of the business, but she's fine getting in my way."

Trace flashed her a wide grin. "That about sums it up." He reached for his son, the child holding out his arms with glee. "Come here, big guy."

As expected, Emma melted at the sight of Trace and his son, so clearly in love with each other. "All right, off you go. Scoot. Trace, he needs to be put down for a nap."

"I'll go run him up." Trace dropped a kiss on Emma's cheek and headed out.

Peyton waited for a moment for Emma's hands to slow down and stuck her plate under the water to rinse it off.

"Don't be too hard on her."

"Hard on who?" Peyton asked, her mind already moving on to the rest of the day's schedule.

"Your sister." Emma took the plate from her and opened the dishwasher. "Tough as nails on the outside, but there's something more going on inside."

Red kept his distance from Peyton the rest of the day in order to mull over the issue of his father. What he would tell Peyton. When. If he should say anything at all. If his warning—and the new locks he'd installed—would be enough to deter his father from trying anything else.

He kept his distance from Peyton for the rest of the day, knowing he wasn't in a position to make rational decisions where she was concerned. But any time she was near, his eyes were drawn to her like a magnet. He couldn't help but watch her from the corner of his eye.

And though she was careful, he caught her watching him, too. His gut told him she wouldn't turn him away tonight. And the truth was, he was dying to hold her. After the long day and his father's abrupt appearance in town, he needed something soft and simple to occupy his mind and erase the filth.

Red waited until the ranch slept. As he crept down and around the garage, he stood still for a moment. Something in the shifting wind warned him to hold off on crossing over the open land to the main house. Something—no, someone—else was out there.

Red's blood boiled. His father. The damn man hadn't even waited twenty-four hours after hitting his son up for money before deciding to take some for himself. But even as Red crept back into the shadow of the garage, he caught sight of what'd stirred his senses. And it most certainly wasn't his father.

Lithe, graceful, and sure, the obviously female form moved with purpose across the dirt driveway from the main house toward the barn. He'd have said Peyton, but the figure was much too tall to be her. And much too fast to be Emma.

Beatrice, the youngest then.

But what the hell was she up to? The youngest, who hated the dirt and the outdoors and thought the horses smelled horrible, going to the barn on purpose. He watched her open the sliding barn door and walk in. Curiosity warred with a need to reach Peyton, but the curiosity won out. He snuck around until he was flattened against the stable wall, using his ears to detect what she was up to.

The sound of the tack room door opening. Soft, feminine murmuring, the wicker and ninny of a horse. Then the unmistakable sounds of a horse being saddled. Leather creaked, brass clanged. And without realizing she was being watched, Bea led the horse through the open door and into the darkness. From close up, he could see she wore jeans that were tight, but not impractically so, boots and a jacket. Her hair, usually fluffed and sprayed, was held back by simple clips from her face.

And as she and her chosen horse—Lover Boy, a responsive but spirited mount—cleared the stable, she placed her left foot in the stirrup, gripped the horn and back of the saddle, and launched herself into the seat with practiced ease. Those mile-long legs were a clear plus when it came to mounting without assistance.

"Okay boy," she said, her voice much softer than the sharp-toned one he'd heard her use before. "Let's have a little fun."

With a click of her tongue and a nudge of her knees, they headed off.

Red debated a moment going out with her, following her to make sure she wasn't going to hurt herself. But that little show was not the behavior of a woman unused to riding. Unless he missed his guess, she was more than a little familiar with the practice. Not to mention, she technically owned a third of the place, and that included the horses. If she wanted to go out riding in the middle of the night with one of the Muldoon horses, who was he to question it?

He shook his head and kept on toward the main house. But even as he reached the porch, another figure exited the kitchen door.

This time, he was sure, it was Peyton sneaking off into the dark.

"Out for a midnight ride, sweetheart?"

She gasped and covered her mouth with her hand. "Oh, my God. Don't do that!" With her other hand over her heart, she turned her back to him a moment. After composing herself, she looked over her shoulder. "What are you doing out here?"

"Same as you, I suppose." When she cocked her head to one side, he smiled, though he doubted she could see it. "Practicing my breaking and entering skills."

Peyton started to laugh, then swallowed the sound and slapped at his arm. "Stop that." She glanced around as if she were being followed. "Come on. Back to your place."

"I like a forward woman." He tucked his hands in his pockets and easily caught up, thanks to the fact that it took her two steps to make one of his.

"I'm not forward, I'm discreet. Something we can't be if we're in the house, with Emma and Trace and Bea in there."

"Bea's not—" He stopped himself short.

"Bea's not what?" She didn't look up at him, concentrating instead on the ground and not tripping over anything in the dark.

"Bea's not . . . like you," he finished lamely. If Bea didn't want her family knowing she went for joyrides in the middle of the night, it wasn't his business to bring it up. He'd check on Lover Boy in the morning, but as long as she groomed him well and settled the tack back in the proper spots, then he wouldn't say anything.

Peyton snorted. "She never was. Barbie doll and tomboy, we couldn't be more different if we tried."

"Who gave you those labels?" Red followed her up the stairs to his apartment and opened the door around her. As she shuffled inside, he watched her make herself at home in his small place. Boots came off and settled by the door, just as if Emma would come bursting in to scold her otherwise. She hung her jacket on the back of a kitchen chair, walked to the fridge and grabbed his pitcher of water, then started looking through cabinets for a cup.

"Above the stove," he said helpfully.

"They should go by the fridge. That's where they make the most sense." But when she reached for the cabinet, she couldn't quite make it. "Why don't you have a stool in this place?"

He walked up behind her, raised his arm, and pulled down a cup without a word. As he handed it to her, she scowled. "Not all of us can be freak-of-nature tall, you know."

"Of course not." He waited until she had a drink and asked again, "Who named you the tomboy and your sister the Barbie doll?"

"You just assume I was the tomboy? Why couldn't I be the Barbie?"

Red just stared at her.

"Oh, fine. My mother. Sylvia."

He waited patiently.

"Trace is the oldest. And he was all boy from the start. Which was a good thing. But when I came along, I think my mother just saw me as a plaything. Trace was already Dad's little helper, following him around the ranch like they were joined at the knee. So a girl? As far as she was concerned, I was practically begging to be decked out in lace and ribbons and bows simply because I was born female."

Red tried—he really did try—to hold back a laugh at the thought of a little mini-Peyton all dressed up in her Sunday finest on a daily basis. And he could perfectly picture the little brunette cutie sulking in a corner with her frills, a pretty pout on her face because she would rather tear the whole thing off and go roll in the dirt.

Peyton's mouth curved, as if she knew exactly what he was thinking. "Uh huh. Obviously you see this didn't work out. Much to my mother's dismay, I was just as determined to be outside with Daddy as Trace was. We were three peas in a pod. Then came Bea."

Peyton shifted to stare out the small window behind his kitchen table. "She was the little princess my mother had been waiting for. All baby-fine blond hair and those big blue eyes. The doll she could dress up and show off to her friends. Perfection, really." Peyton shrugged, like it didn't matter. Red wasn't buying it. "Trace was Daddy's protégé. Bea fell right in line with Mama's girly plans. I sort of just . . . hung in limbo. Wasn't a fun place to be sometimes."

"Why weren't you your father's protégé?"

She sighed. "I was still a girl. I loved my father so much. And he taught me what he knew about horses, which was plenty." As if reading his mind, she shrugged her shoulders. "It was his business sense he struggled with. But anyway, he didn't mind teaching me how to ride, handle life in the barn. But I was still a girl, and he never quite let go of the idea that Trace would step into his boots. Between being the oldest and being male, well . . ."

"And you never mentioned you wanted to learn how to run the ranch?"

"I didn't want to upset the balance." Peyton cleared her throat and shot him a sultry look. "But that's enough of that. How about you and I see what your bed feels like?"

He let her lead him to his bed, small though it was. He had more than a few creative ways to get around the lack of square footage. But in the back of his mind, he mentally made a note to think about how upset she was with her mother and the lot she'd been handed in life. Nobody thought Peyton gave two shits about her mother. And God knew, it seemed her mother hadn't care a damn for Peyton. Or the ranch, come right down to it. Probably didn't care about anyone but herself. But Peyton cared. Or at least, the little girl Peyton had once been cared.

He ached for that little girl, the one in the frilly dress who wasn't enough for her mother just by being herself, nor her father who loved her, but didn't know what to do with her. He hated that she felt the weight of restrictions placed on her shoulders, a conditional sort of love. And he sympathized with her for that, since his own father's affections could be bought and sold for a few grand and a good bottle of Jameson.

But Peyton wasn't ready to bond over childhood memories. Not yet. He was prepared to wear her down though. Prepared to wait her out. He was a patient man. It made him damn good at his job. So he could afford the same sort of patience with the woman he was becoming more and more sure he wanted to spend forever with.

Taking her hand, Red led Peyton to the bed, a whole seven steps in the other direction. When her knees hit the mattress, he used one hand to guide her down gently until her feet dangled over the edge of the bed. He sat beside her, but ignored her outstretched arms. First things first. He gripped one boot and pulled until it slid off her foot, then massaged her instep a moment. Peyton groaned in response, her back arching.

"Oh my God, that is unbelievable."

"I hear that a lot. Ouch." He rotated his shoulder where she whacked him. "This is the treatment I get?"

"You mention other women, it's what you get." She only melted farther into the mattress when he switched feet. "Okay, you can say whatever you want, just don't stop doing that."

He laughed. "You're making it too easy on me."

She cracked one eyelid. "I think that's the first time a guy has ever complained about having it easy."

Red almost tossed her words back at her, but then his gut clenched at the thought of Peyton with another man. Call him a caveman, but he didn't want to think about it. To take both their minds off the conversation, he worked the button to her jeans until it popped free, then the zipper. The rasp of the metal teeth giving was almost drowned out by Peyton's accelerated breathing.

She was definitely not as immune to their chemistry as she wanted to make him believe, wanted to believe herself. She was a woman who would go to her grave attempting to convince herself one thing while feeling another. But there was no mistaking her sharp breath when he hooked his thumbs in the top of her jeans and pulled. The denim caught at her knees, then slithered to the floor with just a small push from him.

Creamy skin covered with practical cotton underwear had him smiling. He liked her simple underwear. Showed she wasn't interested in fooling around with the frilly stuff. A woman after his own heart.

But after those panties were on the floor with her jeans and boots, he was smiling for a whole different reason.

"I hate when you look like that," she grumbled.

"Like what?" Red let his fingers trail down her center, pausing with every shiver of her body.

"Like right now. You look like a wolf stalking a helpless sheep."

He did a quick roll that put Peyton on top. "Helpless, my ass."

And with a wolfish grin of her own, Peyton took to her newfound advantage like a duck to water. She ripped at his shirt, shoving aside the material so fast he was sure he heard seams pop. But he'd have gladly torn the thing to shreds himself to help her once she put her mouth on his skin.

Her tongue traced around his belly button, then down the happy trail to his waistband. Then the pink tip darted under the elastic of his boxers and he nearly lost it.

"Jesus, Peyton. Take them off or just kill me already."

She laughed, enjoying her power a little too much. "Anxious, cowboy?"

"Honey, I can't think straight, I want you so much."

Her eyes shifted to a dark, almost blue-black, color, and she tugged hard at his belt and the button of his jeans. While she finished undressing him, he reached into the bedside drawer for the box of condoms, tossing one onto his stomach. Before he could sit up to roll it on, she grabbed it and did the deed herself.

God, her hands around his cock, even with something so practical as protection, hammered him with sensations he needed to lock down if he was going to make this last longer than five seconds. He rolled once more so she was under him, then had the satisfaction of watching her eyes go glassy when he pushed into her, pulsed fully inside her.

When he didn't move, didn't set the pace, Peyton's

hands streaked up and down his back. "Red, I can't wait. Don't make me wait."

Her small plea broke his need to take it slow, and he gave up all hope of lasting. He pulled back, pushed in again, and shuddered when she tightened around him. Jesus God, the woman could drive him crazy on every level.

He breathed her name as he thrust again and again. The satisfied sound of her climax barely had time to register in his mind before he fell over the cliff of completion himself.

The last thing he thought before they both drifted to sleep, with Peyton tucked firmly beside him, was that there was no way he would willingly give this up.

Hours later, Red kissed the top of Peyton's head and opened the side door to the main house. "Good night."

She smiled back up at him and bumped his arm with her shoulder. "You didn't have to walk me back. This isn't a date or anything."

"No, not a date." At least, none of his dates before had ever been so much fun. "But it's still my job to make sure you get home safely."

She rolled her eyes in the weak light, but the corners of her mouth twitched. Answering the temptation, he swooped down and kissed her once more, hard and fast. "Go to bed. Boss needs to be in top condition tomorrow."

She rolled her eyes again, but scooted out of reach when he made a lunge for her. "You go to bed. My prize trainer needs to perform." With a wink that left him a little dumbfounded—did Peyton really just wink?—she closed the door behind her, and he heard the dead bolt slide home.

Grinning like the fool he was, Red shoved his hands in his pockets and walked back across the dirt path toward his apartment. Somehow he managed to resist the urge to whistle. He couldn't remember a time when he'd ever felt like things were going so right in his life. It wasn't ideal, he admitted. Sneaking around like horny teenagers trying not to get caught by mom and dad wasn't really how a man in his thirties wanted to handle his love life. But for the moment, it was what Peyton was comfortable with.

Eventually he could ease her into a more open relationship. But he knew it'd take some time. Pushing her would be a surefire way to have his ass kicked off the property pronto.

A movement, a shift of shadow, caught his eye and he turned toward the barn. Someone stood in the dark shade of the overhang of the side door that led to Arby's office. Immediately the hairs on the back of his neck stood up. Definitely not Beatrice, and not one of his guys either.

But it was definitely a man. A man Red shared DNA with. Before he could decide whether to try to sneak around the side and catch his father unaware or sprint full out at him, the shadow turned and ran in the opposite direction. Red ran after him, doing his best to make up for the head start, ready to tackle his father to the ground, but as the man rounded the corner of the workout arena, it was as if he disappeared into thin air.

Dammit, Mac. Red halted, knowing the chase would do no good. Instead, he turned on his heel and raced back to the barn to see how far his father had gotten in the process of breaking into the barn. The lock still looked intact. Going around to the front, where the large sliding door wouldn't be locked, he stepped onto the concrete floor. One lazy head poked out from her stall to give him a soulful look, begging for a late-night snack.

"Sorry sweetheart." He scratched the mare between her ears. He headed a little farther in to find Steve sitting in a folding chair, boots propped up on a bucket, reading a worn paperback. "All well in here?"

Steve folded down the corner of the page and closed the book. He didn't appear at all disturbed. "Yup. No activity, they're all quiet."

Red glanced around, but nothing was out of place. "Nothing weird, no strange sounds?"

"Nope." Steve eyed him and checked his watch, pressing a button on the side to illuminate the face. "Kinda late to be making a round. Everything okay?"

Red paused, listening again to the comforting sounds of a barn at peace. Deep breathing of sleeping equines, the soft rustle of hay beneath feet, the low hum of the one overhead light kept on for Steve. "No, everything's fine." He gave Steve a nod and headed back out.

So his father intended to slip in to the office and slip out again. Must have figured on the ranch having twenty-four watch. It was the only reason he'd go in through a locked door rather than the easy way.

One thing was for certain. Red wasn't about to let Peyton roam around the grounds in the dead of night. No way was he giving his father a chance to get to her.

Chapter Seventeen

She really had to stop doing this. Night after night of slipping out in the dark to meet with Red, then getting up earlier than normal to sneak back in was wearing on her.

But God, what a good week and a half it'd been. She smiled as she set her boots down on the floor by the door and tiptoed up the stairs in her socks, counting down the minutes she still had left to catch some sleep in her own bed before she'd have to start her day. And as she hit the top landing, she ran straight into something that squeaked.

"Oh my God!" Bea's voice cried out in the dark. "Who's th— Peyton?" Her sister's hands gripped her upper arms. "Is that you?"

"Yeah. It's me." Peyton took a step back in case Bea could tell she was chilled from being outside. "What are you doing up?"

Bea took a step back herself, sliding closer toward her own bedroom door. "Bathroom."

"You have your own bathroom in your room."

"Right. Yeah." Bea tapped her head and shook it. "Sorry, sleep fog. I meant water. I went downstairs for some water."

Peyton surveyed her sister's attire. Jeans and a sweater,

though the details were difficult to make out in the dark. All that for a trip downstairs. But she wasn't about to ask questions, which might only prompt Bea to ask where she'd been herself. So she nodded and slid to her room and shut the door behind her.

And within seconds, she was lying in her own bed, ready for a few moments of shut eye.

But her body was too wired, her nerves still singing from the delicious treatment she'd received in Red's apartment.

The man's hands were a gift from God.

A gift Peyton wanted to keep receiving. But each time, each night they were together, it was just another chance to get caught. Could she seriously risk being outted as sleeping with her trainer? It hadn't exactly worked well for her mother's reputation. That's just what she needed . . . people thinking she was a carbon copy of Sylvia. Peyton had too much to risk. An entire staff of employees, not to mention Emma, who was more family than employee herself. Plus Trace was now on payroll, and Seth's well-being was wrapped up in his.

And she couldn't very well buy out Bea's share if the place tanked.

Time to stop the nonsense, she lectured herself as she rolled over and punched her pillow into shape. Time to stop sneaking around, stop dancing with the devil just because it feels good. Time to grow up.

But oh God, she was going to miss those stolen moments with Red. All of them, not just the naked ones.

And that was the worst part of all.

An hour later, Peyton settled down to breakfast, a plate of Emma's infamous blueberry pancakes and crispy bacon in front of her.

"You're up early," Emma commented lightly. "Normally you'd be rolling one of these pancakes dry and shoving it in your mouth as you ran to the barn. Couldn't sleep last night?"

Peyton kept her eyes on the syrup as she dribbled it in a delicate pattern over the stack. "I slept fine."

Emma's form hovered for another moment; then she sniffed and headed back to the kitchen. "Drink your milk," was all she hollered back over her shoulder.

Peyton blew out a breath and dug in, moaning in ecstasy around the fluffy warm mouthful.

"Sinful, aren't they, sis?"

Peyton almost choked on her bite, grabbing the glass of milk and taking a swallow before blinking rapidly to clear the tears from her eyes. Her sister sat in the chair across from her, chin in her hand, smiling catlike at her.

When she could breathe without coughing, she pushed the platter toward her. "Want a taste?"

Bea glanced longingly at the offering, then shook her head. "That was hateful. I'll make my smoothie in a minute."

"All that alfalfa and grass in drinkable form. Yum. Maybe I should try that when the horses go lame."

Peyton waited for her sister to shoot another barb back at her, like normal. But instead, her smile just grew. "Speaking of sin . . ."

"Hmm?" Peyton snapped a piece of bacon in two, popped one half in her mouth.

"I'm just curious where you were coming from last night."

The bacon turned to dust in her throat, and she once again scrambled to take a gulp of milk before she stopped breathing. "What the hell are you talking about?"

"Oh, come off it. I'm not an idiot, despite that bimbo I played on TV." Bea snuck a peek toward the kitchen, then, satisfied Emma was busy, leaned over the table. Her voice dropped a few levels. "I know you're seeing someone. So spill."

Peyton shook her head, then realized that might look like she was admitting something. "I'm not seeing anyone." At least, not on a permanent basis.

Bea looked annoyed. "Peyton, you are the closest thing I have to a girlfriend in this godforsaken town. So stop being selfish and share."

"Well, with an invitation like that . . ." Peyton rolled her eyes. Once again, it was all about Bea. "Why are you here?"

Her sister sat up, spine straight. "I don't know what you mean. Mama died."

"Months ago. Mama died months ago. So why are you here now?"

"If I'm such an inconvenience, I can always pack up and go." Bea flattened her palms on the table as if ready to push back in outrage. Peyton managed to keep from rolling her eyes again. But years with her sister had taught her to watch for the melodramatics. It made her sister a shoe-in for the soap operas. But having a serious conversation was a bit of a trial.

Playing her part in the whole farce, Peyton covered one of Bea's hands with her own. "That's not what I meant. You're not an inconvenience. It's just . . . this is the first time you've come back on your own since you left. Don't the viewers wonder where you are?"

Bea scoffed and settled down. "Since Trixie West was electrocuted before falling down an elevator shaft to her death, I doubt they're curious where I'm at."

Peyton's mind spun for a minute, but she came up blank. "I'm sorry. Who the hell is Trixie West? And how did she fall down an elevator shaft?"

Bea stared for a moment, her perfectly shaded mouth hanging open. "Trixie West was my character's name on *The Tantalizing and the Tempting.*"

Well, crap. "Oh, right. Of course." Who the hell would name someone Trixie West?

"Right now negotiations are working to see if Trixie's long lost twin sister will make an appearance. Also played by me, naturally." When Peyton stared, baffled, Bea's eyes watered on command and her lower lip quivered. "You never watched while I was on, did you?"

"I'm always outside, working." It was a weak defense, and they both knew it. She could have at least DVRed one or two episodes. But she hadn't. Why? Even now, she wasn't entirely sure. The show probably would have put her to sleep. But to catch a glimpse of her sister's job . . . She always caught up with Trace, tried to watch for him when she knew he'd be riding in a televised event.

Maybe her childhood resentment of the Barbie doll went deeper than she thought.

"I'm sorry, Bea. I should have. I was wrong."

Hearing that soothed whatever insult—real or imagined—Bea had stacked against her. "Yes, you should have. Some of my best work was on that show."

"And now you're dead. Hmm." Peyton went back to her pancakes, expecting her sister to leave. But she didn't. So Peyton took a chance. "Did it hurt?"

"What, being let go?"

"Being electrocuted."

Bea's lips twitched. "Stung less than being let go in the first place. But a death scene is always appreciated. And who knows. Maybe my evil twin will pop up next season to stir the pot."

Peyton laughed at that. It felt good, laughing with her sister. Maybe they could try it again tomorrow.

"So you really aren't going to tell me who the guy was?"

Peyton sobered and stared out the window. "Don't know what you're talking about."

Bea rolled her eyes and broke a piece of bacon off Peyton's plate. "It doesn't count if it's not from your own plate," she said quickly before Peyton could snark at her. "And I know that look. That satisfied, loose look. You're getting some attention from someone, and I'm jealous." Bea chewed the tiny piece of stolen bacon. "Though around here, I don't know who you would be with. Knowing you, you'd have some sort of weird rule about sleeping with any of the employees. Too Sylvia for you."

Though it was a joke, Peyton's throat closed.

"I doubt you went into town, since I didn't hear the Jeep drive back up, unless you parked farther away and walked. Oh!" Bea's eyes widened. "Morgan Browning. The Brownings still live down the road, right? Was it him?"

"No. Definitely not Morgan." The finality in Peyton's voice was convincing, especially since it was true.

"Definitely not Morgan, which means it's definitely someone else." Satisfied she'd pried that much from her tight-lipped sister, Bea stood and walked toward the kitchen. "I'm just glad you're loosening up a bit. We all have more fun when you're not so wound up."

Peyton waited until she heard the blender start and let her head drop into her hands. How could she have thought for a moment sleeping with someone who worked on the ranch was okay? Even Bea had made the Sylvia connection. If someone as unobservant as Bea could put two and two together . . .

Pushing away her mostly uneaten breakfast, she stood and hurried to the front door to grab her boots and get to work. She needed a distraction from that thought.

* * *

"Peyton, you've got a visitor." Trace laid a hand on her shoulder as she stood in the middle of the birthing barn.

"Who is it?" she asked without turning around. Red was working out a three-year-old in the training arena, and she was mesmerized.

Red's shirt pulled across his back as he leaned over the horse's neck for a moment to rub his neck. His hat was tipped back, enough that she could see the fierce concentration on his face. She could have stripped naked and he wouldn't have noticed. In Red's world, he and the horse existed alone, in a vacuum.

Red shifted, using his legs to maintain balance and then guide the reluctant horse in the direction he wanted. There were several hundred pounds difference between man and horse, but the man was in control, always. His hands, covered in their worn leather gloves, kept their loose grip on the reins, never pulling, but keeping firm pressure.

The thought of his hands brought up reminders of his touch, how his fingers skimmed over her body so gently, so tenderly. Almost reverent in his touch. And then more roughly when she raced him to the finish line, gripping and kneading and telling her without words that he was as lost as she was when they were together. Unable to stop reaching for each other at all hours of the night.

"Peyton."

She worked hard to contain the flush. "Sorry, what?"

Trace eyed her a moment, then shrugged. "Your visitor, a guy named Peterson. Said you weren't expecting him, but he's here all the same."

Peyton nodded. "Thanks." A quick jog to the house and a stop in the kitchen to rinse her hands off took her all of five minutes. Luckily she saw Emma had played hostess for her in the living room. A wiry man with light brown hair going gray at the temples sat with a glass of lemonade in his hand.

"Sorry to keep you waiting. I'm Peyton Muldoon." She held out a hand and the man stood.

"Chuck Peterson. Pleased to meet ya." He set the glass on the coffee table on a coaster. "Wondered if we might talk a little business. I'm in the market for a stud, and I've heard you might just be the place for it."

"Have you?" She guided the man to her office, her heart doing a giddy skip-dance in her chest. Word of mouth was the golden ticket in the horse world.

"Yup. Came over from Wyoming, so I'm glad you could see me with no notice. Was at an event a few weeks ago, saw your brother Trace competing. Asked around, heard he was a top-notch competitor."

"Absolutely. He's my brother, and I love him. But I don't mind saying it pains just a little to say when he's on, he's unbeatable." She grinned when the man chuckled. If only all business meetings started so promisingly.

They sat, Peyton behind her desk and Peterson in the comfortable chair across from it. He asked good, solid questions, and she had an answer ready for each one. What's more, he asked the right questions. Ones that showed he was aware nobody could give an absolute guarantee of a winner or a champion simply because of breeding. He was fair-minded, intelligent, and on the mark. Peyton all but salivated at the thought of claiming him as a customer.

As his questions dried up, Peterson sat back and laced his hands over his stomach. "So you're the brains behind the operation after all, huh?"

Peyton smiled a little, confused. "I'm sorry?"

He shook his head. "When they told me a young woman ran the operation, I thought they joked, exaggerated. Figured either the father ran the operation, or Trace did and just needed someone to babysit the place while he was gone."

Peyton felt the smile slide off her face.

He held up his hands in a hold-on-a-minute gesture. "I know, I know. Sexist of me. But I don't mind admitting I was wrong. You've got the knowledge and the goods to back it up. And I don't mind mentioning hearing Red Callahan worked here was another big item in the plus column."

A month ago, it would have burned her raw to hear it, even if it was the truth. Now? She just felt grateful she could call Red an ally. "Are you satisfied so far, Mr. Peterson?"

"More than. I worried when Trace went to get you that you'd be a sort of ornamental figurehead. Little to do with the actual business, but someone they trotted out for show every now and again. I can see I was incorrect with that. I'm glad you're not one of those flighty females." He smiled sadly. "Don't make a very good impression for their gender. And the opposite is the truth here. So. Let's talk details."

As Peyton led Peterson out to the barn to see the setup, she reassured herself that cutting the physical relationship with Red was truly the best thing. Her reputation meant everything in this business, and she wasn't about to screw her entire family over for a little late-night fun.

Which was all easy to say in the light of day. At night when she instinctively reached out for him beside her in bed, it was so much harder.

Red snuck past the barn, noticed the sliding door standing slightly ajar. Though he wanted to get to Peyton as fast as he could, he took a moment to peer in. His entire body was on high alert after his father's attempt to get in the barn. But his father's stocky frame didn't appear. To his relief, the same slim, long outline he was coming to know as Bea Muldoon 2.0 stood by Lover Boy's stall, talking softly to the gelding. Satisfied it was only she, he crept on toward the house.

How long would Bea manage to pull off these midnight rides without anyone knowing? Surely the ranch hands playing night guard had to know. Did she bribe them to stay quiet? Peyton would find out eventually. And wouldn't that be interesting. To be a fly on the wall for that revelation . . .

As she had the past few nights, Peyton slipped through the kitchen door silently. Over a week now they'd been meeting in the night. She never attempted to make plans with him, but he wasn't about to let her creep around alone. So every night he snuck over and waited outside like a lovesick teenager waiting for his high school girl-friend to climb out her window to sneak away while her parents slept.

The things a man did to get a little quality time with his woman.

"Red?" Peyton's voice cut through his mental wanderings. "Are you there?"

"I'm here." He let a bush rustle just a little to give her some bearings. As she approached, he stepped out of the shadow of the tree and grabbed her upper arms. Swinging her around, he planted her back against the trunk and took her mouth with a kiss that left no doubt how badly he wanted her. Needed her.

Instinctively, she struggled a moment against his firm hold, but she melted into him after the token resistance. Wound her arms around his neck and showed him with-out words, she needed him, too.

But then she broke off with a gasp, stumbling out of his arms and out of reach.

"No. Can't."

Ah, she was going to do that bullshit thinking-too-hard thing again. "Yes, we can." He kept his voice gentle, soft. "We're pretty good at it, actually."

She laughed and rubbed a hand over her face. But the laughter held no humor. More like self-mockery. "Yeah. Pretty good, all right. For what that's worth."

For what what's worth? Red stood still, wondering if he was missing parts of the conversation. "What's up, dar-lin'?"

"Peyton," she corrected automatically, and he smiled. Some things never changed. "And what's up is we can't do this anymore."

Another day, another way for Peyton to put up walls. "Why not?" He wanted to ask *why not this time?* But he decided to keep that part to himself.

"If this ever got out? I would be the laughingstock of the community. Nobody would take me seriously. I've al-ready got one strike against me because I'm female, and I can't change that. But this, I can change."

"Peyton . . ."

"I will not be my mother," she hissed, then deflated like a balloon. "I can't be...I just don't want . . ."

He gathered her gently in his arms, waiting for the smallest sign of resistance. But she came willingly, eagerly into the embrace. "You're not your mother. Finding one man you respect and want to spend time with is not the same thing as landing on your back whenever you want to manipulate someone."

She rubbed her cheek against his jacket. "I know that. What everyone else would see though, that's another story."

"Screw everyone else."

She laughed, then slapped a hand over her mouth, swal-lowing a few more giggles. "Easy for you to say. A man takes a lover and no matter who she is, he's slapped on the back and winked at. A woman choses to have someone in her bed, and the whole thing is analyzed. Plus, it's not your name on the sign. You pick up and go wherever you want when you're ready to move on." She fell silent then, and he could almost see her mind taking that new direction.

The one where he would eventually pick up and leave. Just another wall in a maze full of walls on his way to convincing Peyton this wasn't a simple fling for him. Or her.

"Tell you what." He took one of her hands in his, chafed it to warm the tips. "Why don't we take things one day at a time? There's been no mention of this in the stables, right?"

"No," she said slowly.

He brought her hand to his mouth, blew warm air over her fingers. "So how about we worry about tonight, tonight. And when tomorrow gets here, we'll deal with that then."

She watched him for a bit, as if trying to read whether he was bullshitting her or not. Then she shrugged. "Guess I can't argue with that."

When he slipped his hand around hers and pulled gently, she followed like a docile mare being led in circles for a kiddie ride. He wasn't a stupid man, though. Docile didn't exist in Peyton's DNA. She was biding her time, thinking things through. And when she wanted to break away, he couldn't hold her back with steel bars if he wanted to.

So he'd take it one day at a time, like he'd suggested for her, and see how that played out.

Chapter Eighteen

Red polished up his last order form for the day and set it in the Outbox for Billy to call in tomorrow morning. Damn, paperwork sucked. But it was just a part of the job. Or, rather, part of this job. Drifting from one stable to another, he hadn't been responsible for most of the paperwork. His focus was the animals and the riders.

His cell phone rang, and he jumped at the chance to clear his mind from numbers and order sheets. "Callahan."

"Red—" Arby's voice was tense. "Get to the stables. Now."

"What?" Red's boots hit the floor and he slammed the office door behind him, glad he'd changed the lock to the office for one that automatically locked every time the door closed. "Is it one of the mares? Peyton? What?"

"Your father," was all Arby said, then hung up.

Shit. Red shoved the cell in his pocket and kicked up his speed from a fast walk to a jog. It'd been twelve days since Red had seen Mac at the feed store. With forty-eight hours left on his deadline to get the hell out of town, his father should have been too busy packing and gassing up his truck to come over and cause trouble.

His father's laughter met him before he set foot in the stable. Mac laughed like a man with nothing to hold back. Usually because Mac didn't believe in holding back. Red's boots clicked over the concrete as he worked his way back to the tack room where Mac and a few hands were polishing hardware.

"So anyway, there Red was, scared spitless over this bucking bronc, and I had to pull his ass out of the way before he got himself trampled to death. You'da thought the boy was slow the way he just watched, begging to get kicked in the head."

The hands shook their heads, as if unable to believe it.

"I took that scared kid and turned him into a horseman, I did." Mac's pride—however false—resonated in his voice.

"Great story, Dad." Red crossed his arms over his chest and stared. "You came to see me?"

Mac grinned and dropped his rag. "Sure did. These boys here were just keeping me company. Say, remember the time you—"

"No, can't say that I do." Red grabbed his father's bicep and pulled until the man started to move. "Let's go talk in my office." Talking was the last thing Red wanted to do, but getting him out of the stable was the first priority.

Mac let his son pull him a few feet, then planted his heels. Though Red wasn't weak, his father was a big man. Short of finding a wheelbarrow, he wasn't going to move him without some cooperation.

"I rather like the atmosphere in here." Mac's eyes roamed over the stables, taking in the clean floors, the high ceiling, the few curious horses who were watching. "Nice setup. Classy joint."

"Agreed. I can give you the grand tour, starting with my living quarters." Desperate to move the man, Red threw one arm around his father's shoulder as if hugging him from the side, trying to step forward. But Mac didn't budge.

"Nah. I like it here. I was just telling your boys back

there how glad I was we were living in the same town now. We haven't been close for a while, nice that we have this time to catch up."

The boys, as Mac called them, were listening with poorly concealed curiosity, soaking up every word, every bit of body language. Red nodded. "But since you're heading out of town soon—"

"Oh, no. Where'd you get an idea like that?" The gleam in Mac's eyes sent red flags flying through Red's brain. "I've got plans to plant some roots, I do. Make a name for myself here. You've already started. The Callahans of Marshall, South Dakota. Has a nice ring to it."

From the corner of his eye, Red caught Arby leaning in a doorway, watching silently. Another hand stood with him. The crowds were slowly gathering. Drama in the stables brought all the ants to the picnic.

Dammit. He didn't want to actually use the threat he'd given his father, but he was left with no choice. "Dad," he said softly, angling his back to the onlookers. "Your deadline's almost up, in case you forgot."

Mac nodded. "Sure, sure. Deadline. About that, though." Mac scratched at his week-old beard as if thinking things through on the fly. "See, I've got a bit of a problem with how you tried to push me out of town. Made me wonder if you had something to hide."

No. Not here. Please, God, anywhere but here. "Dad, don't make me do this. Go somewhere else, start fresh, and move on."

"I think not. I think I'd rather stick around." Mac took a step back, out of Red's reach. "Shouldn't hold threats over someone's head unless your own nose is squeaky clean."

What the hell could he possibly be talking about? Red had no criminal history, had no problems with previous employers. He was bluffing. "No problems there, then."

Mac stared at him, judging, considering a long moment. Then he shrugged. "Maybe there isn't a problem after all. I didn't realize everyone around here was good with you screwing the Muldoon gal." Slapping a thick hand on Red's shoulder, he said, "Take what ass you can, when you can, right? Though banging the boss is a bit of a cliché, even for us Callahans."

Something behind him dropped, a piece of brass hitting the concrete. Boots shuffled over the floor, edging away, as the men finally realized this was the wrong conversation to be listening in on.

Fuck.

One corner of his father's mouth twitched, as if holding back a satisfied smile. "I think some of the local business-men might be interested to know what all goes into a Muldoon business deal."

Red shrugged his father's hand off, resisting the urge to plow his fist through his father's face. Satisfying, yes. Help-ful, not in this case. "I don't know where you get off mak-ing up shit like that," he growled, feeling the heat creep up his neck. Heat from temper as much as embarrassment. "But you need to get the hell off the property. Now."

Mac smiled and shook his head. "Manners. I keep telling ya, you've got no manners. But I'll head out for now. Call if you want to grab a bite to eat or something, or stop on by. You know where I work."

Sauntering away, as if he'd just scored big at the craps table, Mac headed out the stable doors. A moment later an engine started up, and tires crunched down the driveway.

Red swiped his hat off and ran a hand down his face. So his father had seen more than Red could have guessed the other night. It made Red's stomach turn to think about his father spying on that intimate moment with Peyton. And his entire body clenched at the thought of what his father's little show would mean for them both.

Peyton wasn't about to see this as anything more than an excuse to end what they had together. The truth was out there, though not everyone knew whether it was really fact or fiction. And even if he and Peyton both denied it, the hands would always wonder.

Goddamnit.

He took a few steps, then realized everyone was still staring at him, frozen in time. "You see that man on the property again, you boot his ass out." When nobody moved, Red barked, "Get back to work!"

The scurry of boots grated over his nerves as people beat a hasty retreat to, well, anywhere that wasn't in his line of vision. Red ignored them, waiting until the sounds calmed before walking out into the sunlight. He needed quiet, peace, a moment to himself to figure out how he would break the news to Peyton. Because he had to tell her. Hearing from someone else—and she would, he had no doubt—would be worse. But how to do it without pissing her off . . . that was something he needed to think about.

As he headed through the barn doors and into the sunlight, he caught movement from the corner of his eye. Peyton, standing with Arby, locked deep in conversation. She kept shaking her head, hat angled so he couldn't see her face. But when Arby saw him, he shook his head, mouth pulled down in a frown.

Shit.

Peyton nodded and placed one hand on the older man's arm. Then she nodded and headed his way. "Arby says you need to talk to me."

He tried to ask for a few minutes, but his tongue swelled and trapped him.

She raised a brow. "He said it's important?"

Red nodded.

Peyton glanced around the yard, noting the not-so-subtle presence of several hands who just happened to be working quietly within earshot. "Do we need to head to the office, then?"

"My place," he managed to choke out. The office seemed so . . . final. So official. He needed to talk to her somewhere personal.

She shrugged and walked ahead, still unaware of exactly what was in store. Red only prayed she would be as calm ten minutes from now.

As they walked around the garage, Peyton bounded up the first few steps and sat down. "It's nice, let's stay out here."

"Okay then." He checked around, but the garage door was down and he knew nobody had any reason to be out their way at that point in the day.

Peyton smiled. "Stop pacing, Red. You're making me dizzy."

He glanced down, saw the boot marks in the dirt and realized he'd started walking in a circle without any thought. He propped one boot on the bottom step, took his hat off and ran a hand through his hair. "Peyton . . ." How the hell did he start this conversation?

"Okay, you're starting to scare me." Peyton's face morphed from amused to confused. "What's up? Is it one of the mares? The Jacobson mare?"

"No, no. Nothing with the animals." He was screwing this up, big time. "Peyton, my dad came by today."

Her brows rose in surprise. "I didn't know your dad was in the area."

"He shouldn't have been," Red muttered. "He is, but not for long." *I hope.* "The problem is, my dad's not . . . I mean, he's not what you'd think . . ." He sighed. Talking about his father wasn't something he did, ever. Breaking the habit was harder than he'd thought. "He's just not a good guy. He won't win any Father of the Year awards."

Peyton smiled sadly. "I get what you mean. Sylvia was the same way. No Mama awards for her. Sucks sometimes, when parents are less responsible than the kids."

"Sucks. That's one word for it." He slammed his hat back on his head and started pacing. Too bad if it made her dizzy. He needed to think. "My dad was in the barn when I got there. I didn't invite him. I didn't want him here. But he was in there. And he said . . . things. He said things he shouldn't have."

Peyton leaned back, elbows propped on the step behind her. "Such as?"

"He said things about you. And me." When she didn't respond, he added, "Together."

Understanding lit her face. Her body froze, and he would have sworn she stopped breathing. "He knows?" she whispered.

The horrified look on her face said more than any words. "He doesn't know," Red said firmly. "He played the odds, I'd bet anything. Guessed. Took a chance that he'd embarrass me and get me to back off." And it worked. At least for the moment. For once, Mac Callahan had come up with the right cards at the right time.

"Back off from what?"

But Red wasn't done yet. "He took a gamble and said something about us"—he wasn't about to repeat the actual words used—"and the hands overheard every word. Every goddamn word," he muttered.

"So, now they know." Peyton's voice became soft, almost too calm for the situation. Her hands clenched and unclenched, as if holding an imaginary stress ball.

"They don't know. Peyton," he said when she wouldn't look at him. "They don't. They heard one man they've never met before blowing smoke. If I just take the time to tell them my father's a jackass who likes to stir up trouble—"

"But they'll know." Peyton rubbed her palms over her jeans. "I don't hire stupid men. You might tell them it's not true—which is a lie in itself, and I hate even the thought of lying to my staff—and they might nod and agree and say it's too bad we all had to deal with that man. But the seed was planted. It'll always be in the back of their minds now, won't it?" She looked up at him, almost begging him without words to disagree with her, tell her it wouldn't happen, tell her everything would be all right.

He couldn't. "Yeah. It will."

"And now they'll be watching closer, looking to see if there are any subtle signals between us. Which there probably are," she added, almost biting the words off. "Because I can't get within ten feet of you and not get flushed."

"Really?" Hope sparked for a moment. "Peyton—"

"And your dad is mad at you for some reason I don't know or understand, and he might go spreading this to other people. People I do business with. People I depend on for their loyalty. God, just when I thought things were starting to get better." She clenched her fists and pounded against the side of the garage, metal ringing dully.

"Peyton, come on—"

"Stop." She let her head droop for just a moment until her forehead touched her knees, like a child in protective mode. "Just give me one moment, please."

He heard a gate opening in the distance, closing again. The almost inaudible sounds of men speaking to their mounts, speaking to each other. The ranch hummed with activity beyond the walls of the garage.

"Okay. All right. Okay." She did that palm-rubbing thing again, bit her bottom lip, then stood with enough force to almost catapult her off the step. "That settles it then."

"Settles what?"

Peyton watched him for a minute, as if she couldn't believe he hadn't put two and two together yet. "What we need to do. We'll deny it, though I hate lying. It's just nobody's business. We'll chalk it up to a guy with a personal grudge spouting off stuff he doesn't know about."

That sounded simple enough. Red nodded.

"You and I will have to keep our distance for a while."

Wait a second. "I don't think that's—"

She rolled right over him. "And eventually, once something else happens in this small town or some other piece of gossip floods the area, you can quietly slip out and move on to your next job."

"Next job?" What the hell? "This was a permanent thing, Peyton."

She huffed out a breath. "You're never permanent, Red. I knew that going in. I hoped you'd stay as long as possible. Hoped I'd keep you. I mean, the ranch." She flushed and turned to the side, looking out past the property line. "I'd hoped M-Star would keep you. But I think in the back of my mind, I knew you wouldn't stay."

Just a slip of the tongue? Or was she sharing more than she wanted to? He shook his head numbly.

"You were going to take off eventually—let's not kid ourselves on that one. So it'll just have to be sooner than later. God knows, with your reputation, you could find a dozen operations in this state alone that would drool all over the chance to snap you up. Give it a week or two and you'll get other offers in the surrounding states."

"I don't want to go." He grabbed her arm, shook her a little. "Stop doing this. We can work around it. Don't push me out the door."

"I'm not pushing. I'm just . . . clearing a path." She stepped back, out of his reach, then slid past him down the stairs. "It'll be fine." Her eyes were a little bright in the late morning sun, but her mouth was firm and her shoulders set. "It will be fine. We can weather this, and we'll do okay."

She turned and left, disappearing around the corner of the garage. Red sat down, butt thumping heavily against the old wood of the stairs, and flicked his hat out of his way.

That couldn't have gone worse if he'd scripted it. She was upset, and he'd known that part would come. But tossing him out on his ear? Sending him on his way? That hurt. That fucking hurt. He thought they had enough time together now to fight for each other.

Apparently not.

With a heavy sigh, he headed upstairs, needing to soak his head, grab some lunch, take a breather. His nerves were too jittery to do any horse any good, and the men would see his mind wasn't in it in a quick minute.

As he reached for his keys, he realized he didn't need them. His door was propped a few inches open. "What the . . ." He listened quietly for a moment, heard nothing, then slowly stepped inside and surveyed the damage.

Whoever had been in his apartment had done a thorough job of making their presence known. Whoever? He rolled his eyes at himself. His father, of course. Mac must have made a quick stop here before heading to the barn to start raising hell.

Chairs were tipped over—one with its legs completely busted off. The small table was tipped on its side. Curtains lay in heaps under the windows where they'd hung, the kitchen cabinets had been emptied onto the small tile floor in front of the stove. The bed, which he'd made out of habit that morning, was stripped bare, the mattress leaning against one wall, box springs angled drunkenly off the frame. And his closet was bare, his things scattered over the length of the apartment.

He shut the door behind him and propped his shoulders up against it. Today was a mother of all days. And now, on top of deciding whether he should convince Peyton to let him stay or sneak out with his pride intact, he had to figure out how to handle his father, and what the hell the man's end game was.

Chapter Nineteen

Peyton was not a crier. Muldoons didn't cry—except for Bea, and usually only when she wanted something. They gritted their teeth, bore down, and got the job done. So the tears that constantly pricked her eyes until the end of the day did more than confuse her. They pissed her off. She wasn't about to cry because some jackass had guessed about her love life and spread it where it didn't need spreading. He didn't deserve her tears, her emotion, her pain.

But even as she gave herself the pep talk, she knew it wasn't Red's father that had her so close to losing her hold on her emotions. It was Red. God. For once, she'd felt safe, and actually wanted, by a man. Not on her toes, not having to play the *you're so much smarter than me, I'm just a silly woman* card. She'd finally found a man who wasn't threatened by her ownership, by her essentially being his boss.

And it was ruined. Their chance at . . .

Their chance at what? She pushed back from her desk and stared out the window into the open field. At nothing. From the start, it'd been a bad idea to get involved. And look what happened.

Though she trusted her ranch employees, something like this just couldn't be stopped. They'd mention it to one person—like a wife or girlfriend—in confidence, and suddenly it was everywhere.

A soft knock sounded behind her.

"Peyton?" Trace stepped into her office hesitantly. "Hey."

"Hey." She uncrossed her arms and sat down in her chair. "What's up?"

"I was coming in to ask you the same. You've been in here all day." Trace looked around the office, anywhere but in her eyes. "I thought maybe you wanted to, you know, talk or something."

Peyton stifled a smile. God love her brother for trying, but he was definitely not the person she wanted to see right now. "Thanks, but I'm good."

"You sure?" Trace wandered over to the bookshelf, grabbed the biggest textbook from the shelf and started flipping through it. One of her old animal husbandry textbooks from college. Riveting stuff.

"Yeah. It's sort of a girl thing." When Trace's eyes widened, she snickered. "Your face right now . . ."

He shut the book with a snap. "I don't do the girl talk thing. That's Bea's area."

"Oh, hell no." Peyton stood up fast enough to send the rolling chair back several feet. "Don't you dare corner me in here with her. I will hunt you down."

Trace smiled wolfishly at her. "Tempting. But I won't take it that far. I like my skin right where it is." He placed the book back and gave her a once-over. "If you're sure . . ."

"I'm sure," she said quickly, pulling the chair back toward her to sit down. She stared at her computer, making a show of reading the completely blank screen until Trace shut the door behind him. Then she let her forehead drop to the desk with a thump.

She was in deep water.

"Knock, knock!"

It only needed this. "I'm busy," Peyton said to her shoes, not raising her head.

"Busy napping? You complain so much about how hard it is to run this damn place, and here you are sleeping on the job. I could do that."

Peyton lifted her head to stare lasers through her sister. "Go. Away."

Bea tsked and sat down softly on the guest chair, legs crossed daintily, foot swinging in some delicate, impractical sandal. "I'm here on official business."

"Business?" That made Peyton do a double take. "What business?"

"Ranch business. I was thinking about making some changes to spruce things up."

Peyton blanched. "What?"

Bea rolled her eyes. "Well, you said I had to wait before I could cash in on my portion, right?"

"Yes. I also said you could wait back in California, since there isn't anything specific you can do here."

"But there is. Something specific," Bea clarified. "I got to thinking, and I'm really not the person to help in the barn."

"Shock among shocks," Peyton muttered.

"I'm ignoring that for now. But my main reason for staying is that I would like to help with the M-Star's image."

"Image." Peyton rolled the idea around her mind a moment like a marble. "Nope. Still don't get it."

Bea stood and then balanced one hip on the edge of the solid desk. "You're selling horses and experience. But you're also selling an image. All businesses have an image. We want ours to reflect the right tone. Professional, knowledgeable, but not ostentatious. You don't want to scare away the novices with something that will intimidate them, but you also don't want grand champions to think we only cater to kids and weekend cowboys. An every-cowboy ranch. Beginners to winners." She grinned at the thought. "That's a good pitch point."

Peyton filed the fact that Bea used the words "we" and "ours" in regard to the business for later thought and went with the more immediate questions. "Exactly what did you have in mind?"

"Oh, just little changes here and there." She waved a hand in the air like that was helpful. "Nothing major, since I'm sure you and Trace would veto me without even giving it a chance."

Peyton thought for a moment, then shrugged. If it gave her sister something to do, then why not? "Nothing major," she repeated again.

"Of course. Now I've got something to do." Bea looked around for a minute. "Hey! Idea time. Let's go grab a drink."

The thought of going into town on purpose, when she had no clue how far the gossip had already spread, made something bitter and vile rise up and choke her. She shook her head.

Bea's face softened. "What was it Emma always used to say about people gossiping about us? When Mama would make a fool out of herself again and kids would tease us at school?"

Peyton rolled her eyes and mimicked Emma's voice. "When people start flinging the shit, pull on some waders and trudge through."

Bea smiled. "Hiding won't make it any better. But showing your face, as if you have nothing to hide, that stops the talk a lot faster."

"You have no clue what this is even about," Peyton shot back.

"You and Red?" When Peyton's face flushed, Bea nodded. "Trace told me, more as a warning to not tease you than anything.

"Trace knows, too?"

Bea nodded again. "So there it is. It's out, it's in the open. Time to deal with it."

"I don't want to just 'deal with it.' " Peyton crossed her arms over her chest, knowing the action was childish. "I want it to go away."

"And it will, if you just show your face, keep your head up, and act like there's nothing to talk about. If a man slept with a woman in his employ, nobody would give a damn."

"No, they wouldn't," Peyton mumbled. Life was so not fair.

"So show them you can take the lumps but you're going to keep going. Show them how tough Peyton Muldoon is. Show them the backbone M-Star was built on."

Peyton stared, openmouthed, at her sister. Her baby sister, the one who she would have sworn had nothing but cotton stuffed between her ears, had just given an amazing, motivational speech that had Peyton wanting to hug her and cry on her shoulder in gratitude.

"Wow. Bea . . ." Peyton shook her head, amazed. "That was something else."

Bea grinned. "I know, right? It was from a scene they cut from my second to last episode of *The Tantalizing and the Tempting*. I just changed a few words."

Ah, there she was. And the world made sense once more. "I'm not going."

"Peyton, please? I am dying for some company other than Emma and the kid. And you're the best thing I've got."

"I feel so loved." Peyton stared at the blank screen of the computer once more. It might have been a scripted speech, but Bea's words sank in, swirling around in her already-busy mind. There was one surefire way to make the whole thing stop.

"Okay, fine."

Bea squealed and clapped her hands.

"But I refuse to drink anything with an umbrella in it or something with sex in the name," Peyton qualified.

Bea rolled her eyes. "As if you could get a good Sex On The Beach in this town. Please. Now go change."

She looked down. "I haven't even been in the barn. My clothes are clean."

"Oh my God. My work is never done with you." Standing up, and with a startling strength for someone who looked like she ate Life Savers for breakfast, Bea hauled Peyton out of the chair and through the office doors. "We're going to find something—anything—in your closet that doesn't scream *cowgirl not-so-chic*. This might be my biggest undertaking yet."

"Feel free to give up now."

Bea glanced over one slim shoulder. "Oh, hell no. You agreed, and I'm not letting you out of the deal now!"

Red stared at the ceiling, wondering if he'd actually be able to die from exhaustion. After Peyton's talk, he knew it was no use going to her that day and asking her to reconsider. So instead, he'd worked his ass off. The hands had given him a wide berth, though whether that was due to the scene earlier that morning or because he worked like someone had cattle prodded him, he had no clue. Didn't matter. He picked the dirtiest, toughest jobs and tackled them, working until his muscles screamed and his mind begged him to stop. Once those were complete, he'd brought out one of their meanest horses and given them both a good workout.

And still, after a shower and changing into a pair of

sweatpants, he flopped on the bed and his mind turned to her. There was something sick and twisted about that. But this obsession was the price of going against his mind and using his gut. He'd known from the get-go working with Peyton Muldoon would lead to something bad. He'd been half in lust for her and they'd barely exchanged more than three minutes of conversation before. Putting himself in close proximity with the female had been asking for trouble.

And he'd gotten it. A double serving.

A knock at the door brought him a welcome reprieve from running through all the mental images of Peyton his brain had stored up. Unless it was Peyton . . . nah. She wouldn't have cooled off that fast. Trudging to the door, he opened and stared, slack-jawed, at Trace Muldoon and his kid, stuffed into that same baby carrier.

"What the . . ."

"Boys' night." Trace shoved in past Red, careful to shield the kid from any contact. "All the girls are gone and I'm dying of boredom."

"Isn't that why you have a kid? To keep you busy?"

"No, I have a kid because the rubber broke." Trace's harsh words were tempered by a gentle hand stroking over his son's head. "As you can see, he's not in a mood to settle down, so I thought we'd go for a walk. We just ended up here."

"I see." Though he really didn't. Resigned to company, he grabbed a shirt from his closet and stuck his arms through, not bothering with the buttons. "Drink?" he asked, shuffling to the kitchen area.

"Sure, I'm not driving."

"Beer for Daddy and . . ." Red popped his head up over the top of the fridge door. "What's little man having, whiskey sour?"

"He's had his nightcap," Trace said dryly.

Twisting the top off the two beers, he met Trace at the table and sat. They both drank silently for a minute. Seth, taking the silence as his invitation to show off, gurgled and blew spit bubbles. Red winced when a little drool ran from his chin down to land in a puddle on Trace's forearm. But the man—a one-time major rodeo contender, total ball buster and overall cowboy badass—simply wiped his arm on his jeans and shrugged.

"It's not the end of the world."

"What's not?" Red couldn't stop watching as Seth's hands flailed around and pounded on the table.

"Having a kid. Wasn't my first choice. Or at least, not the timing of it. I had more shit to do. More to get done, more to see."

Red could understand that.

"But he's here, and I wouldn't give him up for the world." Trace's hand molded over his son's head, thumb rubbing a path between the crown and the tip of his ear. Seth leaned into his father's touch, eyes drooping a little, lulled.

"And the mom? She still off doing that shit she had to do?"

Trace's face closed up tight. "She's irrelevant."

Red shrugged. Not his business. "Just trying to make conversation."

"How about we try this topic on for size then? Peyton."

Red choked on the swallow of beer, leaning over his knees, thumping his chest to dislodge the bubble that formed in his airway. After a few false starts, he glared at Seth, who was chortling with glee at the show. "Think that's funny, huh?"

Trace started unhooking his son from the harness contraption. "Judging by your reaction, you're not real keen on talking about my sister."

"Not with her brother," he admitted. "Not with anyone, right now. That's a . . . sensitive subject."

"Figured it would be. I assume Bea's out with Peyton trying to get the same info I'm trying to get."

"Peyton's out with Bea?" Stunned, he sat back in his chair. "That, I did not see coming."

"Nobody did. Emma all but danced out the door after them, since it's her night off. Said she was going to celebrate the progress with a night out on the town. Which likely means she's going to go pop in on a friend and fall asleep on said friend's couch watching a black and white movie." He leaned over and settled his son down on the floor on his back. "I think Emma's premature in the celebration, since I'm sure those two will come back fighting harder and louder than two she-cats going after the same Tom."

"I'm not the Tom in this scenario, right?" Bea was gorgeous—any man with eyes could tell. But the thought of her chasing after him put chills down his spine.

"All hypothetical and irrelevant to you," Red agreed. "But the fact is, there's something to discuss." He held up a hand when Red started to stand. "I'm not playing big brother on you, believe me. Peyton would kill me for it. I might use that routine for Bea, but with Peyton, it's a lost cause. The girl can take care of herself. And what's more, I've got a pretty good idea you didn't treat her poorly."

"I didn't." *God, I hope not.*

"Then we're squared. I figured you might just want another male to bounce your thoughts off of. Wouldn't be right using one of the hands, and Arby's not really your biggest fan currently."

"Wouldn't be right using one of my bosses, either," Red pointed out, trying another sip of beer and feeling grateful it went down more easily this time.

"Peyton's the boss. I'm as much an employee as anyone else. My name might be Muldoon but I haven't put in the time yet to be in charge of much."

The man's simple acceptance of his role took Red by surprise. "No plans to head back to the rodeo circuit anytime soon?"

Trace looked down at the floor where his son had started the laborious process of rolling over onto his stomach. "Soon? Doubt it. Ever? Can't say. A lot of the future's up in the air right now."

Red lifted his bottle. "On that, we have something in common."

Chapter Twenty

"Oh my God, this place is completely different!" Bea swiveled around once as the sisters walked in through the doorway of Jo's Place.

Peyton had only been a few times herself, but she knew exactly what Bea was envisioning. The bar, as it had been before the current owner took over, had been the stereotypical honkytonk. Smoke-filled air, sticky floors, dark lighting, thirty-year-old country blaring from broken stereos, and the only option for anything edible stale peanuts or stale pretzels. And if you wanted something other than beer, your choices were Jim, Jack, Johnnie, or José.

Though the bar maintained a general western décor and country music in the background, the overall feel was more . . . classy, Peyton decided. Comfortable and classy. Clean, but not sterile. No problem sweeping empty peanut shells on the floor, but no fear in using the restroom either. Enough western hints to keep the locals happy, but not so much that the place was a caricature. The music was current, contemporary country, with some classics thrown into the mix. A small but decent menu was served during normal eating hours, and the drink menu now offered a few choices that women were drawn to in addition to the typical male-driven drink selection.

The perfect blend of old and new.

"This is fantastic." Bea led them over to a round high-top table and settled down. Grabbing a drink menu, she smiled. "And I can have something here other than a water. Excellent." Putting the menu down, she gazed around the room, over toward the back where pool tables still dominated. "Guess some things do change."

Peyton's eye was drawn to a figure moving toward them, and she groaned. "And others stay the same." She stayed seated, knowing the high chair gave her an advantage over standing.

Sam Nylen stopped in front of her, leaning over in a blatant show of intimidation. "Out enjoying the town, Ms. Muldoon?" His voice ended in a sneer, showing her just how much respect he truly had to give.

"Why else would we be seated in a bar, menu in hand?" She turned to Bea, using her shoulder to block the man. "What are you ordering?"

Bea's eyes flicked between her sister and the old trainer. "Uh, I think I'm going to try the—"

"Giving the boyfriend the night off? Maybe you're out trolling for a new stud. Any businessmen here you're hoping to persuade?" The man raised his voice so it carried easily over the soft music.

Bea's eyes rounded in shock.

Peyton rolled her own, though her blood boiled. In spite of her temper, she worked hard to keep her voice calm. "I'm not my mother, so you've got the wrong idea. I don't need my body to do business." Her voice dropped even lower, knowing those at the tables close by were listening. "And besides, you're not really one to throw stones, are you? Not when your glass house was built with siphoned funds."

Nylen snorted and puffed out his chest, invading her

personal space just a little more. "You little bitch, you've got no idea—"

"Nylen." A large hand landed on the ex-trainer's shoulder. "Can I call you a cab?"

Peyton peered around Nylen's body to find a man she recognized by face, but not by name. He was older, in his late fifties she would guess. They'd likely bumped into each other at one of the more recent rodeo events she'd been in. But right now, all she could think was that he was saving her from kneeing Nylen right in the gonads, which would have been a serious showstopper.

Nylen shrugged the hand off and—blessedly—stepped back. The cool air that rushed to meet Peyton was ambrosia. "Taking up for this slut, too, Jacobson? She'll be flat on her back for you in no time. Just take out a few stud fees and you're in."

"Now, Sam, that's just rude. The ladies here are enjoying their night out." Though said pleasantly, the undercurrent of *don't mess around with me* couldn't be missed. The older man squeezed Nylen's shoulder, and he shrugged under the pressure.

Nylen might have been a jackass, but he wasn't slow. Shooting Peyton one more disgusted look, he stalked out the front door. Another man followed closely behind, but she couldn't get a good look at him. Who the hell would be stupid enough to befriend that jerk, anyway?

Mr. Jacobson shook his head sadly, then wiped his palms on the sides of his jeans. Holding one hand out, he said, "Nice to see you again, Ms. Muldoon. We met a few weeks back, at that rodeo in—"

"Of course. How are you, Mr. Jacobson?" Peyton mentally searched her mind and came up with a short, almost inconsequential conversation while waiting for Trace to compete.

"Dan, please." He smiled easily and introduced himself to Bea. "Sorry about the trouble. Sam's never been good for a damn thing, pardon the language."

Bea fluttered her eyelashes at him. "You were wonderful. Thank you for helping, we really appreciate it. Could we offer you a seat and a drink? It's the least we can do."

Though the man was probably a grandfather by now, and married, judging by the ring on his finger, he blushed at her invitation. "Thank you, but no. I'm going to head back, I've got friends waiting." Turning a more serious look to Peyton, he added, "Nylen talks a lot, but not many people listen anymore. Maybe once upon a time . . ." Dan shook his head. "What people do in their private lives is their own business. I don't give two hoots. What I care about is the product and the quality of the business. And Ms. Muldoon? You've got quality. I watched your brother ride, and he and that horse were a thing of beauty. Plus, you have Redford Callahan in your corner, and that man is the definition of quality. I've been telling everyone I know you're the next stop for me when I'm ready for some more stock."

Peyton's tongue felt twice its normal size. She managed to swallow and smile. "Thank you. Thank you very much."

He nodded. "I don't spread around the manure, and I don't like watching others fling it around either. We'll just keep this little convo to ourselves, like the respectable people we are."

She could have hugged him. But instead she held out a hand again, thanked him, and watched him melt into the crowd.

"He was nice." Bea fiddled with the menu. "Wanna talk about it?"

"Nope."

Like an angel of good timing, a short woman with black hair scraped back in a tight ponytail came over and set napkins in front of them. Hopping up on the empty chair, she leaned against the high back, as if getting comfortable for the evening. "Girls night out?"

Peyton stared for a moment. Quite forward for a waitress.

Bea smiled. "Trying to work out some man problems."

The woman nodded, as if she heard this all the time. Heck, maybe she did. "Trying to keep one, or get rid of one? Gotta warn you, I've got no experience in the first, but plenty with the second."

"Neither," Peyton answered before Bea could spill out her life story. "Just spending a nice night out."

The waitress shrugged, her shoulder brushing against one of the large hoops hanging from her ears. Just one of several pairs of earrings, actually. She must have at least four piercings in each ear. "Easy enough. What can I get ya?"

They each ordered, though the woman never wrote anything down. After hopping down from the tall chair— the woman really was quite short—she said, "I'll be back in a minute with those drinks. Just holler for Jo if you need anything."

"Jo, as in . . ." Bea pointed to a sign over the top of the bar declaring the building Jo's Place.

"That'd be me. My name, my place." She disappeared without another word.

"Hmm. She's interesting. Definitely not local, or even from the surrounding area." Bea tapped one finger against her lips. "Wonder what her story is."

"Hey, Nosy, don't worry about it. What's with you and all the curiosity these days? I thought you couldn't wait to get out of this place."

"I couldn't. I can't," she corrected quickly. "I'm just trying to keep busy while I'm here. Might as well get to know people, including you, if I have to stay."

"You don't have to stay," Peyton pointed out.

The ongoing argument was put on hold when Jo returned with their drinks.

"One Bud Lite for everyone's favorite cowgirl," Jo said, placing a cold bottle on Peyton's napkin, "and one Cape Cod." A short glass with pink liquid settled in front of Bea, ice clinking.

"Thank you sweet baby Jesus." Bea grabbed the glass like a drowning man might grab a life preserver and took a sip. "That is fantastic. Jo, you might be my new favorite person in this town."

"Thanks," Peyton said dryly.

"Thanks," Jo answered, a little more pleasantly. Sitting back down on the tall chair, she sighed. "Mind if I take a breather? I like being out on the floor with the customers, but I'm not twenty-one anymore."

Coulda fooled Peyton. Maybe it was the woman's short stature, or her slightly round face, but Peyton wouldn't have put her over twenty-two, max. Obviously that was wrong, since someone in her early twenties wouldn't typically have the cash or know-how to open a bar in a town like Marshall and keep it running well.

"I heard what Dan said before he walked away. I was eavesdropping." She just put that out there, so there was no confusion. "Unlike Dan, sweet man that he is, I have no problem with gossip of all shapes and sizes. So, what's the deal with you and Red Callahan?"

Peyton nearly tipped her beer over. "What? How do you . . ."

"I overheard, remember? It's my place. I figure if someone's talking in here, I've got a right to hear what you're saying."

Bea watched her for a moment. "I think you and I are going to be very good friends."

Peyton sighed. "Before you two start bonding, could we back up a minute?"

Jo set her tray down on the table and stretched her arms overhead, causing her breasts to press against the front of her polo. For a short woman, she had some unexpected curves. "Current chatter is that you, dear Peyton, are involved in a hot, torrid affair with Red Callahan. Which most of the women in this town are green with envy over and the men are split on."

Bea pushed her empty glass toward Jo. "I'm gonna need another one of these when you get a minute. You can drive home, right, Peyton?"

She ignored her sister. "Split? How so?"

"Seems a pretty even divide, truthfully. Half of them are pretty sure it's the downfall of society once owners and trainers start shacking up and doing the nasty. The few who made some disgusting remarks I won't repeat because it won't add to the probably-already-shattered illusion that I'm a lady."

Peyton let her head fall to the table, rhythmically beating her forehead against the wood. "I knew it."

"But the other half seem to think there's nothing wrong. That half is split between people who just don't care, regardless, and those who might have cared, but know you're solid at what you're doing and so they're willing to turn a blind eye to it. A little hypocritical, if you ask me. But a hypocrite's dollar splits into a hundred pennies, just like a righteous man's."

Peyton mulled over that bizarre phrase for a moment before lifting her head. "They don't care?"

"Half, anyway. And I'd say probably more than that; it's just other people are staying mum. And frankly, I think you shouldn't give a damn. You're a strong woman and you run a good business. Do you have any idea how many jackasses tried to tell me I had no business running a bar, especially out here?"

"How many?" Bea asked, leaning in with fascination.

"Too many to count. The point is, I knew I was going to be successful, so I gave them all the middle finger and went right on doing what I wanted. It worked for me. Why can't it work for you?"

"Because Peyton plays by the rules," Bea answered for her.

"I do not."

"Of course you do." Her sister sat back, so smug in her unwrinkled shirt and perfect hair and flawless makeup. "If you didn't play by the rules, you'd do just what Jo said. But instead, I bet you heard the shit was going to hit the fan and you immediately dumped that hot man, didn't you?"

Peyton grumbled and took a sip of beer.

"Which sucks on more levels than one, since I guarantee you wanted him for more than just his riding skills."

She stared at her sister, not sure which part to address first. The idea that she felt more for Red than just lust, or that her sister was making sex puns over cocktails? When the hell had she grown up?

Someone called for Jo, and she held up a finger to signal she'd be a minute. "Look, I don't know you well, but I'll give you advice anyway."

Peyton raised a brow.

"Comes free with the drinks. If you want this guy for more than just a few quick pokes in the hay, then grab the bull by the horn and do the thing."

"Could you insert just a few more cowboy puns in there?" Peyton asked, setting aside her empty bottle.

"Still learning. I'll work on it. I don't have any experience in keeping a man around for more than sex. Never wanted to. Not my thing. But if that's what blows your skirt up, then by all means, go for it. *I'm coming!*" she yelled over her shoulder when someone from the bar called her name again. Hopping down from the chair, she grabbed her tray from the table and nodded. "Think about it."

Bea waited until Jo was gone before asking quietly, "You really are hung up on him, aren't you? You wouldn't be so upset if it was just about business. Pissed, yeah. But not upset."

In one last ditch effort to play it cool, Peyton pointed out, "I do love the ranch, you know."

"Of course you do. God knows why, but you do. Bless you," Bea said to a server who dropped off another round of drinks and took their empties. Peyton stared at the fresh bottle, wondering when she'd polished off the first. "The bigger question is, do you love him?"

Luckily, Peyton hadn't taken a sip yet of her new drink. "I . . ."

Bea smiled softly and reached over to pat her arm. "There, there. It'll be okay."

"Smart ass."

"We share the same genes."

Peyton stared down at her own self, dressed in what Bea had termed barely acceptable jeans and a simple blue shirt, the hair she kept in one braid for practical reasons, the fact that she didn't own makeup at all. Oh yeah, they were two peas in a pod, the Muldoon sisters.

As if reading her mind, Bea sniffed. "Well, sometimes the gene pool is a little shallow. Don't worry, I'll catch you up."

Like hell, Peyton thought. But she smiled in spite of herself and traced a finger through the drops of condensation on the bottle.

Before she could find a lighter topic to move on to, Peyton's phone buzzed. Glancing at it, she saw the envelope icon indicating she had a text message from an unexpected number.

"Billy?" she murmured, then flipped the phone open.

"Billy," Bea repeated, taking a sip of her girly drink from the tiny straw, brow scrunched in concentration. "That cutie high schooler? Honey, I think it's great you're opening yourself up to new experiences. But if you think being with Red would cause negative gossip, then you and—"

"Hush." She mimicked a beak closing with her fingers. "I don't know why he'd send me something this late. Probably a misdial. I think there's someone he's interested in at school. Maybe he . . ." Peyton felt the blood rush from her head as she read the message. "Shit. Bea, we gotta go."

"Now?" Bea stared at her half-full drink. "We just got here."

Peyton tossed a twenty and a ten on the table—likely an overpayment for the drinks, but she wasn't waiting around for the bill—and hopped down. "Haul ass, princess. Something's up at home."

Chapter Twenty-one

"If you don't mind me giving you a little advice . . ." Trace started, rocking back on his heels as he paced through the tiny apartment.

"I do mind," Red answered, knowing it was pointless. Though Trace wasn't drunk, he was slowly but surely plowing through the beer with full steam. No real reason why, it seemed. Red wasn't about to judge. Sometimes a man just needed to let loose with other males.

Even if one of the males in question hadn't celebrated his first birthday yet.

"Too bad. I say screw what people think."

"Including me?" Red chuckled when Trace's face went blank with confusion. "Sorry. You were making a point?"

"Hell yeah. You two thought you were so clever, sneaking around. But Emma knows all."

"Emma?" Red went a little white at the thought. That woman was scarier than a two-ton bull headed right at you in an open field. Nowhere to hide. "Emma knows?"

"Of course Emma knows. Emma's all knowing." Trace looked disgusted Red would even question the thought. "I'd be willing to bet most people knew already around here. They were just keeping their traps shut 'cause they like Peyton and their paycheck."

"Not everyone will keep their traps shut. Not everyone likes Peyton."

"Because she's a girl? Yeah. Fuck them." Trace shot a guilty glance at his son, dead asleep on the makeshift pallet he'd created out of his jacket on the floor. "Sorry, bud."

"I think he's still conked out."

"Yeah, well, the books say to start curbing the language early. They're sponges, you know."

No, he didn't know. But it amused Red that Trace scoured through parenting books looking for answers. He was a good guy, Trace Muldoon. Not at all what he'd expected. But that's what he got for making assumptions based on a profile built up through the rodeo media.

"She's done with me. I'm not going to force myself on her."

"She's not done with you. I know my sister. She's not a quitter. She just hasn't figured out an angle yet. Give her some cool-down time and try again."

Amused, Red crossed his arms and propped one foot up on the chair Trace had evacuated to pace around. "You giving me tips on how to pick up your sister?"

"Hell no. I'd rather you stayed away from her." Trace shrugged. "But it's a little late for that now, isn't it? Might as well be you rather than someone else."

"Better the devil you know?" he mumbled.

Trace saluted him with his bottle. "Got it in one."

Red's phone rang and he glanced at the screen. "I thought you said your sisters went out for some girls' night thing."

"They did."

"Then why is Peyton calling me?" He answered. "Peyton, what's up?"

"Red, thank God. Billy texted me and there's trouble at the house and Trace is there with the baby and I didn't want to call him unless I knew what was going on and—"

"Peyton, slow down." He stood, body going on high

alert at the panic and fear in his woman's voice. "Slow down, baby. Trace and Seth are here in my apartment. They're fine."

"Thank God," she breathed, and he heard her repeat what he'd just said to someone else. A feminine voice echoed her gratitude. Bea's voice.

"Where are you?"

"Driving home. Well, Bea is, I'm riding shotgun. Luckily he texted before we'd drunk too much to drive home. Now listen. Billy said he was out at the barn, staying over with one of the grooms. When he went out to take a leak, he caught movement by the main house, like a person walking around the back, by the kitchen door. Knows it isn't Emma— her car isn't there. I know it's not you or Trace. So it's someone up to no good. I thought Trace might be in there and—"

"Say no more. When you get here, keep the car down by the end of the drive and lock the doors. Don't come out unless you hear the okay from me or Trace. Keep your cell phones ready to call either 911 or one of us for help."

"Dammit, don't shut me out like some incompetent girl. I can help!"

"You'll help more by staying alert and ready to call the cops if I need you." He didn't wait for her answer, just hung up and shoved the phone in his pocket. As he pulled his boots on, he looked at Trace. "Trouble at the main house. I'm gonna go scope it out."

"I'll come with." Instantly looking dead sober, Trace was grabbing his jacket before he looked down once more at his son. "Or, shit. I guess not."

"Guess not," Red agreed. "I've got it. Just keep your phone ready. Maybe stand at the bottom of the stairs, keep the door cracked so you can listen for the kid and you'll hear in case I need you." With a last tug, his boots were on and he headed down the stairs as quietly as he could.

Sound carried far in the dead of night, with nothing else going on and the air so open.

Once his feet hit grass, he hurried as fast as he could, as soundlessly as possible, creeping through the shadows and staying alert. He calculated the best way to approach the house without being spotted. And his mind hovered on the edge, terrified who he would find sneaking around.

He feared it would be his father. Almost knew it would be.

He'd made it to the barn without any problems when a muffled, deep shout cut through the night. Giving up all ideas of stealth, he broke into a sprint and followed the sounds of scuffling, the curses, the dull, unforgettable sounds of fists hitting flesh.

In the dark, as his eyes adjusted, he located two figures brawling in the dirt near the tree he and Peyton had once met under. It was no contest, one man outsizing the other by almost half. He heard a yelp and knew by the tone of the sound the smaller figure was Billy. Immediately he leapt into the fray, doing his best to spare Billy any more blows while prying the other man from the teen's lax body.

"Jesus!" Red fought to knock the man to the ground. Though not as tall as Red, the stranger packed almost as much weight and didn't go down easily. Finally, he managed to wrestle the man to the ground and pin his arms behind him. He whined and yelled like a little girl when Red wrenched his arm a littler harder than necessary. "What the hell are you doing out here, Bill?"

"Trying to keep him from escaping." The teen stood, wiped at his nose with a sleeve. Red could easily guess it was blood he mopped up. "I didn't want him to get away."

Red couldn't see well enough in the shade of the tree to make out any features, not to mention the man was facedown in the dirt. But he knew from the shape of the body, it wasn't his father.

Relief, cool and sweet, swam through his system a moment before anger and rage blocked it out like an eclipse blocked the sun.

"Get. Off."

The voice, now clear and concise, led him to the stranger's identity in an instant.

Sam Nylen.

"What the hell are you doing here?" Red resisted the urge to shove the man's face in the dirt a little harder.

"Why is that kid here?" he shot back, earning him an extra knee to the back. He grunted, then muttered, "This is kidnapping or something. You can't hold me here."

"Bill?"

"Yeah, boss?"

Red smiled a little at that. "Text Peyton again, tell her to call the cops, and that we've got this under control. We've got a trespasser and possible burglar."

"Sure thing." He heard the clicking sounds of the teen's phone as he wandered away to catch a little spare illumination from the front porch lights around the corner.

"Burglar?" Nylen's voice rose to a squeak. "I'm no burglar. I made a mistake. Drove here on accident. I used to live here, you know. Too much to drink. Can't hold that against a man. No harm done, I'll just head on out and—"

Red pushed his knee farther into his back, silencing the poor excuse for an excuse. "Shut up. Save it for the cops. I know it was you in my office, and my apartment, both times. Might as well tell me what you were looking for before the cops get here. I might just forget to mention to the police about the other break ins."

"Your apartment?" He laughed, but the sound was more like a wheeze. "I sure as hell didn't go in there."

"How'd you break in to the office?"

"Had another key made before I got sacked. Idiot woman never changed the locks."

"Shut up," he said absently, leaning harder on his chest. So Nylen admitted the office, but not the apartment break ins. Which meant . . .

"Do you know my father?"

Nylen spit some dirt out the side of his mouth. "Shitty card player. Talks too much when he's drinking."

Pieces fell into place. Of course two lowlifes like his father and Nylen would manage to meet up in a town this small. Magnetic pull of scum to scum, cheat to cheat. Which meant . . .

"Where's your car?"

He didn't say a word.

"Red?" Billy's voice was hesitant. Damn. He'd forgotten Bill was still there. "Arby's heading this way, and Tiny's with him."

"Good." Red stood for a moment, planting his boot in the small of Nylen's back. As the two men approached, he called out, "Hope you brought some zip ties."

Tiny scoffed. "Why bother?" He stepped around Red and sat on the man, causing Nylen to gasp for breath. With a sneer, Tiny bent over to look Nylen in the face. "You can't know how good it feels to finally give you what you deserve, you son of a bitch."

"This all you got?" Arby asked Red quietly.

"All I . . . what?" Red turned to him.

Arby tilted his head toward the main gate. "Thought I saw a car down there. Glint from the spotlight caught on a rear bumper. Mighta been wrong though."

Red clapped a hand on Arby's shoulder and walked around to the front of the house. After a few moments, he started to sprint for the gate. If someone was in the car, he'd never catch it. But he'd have a good look.

He skidded to a halt as he caught sight of his father's own truck parked in the shadows. He'd recognize the truck anywhere. And more, his father sitting in the driver seat. When Mac caught sight of Red, he threw the car in reverse and made a sloppy three-point turn. Gravel flew as he stepped on the accelerator and left M-Star in the dust.

"No honor among thieves," Red muttered to himself, heading back to the main house.

"Peyton said she called the cops; they should be here soon." Bill's face split in a wide grin and he bounced on his toes. "She said we shouldn't do anything heroic and she also wanted me to tell you that she thinks you're a big—"

"That's fine, Bill." He smiled a little. "I get the point." He tilted his head a little, staring at Nylen's completely motionless body. "Can he breathe down there?"

Arby shrugged and leaned against the tree trunk. "I'm not all that inclined to check."

The crunch of boots on gravel had everyone stiffening. But then he heard Bea yell Peyton's name from around the front of the house and they all relaxed. Bill jogged over to direct them.

"He's where? It was who?" Peyton could be heard a mile away with that yell. She rounded the corner, looking like hell on wheels and twice as pretty. He'd never seen her in anything but her work gear. Or, well, nothing at all. But in a pretty top and a pair of clean jeans, with her unbraided hair flowing around her shoulders, she was something to see.

As much as he could see in the dark.

He stared once more at the man on the ground. He'd had a part in catching the bastard red-handed. Maybe, just maybe, this was the opening he could use to work his way back in with her. He'd take all the help he could get at this point.

"Redford Callahan, you big idiot!"

So much for gratitude. "What?"

"You could have been killed!" She walked up and shoved at his shoulders with her hands, anger spitting from her eyes. "You don't know if he was armed or alone or anything! How could you just do that?"

"Bill snuck up on him first," he replied, silently apologizing for tossing the kid under the bus.

"Billy Curry!" she shouted over her shoulder. "You and I are going to have a long talk tomorrow morning!"

"Yes, ma'am," came his resigned reply.

Kneeling down, Peyton squinted at the man. "Is that . . . no. You've got to be . . . Sam Nylen?"

"One in the same," Red agreed.

Peyton laughed harshly. "I see it's just our night to run into each other, isn't it? First you insult me at the bar, now you break into my house?"

"I didn't break in anywhere!" he protested.

"He insulted you?" Red asked at the same time. Leaning down low, he said quietly, "I've got a mind to let you up and give you a running head start, just so I could chase your sorry ass down and kick the shit out of you again."

Tiny laughed at that.

"No point. Bea's already called the sheriff," Peyton said somewhat glumly, as if disappointed she wouldn't get to witness the ass kicking.

"They're on the way!" Bea called cheerfully from the side of the house. "This is way better than drinks and girls night out!"

"Shut up, Bea," Peyton muttered, though there was no way her sister could hear. "Wanna start talking now, Nylen, or wait until you have a bigger audience?"

"Nothing to say."

"Oh, I can guess." Peyton stared at the house for a moment. "Looking for something you left behind when I fired you?"

He stayed silent.

"Or did you just miss us that much? Miss being paid for doing nothing while skimming money from the business?" Peyton shook her head. "Sorry for you, but you wouldn't have found the books anyway. I warned you, didn't I? You piss me off, and I'll take everything I know to the police. Leave quietly and it will all be forgotten. Guess what option I'm going with now?"

Nylen replied, but his words were lost beneath the sound of a siren in the quiet night.

"Ah, here's your ride now." Peyton headed to the front of the house to greet whichever responder had made it to them first.

"Man to man, let's have a quick chat," Red said casually. "Was it you that planted the idea in my father's head about Peyton and me?"

Nylen snickered and wheezed. "Your father's a gullible idiot."

"No argument there."

"He grabbed at the idea of searching your place for cash, maybe even soaking you for more. Then he had to go and blow it and let the story loose too soon. Damn man couldn't even be a proper scapegoat." He spat once more, glaring at Red like he was the one in the wrong. "She should have hired me back."

Red shook his head sadly. "You don't give her enough credit. That's your problem, Nylen. Assuming Peyton's just like her mama. She's smart, she's gutsy, and she's got discerning taste."

"She's rocking the bed frame with you. Can't be too discerning."

That snide comment earned him a bounce from Tiny's large body. "Just keep digging your hole deeper, Nylen. Just keep digging." Tiny patted his head.

Peyton's voice sounded. "They're around here. Hard to see but . . . there."

A bright light swept the area, momentarily blinding Red. Holding a hand up to shield his eyes, he saw Peyton standing with a sheriff's deputy, pointing in their direction. He gave a little wave, then stood up.

"What do we have here?" The deputy walked up and squatted down next to Nylen's body.

"Finally. Took you long enough." Nylen spit out a bit of dirt. "These men attacked me, held me hostage. They need to be arrested."

The deputy glanced between Red and Bill, now holding a bandana to his nose, and Tiny who was brushing dirt from his hands with an innocent *who, me?* look on his face. "Yeah. They sure look ferocious. How about you tell me why you're on private property when you weren't invited first? Then I'll get to your so-called attackers."

Nylen sputtered and sat up, but the deputy quickly cuffed him and hauled him up onto his feet.

"Uh huh, okay, sure." The man led him to his car, which was parked with its light still flashing in front of the main house. "So you're going with the fact that you drove out here, intoxicated, and attempted to enter a residence you never lived in. By accident." He laughed. "That's a new one. I'll have to write that down."

After assisting Nylen—whose low mutters sounded suspiciously like the words "entrapment" and "assault"— into the back of the car, he set up a time to come by the next morning and get statements from Billy, Red, and Peyton.

Red's turn was last, and he knew he had a choice to

make. Cover up for his father—again—and let the pattern of his childhood chase him into the future. Or put his boot down and stop playing into it and give his future a fighting chance.

No contest. He chose the future.

Chapter Twenty-two

A s the deputy's car drove down the gravel drive to the main road, Red's phone buzzed in his pocket and he checked. Trace. "What's up?"

"Is it safe to come out yet?" he asked, voice harsh with frustration.

"Yeah, yeah. Sorry. Bring the kid. It's fine." In the confusion and action, Red had forgotten he'd all but ditched Trace back at his place. "Head over to the main house, we're all here now. I'll explain when you get here."

He hung up and watched as Bea took Billy into the house, rubbing his back with a soothing hand.

"Let's get that nose cleaned up in the kitchen. We can make sure you don't need to see the doctor."

"Yes, ma'am." Even with a bloody nose, the kid looked like he was in heaven with her tender care and attention focused on him. A regular Florence Nightingale come to life. Red shook his head, amused. What were the teen years without a few unrealistic crushes and heartbreaks along the way?

And then there were two. Red watched Peyton shuffle her feet in the dust, stick her hands in her pockets, look anywhere but at him.

Speaking of heartbreak . . .

Red smiled, fighting the urge to grab her, toss her over

his shoulder and storm back to his place for a come to Jesus moment. "Guess we figured out who's been snooping through my stuff."

"Guess so." Her voice was distant, and she wouldn't look at him.

"Peyton . . ." He ran a hand through his hair, gripping the ends and pulling. Didn't clear his head nearly as fast as he'd hoped. "I'm sorry."

"Sorry?" She did look at him now, surprise filling her wide eyes. "For what?"

"It was my father who started all this. Played Nylen's pawn."

Her eyes widened, but he plowed on without waiting for her comments.

"I caught him snooping around the other night. Chased him off, and was trying to figure out how to tell you. I should have said something sooner."

Her eyes narrowed. "Yes, you should have."

No excuse for it. "Then tonight, I saw his truck at the end of the drive. He drove Nylen here."

Her lips curved. "Are you going to mention that to the police?"

He wiped a hand over his brow, pushing back his hair. "Would you let me make the choice?"

"Yes," she whispered.

Hope bloomed in his chest. "Well, I already chose to say something. I added it to my statement to the deputy. What they do with it, I can't control. But I'll do what I can to make sure he's never close to you, or the ranch, again. And I'm so . . ." He turned to look out at the sky, turned back again and swallowed hard. "I'm so sorry. I didn't mean to bring this to you."

She shook her head. "Not your fault. God knows, I know enough about the sins of the parent not being the child's load to bear. Sylvia taught me that much. Probably the only thing she did teach me. We're responsible for ourselves."

Promising. He chanced a step toward her and she didn't back away. "He might spread it around about us. People would know."

"People already know. I learned that much in town tonight. This evening was very . . . educational." She shrugged. "It's out."

Despite her casual stance and nonchalant tone of voice, he could see it hurt. The fact that people would think poorly of her, less of her. "I'm sorry."

"I made my choice. And I'm coming around to accepting the consequences." She took a deep breath and pushed back some hair that fell over her eyes. He smiled at the frustrated gesture. The outside package might be all woman, but the inside was pure tomboy. Just how he liked her.

"So where does that leave us?"

Peyton bit her lip and shrugged. "I—"

"Peyton!"

She cut off, and they both looked over to see Trace hustling over the dirt driveway as fast as he could without jostling Seth on his shoulder. He stepped up and reached around her with his free arm, pulling her in close for a hug. "Are you okay?"

"I'm fine. Red and Billy had it all settled before I could even get in any of the action." She sounded so disgruntled and put out by the fact that she didn't get to swing at Nylen, Red had to laugh.

"Sorry to ruin the fun. I was a little busy making sure the bastard didn't get away." Red smiled. "Next time, I'll let you have a turn."

"Thank you."

Trace looked back and forth between them. "So is someone going to clue me in on what happened?"

Peyton laughed shortly. "Forgot you've been in the dark. It was Nylen." She shot a quick glance at Red, but didn't mention his father. Protecting him? "We'll talk about it more, but he's in custody and the major threat is gone."

"But—"

"Later," Peyton said firmly. She turned to smooth a hand over Seth's head, and her voice softened as she spoke to the child. "Hey, guy. Lot of action past your bedtime, huh? Soon enough you'll be running around here with the rest of these boys, fighting crime."

"Not likely." When Seth cooed, Trace jiggled him a little. "Let's head to bed, little man. Auntie Peyton's got some business to attend to out here." With a significant glance Red's way, Trace headed into the house behind Bea and Billy.

And then, once more, they were alone.

Red figured he had two choices. He could walk away and pretend that nothing had happened and keep his pride intact. Or he could ask her for another chance, fight for the opportunity. Beg if necessary, pride be damned.

No choice, really. What was pride without the woman he loved? A cold consolation. But before he dropped to his knees, Peyton's hand landed on his shoulder.

"Go home, Red."

What? "No. We need to talk."

"We will. I just need . . ." She sighed. "Time. I need some time. So much in the last few hours to process. Too much. Give me just a little bit."

He had the distinct idea that walking away now would be the mistake of a lifetime. "Peyton, I can't just walk away right now. Process it with me."

"Give me time." Her answer was firm, unyielding. He'd say that much for his Peyton. She made up her mind, and it was set in concrete. Stubborn woman.

And wasn't that one of the things he loved about her?

He battled once more against the urge to pull that *hauling her over his shoulder* trick. But if pushing her to talk now would be a bad idea, kidnapping her caveman style would just be the last nail in their coffin. With every muscle in his body screaming in protest, Red stepped back and headed toward his apartment.

He'd give her time. But not much. Because he wasn't about to leave his woman with the idea that they wouldn't be together in the end for long.

Peyton watched Red's figure disappear in the night and rubbed at her forehead. Damn, this was a mess. The entire thing, from Nylen down to poor Billy's nose and back up again to her . . . whatever with Red.

Relationship? She wanted to call it that. But . . .

No. No buts anymore. First to see about her family. As she entered through the front door, Bea stood, arms crossed, foot tapping in her too-high heel. Peyton raised a brow at her sister's obviously impatient stance. "What?"

Bea pointed at the door. "Go."

"Go where? It's almost midnight."

"Are you really going to make him wait until tomorrow?" Bea frowned. "Are you going to make yourself wait?"

Peyton wanted to rub at her head again, but resisted. "Yes. I need to . . ."

"Think? Thinking's what got you into this mess. If you had just done what Jo said and not cared at all what everyone else thought, then people would already be moving on, and not caring right back. Problem solved."

"You know, for someone whose entire career revolves around what people think of her, you sure are pushy about this."

"I know what I'm doing, then." Bea tossed her head, short hair fluttering around her neck. "I'm an expert."

"So you're saying I should not think?"

Bea smiled and performed a slow, mocking clap. "Exactly. The pupil, she learns. Now go."

Peyton could ignore her. Bea might be taller, but Peyton had more muscle. Shouldering past her and heading upstairs to her own bed would be no challenge.

But she didn't want her own bed. She wanted Red.

Dammit. Pointing a finger up, she scowled. "This does *not* mean you were right. It just means I'm changing my mind."

Before she could slam the door behind her, Bea's laughter rang in her ears, the sound haunting her all the way across the ranch.

Red's head hit the door the moment it closed behind him. By his watch, he had about four hours of worthless sleep ahead of him before the start of the workday. Four hours to obsess over what the hell he was going to say to Peyton to make her change her mind. Make her let him stay. Give them a chance.

His body jerked in surprise when someone knocked on the wood panel behind his back. Whirling, he opened the door and prayed his eyes weren't playing tricks. "Peyton?"

She smiled hesitantly, then the smile slid off her face. "Bad time?"

He realized he was looming over the doorway like a guardian. "No, no. Just surprised. It's never a bad time. Come on—" The rest of his sentence was smothered by her lips, her body, her everything pressed against his.

Red might be a lot of things, but stupid wasn't one of them. He wasn't about to continue talking when kissing worked even better. He grabbed hold, twirled her around and closed the door behind them. Peyton all but climbed up his body, legs squeezing around him, and he gripped her thighs and carried her to the bed.

But as he lowered her down on her back, a warning flashed in his mind. He raised his head from hers and looked her in the eyes. "This isn't good-bye sex, right?"

"What?" Peyton stared, openmouthed, then cracked up laughing. "Good-bye sex? Are you going to turn me away if I say yes?"

"No." He grinned, feeling more confident now. "I'd just make it last a damn long time. Long enough to have you changing your mind."

"I don't need it changed. I did that on my own." She gripped either side of his face and tugged him down until her breath fanned against his lips. "I want you. Us. If people don't like that, or make a big deal about it, then that's their problem."

"Even if it costs you business?"

"It won't," she said firmly. "I've got a failsafe plan."

"What's that?"

"You." She kissed him quick and hard.

He lengthened the kiss, deepened what she tried to keep shallow. "So I'm being used for my skills."

"Well, I can't deny you know how to . . . ride." She emphasized her words with a pulse of her hips up until she brushed against his erection.

He rolled until she was on top of him, straddling him. "I'm a better coach. How about you take a turn in the saddle."

She reached for the buttons on his jeans, then stopped. One hand pushed her hair back from her face, the other tracing the ridge of her jeans by her knee. "I love you."

The words, unexpected, sweet and pure, struck him right through the heart. "Thank God." Flipping them again, he leaned over her on his elbows. "Thank God," he muttered against her neck, nuzzling until she shifted rest-lessly. "Thank you, God." He pressed kisses down her col-larbone, pushing aside the collar of her shirt.

"Is that all you can say?"

"What was I supposed to say? Okay!" he shouted on a laugh as she tugged on his hair. "Okay. Uncle." When she soothed the sting with her nails, scratching at his scalp, he leaned into the touch. "I love you, too. I fought it, and I avoided you like the plague because I knew we'd end up here. Somehow, I knew it'd come to this, and my heart wouldn't hold out against you."

"I thought you were just an arrogant, elitist jerk."

"I might still be." When her brows dropped, he kissed her nose. "But I'm *your* arrogant, elitist jerk. Isn't that so much better?"

She sighed and laughed. "Shockingly, I think it might be." One finger traced behind his ear, down his neck and toyed with the hollow of his throat. "Got any plans for the rest of the night?"

With one last roll, he positioned her on top once more. "Take the reins, Peyton. We've got until morning."

If you love all things Western, especially those hot cowboys, don't miss these contemporary Western romances from Kensington!

Available from eKensington wherever ebooks are sold

TUCKER'S CROSSING by Marina Adair

"A perfect mix of heart and heat, Adair keeps the pages turning."
—*New York Times* bestselling author Jill Shalvis

Sweet Plains, Texas, wasn't so sweet to Cody, Noah, and Beau Tucker. But now the Tucker boys are men, ready to take on the questions that have haunted them since they left home. . . .

Cody Tucker shook the dust of his two-bit hometown off his boots ten years ago—right about the time his college sweetheart, Shelby Lynn Harris, married his so-called best friend. But when his dad dies, Cody finds himself home again and knee-deep in the past. Except now his rowdy beer buddy is the sheriff, his housekeeper is a blue-ribbon chili chef, and the family ranch is in the red. The only thing that hasn't changed is Shelby Lynn. . . .

Shelby Lynn has gone through a lot of heartache thanks to Cody. But that's all over now. She just wants a chance to live the life she's made for herself in peace. The trouble is, the Sweet Plains chili cook-off is heating up, the Ladies of Sweet are as riled as hornets, and as soon as Cody gets near, she forgets all about peace. Cody is pure temptation—and she knows just how good it feels to give in. . . .

RIDE 'EM

Cabe Dawson is a cowboy at heart. He's devoted a lifetime to running Blackhawk Ranch, carving out a Northern California empire for his family. When the cattle ranch's wells run dry, he knows what he needs to do. Foreclose on the Jordan place and drill deep for water there. It's just business. Nothing personal.

But, as summer heats up, keeping his mind on business just might be impossible. Rose Jordan left Lonesome, California, eight years ago and never looked back. Back then, she'd challenged Cabe's authority—and his control. Though he wanted her fiercely, she was too young. Too rebellious. Now, with Rose back in Lonesome, business is getting very, very personal. She wants to keep her home, but can Cabe convince her to keep him instead?

Katie Harris loved growing up on a ranch. She had her horse, the beautiful Texas prairie, and Cole Logan, the cowboy next door. But there are a lot of secrets hidden under a Texas sky. . . .

Katie was always sure she'd marry Cole Logan someday—until he kicked away her pretty dreams like so much horse pucky. So she wised up and moved to the big city. And she was happy there. That is, until her daddy got sick and she found herself back on the wrong side of Cole's corral.

Cole knows Katie doesn't want anything to do with him. But after so many years, he can't pretend she's no more than a neighbor. Not when thinking about her cherry lip gloss and hell-for-leather passion is keeping him up all night. Holding his ground was hard enough when she was seventeen. Now that she's her own woman, Cole's heart doesn't stand a chance. . . .